Bealby; A Holiday

H. G. Wells

Alpha Editions

This edition published in 2021

ISBN : 9789354595202

Design and Setting By
Alpha Editions
www.alphaedis.com
Email - info@alphaedis.com

As per information held with us this book is in Public Domain.
This book is a reproduction of an important historical work. Alpha Editions uses the best technology to reproduce historical work in the same manner it was first published to preserve its original nature. Any marks or number seen are left intentionally to preserve its true form.

Contents

CHAPTER I YOUNG BEALBY GOES TO SHONTS	- 1 -
CHAPTER II A WEEK-END AT SHONTS	- 13 -
CHAPTER III THE WANDERERS	- 33 -
CHAPTER IV THE UNOBTRUSIVE PARTING	- 57 -
CHAPTER V THE SEEKING OF BEALBY	- 79 -
CHAPTER VI BEALBY AND THE TRAMP	- 114 -
CHAPTER VII THE BATTLE OF CRAYMINSTER	- 135 -
CHAPTER VIII HOW BEALBY EXPLAINED	- 156 -

CHAPTER I
YOUNG BEALBY GOES TO SHONTS

§ 1

The cat is the offspring of a cat and the dog of a dog, but butlers and lady's maids do not reproduce their kind. They have other duties.

So their successors have to be sought among the prolific, and particularly among the prolific on great estates. Such are gardeners, but not under-gardeners, gamekeepers, and coachmen—but not lodge people, because their years are too great and their lodges too small. And among those to whom this opportunity of entering service came was young Bealby, who was the stepson of Mr. Darling, the gardener of Shonts.

Everyone knows the glories of Shonts. Its façade. Its two towers. The great marble pond. The terraces where the peacocks walk and the lower lake with the black and white swans. The great park and the avenue. The view of the river winding away across the blue country. And of the Shonts Velasquez—but that is now in America. And the Shonts Rubens, which is in the National Gallery. And the Shonts porcelain. And the Shonts past history; it was a refuge for the old faith; it had priest's holes and secret passages. And how at last the Marquis had to let Shonts to the Laxtons—the Peptonized Milk and Baby Soother people—for a long term of years. It was a splendid chance for any boy to begin his knowledge of service in so great an establishment, and only the natural perversity of human nature can explain the violent objection young Bealby took to anything of the sort. He did. He said he did not want to be a servant, and that he would not go and be a good boy and try his very best in that state of life to which it had pleased God to call him at Shonts. On the contrary.

He communicated these views suddenly to his mother as she was preparing a steak and kidney pie in the bright little kitchen of the gardener's cottage. He came in with his hair all ruffled and his face hot and distinctly dirty, and his hands in his trousers pockets in the way he had been repeatedly told not to.

"Mother," he said, "I'm not going to be a steward's boy at the house anyhow, not if you tell me to, not till you're blue in the face. So that's all about it."

This delivered, he remained panting, having no further breath left in him.

His mother was a thin firm woman. She paused in her rolling of the dough until he had finished, and then she made a strong broadening sweep of the rolling pin, and remained facing him, leaning forward on that implement with her head a little on one side.

"You will do," she said, "whatsoever your father has said you will do."

"'E isn't my father," said young Bealby.

His mother gave a snapping nod of the head expressive of extreme determination.

"Anyhow I ain't going to do it," said young Bealby, and feeling the conversation was difficult to sustain he moved towards the staircase door with a view to slamming it.

"You'll do it," said his mother, "right enough."

"You see whether I do," said young Bealby, and then got in his door-slam rather hurriedly because of steps outside.

Mr. Darling came in out of the sunshine a few moments later. He was a large, many-pocketed, earthy-whiskered man with a clean-shaven determined mouth, and he carried a large pale cucumber in his hand.

"I tole him," he said.

"What did he say?" asked his wife.

"Nuthin'," said Mr. Darling.

"'E says 'e won't," said Mrs. Darling.

Mr. Darling regarded her thoughtfully for a moment.

"I never see such a boy," said Mr. Darling. "Why—'e's *got* to."

§ 2

But young Bealby maintained an obstinate fight against the inevitable.

He had no gift of lucid exposition. "I ain't going to be a servant," he said. "I don't see what right people have making a servant of me."

"You got to be something," said Mr. Darling.

"Everybody's got to be something," said Mrs. Darling.

"Then let me be something else," said young Bealby.

"*I* dessay you'd like to be a gentleman," said Mr. Darling.

"I wouldn't mind," said young Bealby.

"You got to be what your opportunities give you," said Mr. Darling.

Young Bealby became breathless. "Why shouldn't I be an engine driver?" he asked.

"All oily," said his mother. "And getting yourself killed in an accident. And got to pay fines. You'd *like* to be an engine driver."

"Or a soldier."

"Oo!—a Swaddy!" said Mr. Darling decisively.

"Or the sea."

"With that weak stummik of yours," said Mrs. Darling.

"Besides which," said Mr. Darling, "it's been arranged for you to go up to the 'ouse the very first of next month. And your box and everything ready."

Young Bealby became very red in the face. "I won't go," he said very faintly.

"You will," said Mr. Darling, "if I 'ave to take you by the collar and the slack of your breeches to get you there."

§ 3

The heart of young Bealby was a coal of fire within his breast as—unassisted—he went across the dewy park up to the great house, whither his box was to follow him.

He thought the world a "rotten show."

He also said, apparently to two does and a fawn, "If you think I'm going to stand it, you know, you're **JOLLY**-well mistaken."

I do not attempt to justify his prejudice against honourable usefulness in a domestic capacity. He had it. Perhaps there is something in the air of Highbury, where he had spent the past eight years of his life, that leads to democratic ideals. It is one of those new places where estates seem almost forgotten. Perhaps too there was something in the Bealby strain....

I think he would have objected to any employment at all. Hitherto he had been a remarkably free boy with a considerable gusto about his freedom. Why should that end? The little village mixed school had been a soft job for his Cockney wits, and for a year and a half he had been top boy. Why not go on being top boy?

Instead of which, under threats, he had to go across the sunlit corner of the park, through that slanting morning sunlight which had been so often the prelude to golden days of leafy wanderings! He had to go past the corner of the laundry where he had so often played cricket with the coachman's boys (already swallowed up into the working world), he had to follow the laundry wall to the end of the kitchen, and there, where the steps go down and underground, he had to say farewell to the sunlight, farewell to childhood, boyhood, freedom. He had to go down and along the stone corridor to the pantry, and there he had to ask for Mr. Mergleson. He paused on the top step and looked up at the blue sky across which a hawk was slowly drifting. His eyes followed the hawk out of sight beyond a cypress bough, but indeed he was not thinking about the hawk, he was not seeing the hawk; he was struggling with a last wild impulse of his ferial nature. "Why not sling it?" his ferial nature was asking. "Why not even now—*do a bunk*?"

It would have been better for him perhaps and better for Mr. Mergleson and better for Shonts if he had yielded to the whisper of the Tempter. But his heart was heavy within him, and he had no lunch. And never a penny. One can do but a very little bunk on an empty belly! "Must" was written all over him. He went down the steps.

The passage was long and cool and at the end of it was a swing door. Through that and then to the left, he knew one had to go, past the stillroom and so to the pantry. The maids were at breakfast in the stillroom with the door open. The grimace he made in passing was intended rather to entertain than to insult, and anyhow a chap must do something with his face. And then he came to the pantry and into the presence of Mr. Mergleson.

Mr. Mergleson was in his shirt-sleeves and generally dishevelled, having an early cup of tea in an atmosphere full of the bleak memories of overnight. He was an ample man with a large nose, a vast under lip and mutton-chop side-whiskers. His voice would have suited a succulent parrot. He took out a gold watch from his waistcoat pocket and regarded it. "Ten minutes past seven, young man," he said, "isn't seven o'clock."

Young Bealby made no articulate answer.

"Just stand there for a minute," said Mr. Mergleson, "and when I'm at libbuty I'll run through your duties." And almost ostentatiously he gave himself up to the enjoyment of his cup of tea.

Three other gentlemen in deshabille sat at table with Mr. Mergleson. They regarded young Bealby with attention, and the youngest, a red-haired, barefaced youth in shirt-sleeves and a green apron was moved to a grimace that was clearly designed to echo the scowl on young Bealby's features.

The fury that had been subdued by a momentary awe of Mr. Mergleson revived and gathered force. Young Bealby's face became scarlet, his eyes filled with tears and his mind with the need for movement. After all,—he wouldn't stand it. He turned round abruptly and made for the door.

"Where'n earth you going to?" cried Mr. Mergleson.

"He's shy!" cried the second footman.

"Steady on!" cried the first footman and had him by the shoulder in the doorway.

"Lemme *go*!" howled the new recruit, struggling. "I won't be a blooming servant. I won't."

"Here!" cried Mr. Mergleson, gesticulating with his teaspoon, "bring 'im to the end of the table there. What's this about a blooming servant?"

Bealby, suddenly blubbering, was replaced at the end of the table.

"May I ask what's this about a blooming servant?" asked Mr. Mergleson.

Sniff and silence.

"Did I understand you to say that you ain't going to be a blooming servant, young Bealby?"

"Yes," said young Bealby.

"Thomas," said Mr. Mergleson, "just smack 'is 'ed. Smack it rather 'ard...."

Things too rapid to relate occurred. "So you'd *bite*, would you?" said Thomas....

"Ah!" said Mr. Mergleson. "*Got* 'im! That one!" ...

"Just smack 'is 'ed once more," said Mr. Mergleson....

"And now you just stand there, young man, until I'm at libbuty to attend to you further," said Mr. Mergleson, and finished his tea slowly and eloquently....

The second footman rubbed his shin thoughtfully.

"If I got to smack 'is 'ed much," he said, "'e'd better change into his slippers."

"Take him to 'is room," said Mr. Mergleson getting up. "See 'e washes the grief and grubbiness off 'is face in the handwash at the end of the passage and make him put on his slippers. Then show 'im 'ow to lay the table in the steward's room."

§ 4

The duties to which Bealby was introduced struck him as perplexingly various, undesirably numerous, uninteresting and difficult to remember, and also he did not try to remember them very well because he wanted to do them as badly as possible and he thought that forgetting would be a good way of starting at that. He was beginning at the bottom of the ladder; to him it fell to wait on the upper servants, and the green baize door at the top of the service staircase was the limit of his range. His room was a small wedge-shaped apartment under some steps leading to the servants' hall, lit by a window that did not open and that gave upon the underground passage. He received his instructions in a state of crumpled mutinousness, but for a day his desire to be remarkably impossible was more than counterbalanced by his respect for the large able hands of the four man-servants, his seniors, and by a disinclination to be returned too promptly to the gardens. Then in a tentative manner he broke two plates and got his head smacked by Mr. Mergleson himself. Mr. Mergleson gave a staccato slap quite as powerful as Thomas's but otherwise different. The hand of Mr. Mergleson was large and fat and he got his effects by dash, Thomas's was horny and lingered. After that young Bealby put salt in the teapot in which the housekeeper made tea. But that he observed she washed out with hot water before she put in the tea. It was clear that he had wasted his salt, which ought to have gone into the kettle.

Next time,—the kettle.

Beyond telling him his duties almost excessively nobody conversed with young Bealby during the long hours of his first day in service. At midday dinner in the servants' hall, he made one of the kitchen-maids giggle by pulling faces intended to be delicately suggestive of Mr. Mergleson, but that was his nearest approach to disinterested human intercourse.

When the hour for retirement came,—"Get out of it. Go to bed, you dirty little Kicker," said Thomas. "We've had about enough of you for one day"— young Bealby sat for a long time on the edge of his bed weighing the possibilities of arson and poison. He wished he had some poison. Some sort of poison with a medieval manner, poison that hurts before it kills. Also he produced a small penny pocket-book with a glazed black cover and blue edges. He headed one page of this "Mergleson" and entered beneath it three black crosses. Then he opened an account to Thomas, who was manifestly destined to be his principal creditor. Bealby was not a forgiving boy. At the village school they had been too busy making him a good Churchman to attend to things like that. There were a lot of crosses for Thomas.

And while Bealby made these sinister memoranda downstairs Lady Laxton—for Laxton had bought a baronetcy for twenty thousand down to the party funds and a tip to the whip over the Peptonized Milk flotation— Lady Laxton, a couple of floors above Bealby's ruffled head mused over her approaching week-end party. It was an important week-end party. The Lord Chancellor of England was coming. Never before had she had so much as a member of the Cabinet at Shonts. He was coming, and do what she would she could not help but connect it with her very strong desire to see the master of Shonts in the clear scarlet of a Deputy Lieutenant. Peter would look so well in that. The Lord Chancellor was coming, and to meet him and to circle about him there were Lord John Woodenhouse and Slinker Bond, there were the Countess of Barracks and Mrs. Rampound Pilby, the novelist, with her husband Rampound Pilby, there was Professor Timbre, the philosopher, and there were four smaller (though quite good) people who would run about very satisfactorily among the others. (At least she thought they would run about very satisfactorily amongst the others, not imagining any evil of her cousin Captain Douglas.)

All this good company in Shonts filled Lady Laxton with a pleasant realization of progressive successes but at the same time one must confess that she felt a certain diffidence. In her heart of hearts she knew she had not made this party. It had happened to her. How it might go on happening to her, she did not know, it was beyond her control. She hoped very earnestly that everything would pass off well.

The Lord Chancellor was as big a guest as any she had had. One must grow as one grows, but still,—being easy and friendly with him would be, she knew, a tremendous effort. Rather like being easy and friendly with an elephant. She was not good at conversation. The task of interesting people taxed her and puzzled her....

It was Slinker Bond, the whip, who had arranged the whole business— after, it must be confessed, a hint from Sir Peter. Laxton had complained that the government were neglecting this part of the country. "They ought to show up more than they do in the county," said Sir Peter, and added almost carelessly, "I could easily put anybody up at Shonts." There were to be two select dinner parties and a large but still select Sunday lunch to let in the countryside to the spectacle of the Laxtons taking their (new) proper place at Shonts....

It was not only the sense of her own deficiencies that troubled Lady Laxton; there were also her husband's excesses. He had—it was no use disguising it—rather too much the manner of an employer. He had a way of getting, how could one put it?—*confident* at dinner and Mergleson seemed to *delight* in filling up his glass. Then he would contradict a good deal.... She felt that Lord Chancellors however are the sort of men one doesn't contradict....

Then the Lord Chancellor was said to be interested in philosophy—a difficult subject. She had got Timbre to talk to him upon that. Timbre was a professor of philosophy at Oxford, so that was sure to be all right. But she wished she knew one or two good safe things to say in philosophy herself. She had long felt the need of a secretary, and now she felt it more than ever. If she had a secretary, she could just tell him what it was she wanted to talk about and he could get her one or two of the right books and mark the best passages and she could learn it all up.

She feared—it was a worrying fear—that Laxton would say right out and very early in the week-end that he didn't believe in philosophy. He had a way of saying he "didn't believe in" large things like that,—art, philanthropy, novels, and so on. Sometimes he said, "I don't believe in all this"—art or whatever it was. She had watched people's faces when he had said it and she had come to the conclusion that saying you don't believe in things isn't the sort of thing people say nowadays. It was wrong, somehow. But she did not want to tell Laxton directly that it was wrong. He would remember if she did, but he had a way of taking such things rather badly at the time.... She hated him to take things badly.

"If one could invent some little hint," she whispered to herself.

She had often wished she was better at hints.

She was, you see, a gentlewoman, modest, kindly. Her people were quite good people. Poor, of course. But she was not clever, she was anything but clever. And the wives of these captains of industry need to be very clever indeed if they are to escape a magnificent social isolation. They get the titles and the big places and all that sort of thing; people don't at all intend to isolate them, but there is nevertheless an inadvertent avoidance....

Even as she uttered these words, "If one could invent some little hint," Bealby down there less than forty feet away through the solid floor below her feet and a little to the right was wetting his stump of pencil as wet as he could in order to ensure a sufficiently emphatic fourteenth cross on the score sheet of the doomed Thomas. Most of the other thirteen marks were done with such hard breathing emphasis that the print of them went more than halfway through that little blue-edged book.

§ 5

The arrival of the week-end guests impressed Bealby at first merely as a blessed influence that withdrew the four men-servants into that unknown world on the other side of the green baize door, but then he learnt that it also involved the appearance of five new persons, two valets and three maids, for whom places had to be laid in the steward's room. Otherwise Lady Laxton's social arrangements had no more influence upon the mind of Bealby than the private affairs of the Emperor of China. There was something going on up there, beyond even his curiosity. All he heard of it was a distant coming and going of vehicles and some slight talk to which he was inattentive while the coachman and grooms were having a drink in the pantry—until these maids and valets appeared. They seemed to him to appear suddenly out of nothing, like slugs after rain, black and rather shiny, sitting about inactively and quietly consuming small matters. He disliked them, and they regarded him without affection or respect.

Who cared? He indicated his feeling towards them as soon as he was out of the steward's room by a gesture of the hand and nose venerable only by reason of its antiquity.

He had things more urgent to think about than strange valets and maids. Thomas had laid hands on him, jeered at him, inflicted shameful indignities on him and he wanted to kill Thomas in some frightful manner. (But if possible unobtrusively.)

If he had been a little Japanese boy, this would have been an entirely honourable desire. It would have been Bushido and all that sort of thing. In the gardener's stepson however it is—undesirable....

Thomas, on the other hand, having remarked the red light of revenge in Bealby's eye and being secretly afraid, felt that his honour was concerned in not relaxing his persecutions. He called him "Kicker" and when he did not answer to that name, he called him "Snorter," "Bleater," "Snooks," and finally tweaked his ear. Then he saw fit to assume that Bealby was deaf and that ear-tweaking was the only available method of address. This led on to the convention of a sign language whereby ideas were communicated to Bealby by means of painful but frequently quite ingeniously symbolical freedoms with various parts of his person. Also Thomas affected to discover uncleanliness in Bealby's head and succeeded after many difficulties in putting it into a sinkful of lukewarm water.

Meanwhile young Bealby devoted such scanty time as he could give to reflection to debating whether it is better to attack Thomas suddenly with a carving knife or throw a lighted lamp. The large pantry inkpot of pewter might be effective in its way, he thought, but he doubted whether in the event of a charge it had sufficient stopping power. He was also curiously attracted by a long two-pronged toasting-fork that hung at the side of the pantry fireplace. It had *reach*....

Over all these dark thoughts and ill-concealed emotions Mr. Mergleson prevailed, large yet speedy, speedy yet exact, parroting orders and making plump gestures, performing duties and seeing that duties were performed.

Matters came to a climax late on Saturday night at the end of a trying day, just before Mr. Mergleson went round to lock up and turn out the lights.

Thomas came into the pantry close behind Bealby, who, greatly belated through his own inefficiency, was carrying a tray of glasses from the steward's room, applied an ungentle hand to his neck, and ruffled up his back hair in a smart and painful manner. At the same time Thomas remarked, "Burrrrh!"

Bealby stood still for a moment and then put down his tray on the table and, making peculiar sounds as he did so, resorted very rapidly to the toasting fork.... He got a prong into Thomas's chin at the first prod.

How swift are the changes of the human soul! At the moment of his thrust young Bealby was a primordial savage; so soon as he saw this incredible piercing of Thomas's chin—for all the care that Bealby had taken it might just as well have been Thomas's eye—he moved swiftly through the ages and became a simple Christian child. He abandoned violence and fled.

The fork hung for a moment from the visage of Thomas like a twisted beard of brass, and then rattled on the ground.

Thomas clapped his hand to his chin and discovered blood.

"You little—!" He never found the right word (which perhaps is just as well); instead he started in pursuit of Bealby.

Bealby—in his sudden horror of his own act—and Thomas fled headlong into the passage and made straight for the service stairs that went up into a higher world. He had little time to think. Thomas with a red-smeared chin appeared in pursuit. Thomas the avenger. Thomas really roused. Bealby shot through the green baize door and the pursuing footman pulled up only just in time not to follow him.

Only just in time. He had an instinctive instant anxious fear of great dangers. He heard something, a sound as though the young of some very large animal had squeaked feebly. He had a glimpse of something black and white—and large....

Then something, some glass thing, smashed.

He steadied the green baize door which was wobbling on its brass hinges, controlled his panting breath and listened.

A low rich voice was—ejaculating. It was not Bealby's voice, it was the voice of some substantial person being quietly but deeply angry. They were the ejaculations restrained in tone but not in quality of a ripe and well-stored mind,—no boy's thin stuff.

Then very softly Thomas pushed open the door—just widely enough to see and as instantly let it fall back into place.

Very gently and yet with an alert rapidity he turned about and stole down the service stairs.

His superior officer appeared in the passage below.

"Mr. Mergleson," he cried, "I say—Mr. Mergleson."

"What's up?" said Mr. Mergleson.

"He's gone!"

"Who?"

"Bealby."

"Home?" This almost hopefully.

"No."

"Where?"

"Up there! I think he ran against somebody."

Mr. Mergleson scrutinized his subordinate's face for a second. Then he listened intently; both men listened intently.

"Have to fetch him out of that," said Mr. Mergleson, suddenly preparing for brisk activity.

Thomas bent lower over the banisters.

"*The Lord Chancellor!*" he whispered with white lips and a sideways gesture of his head.

"What about 'im?" said Mergleson, arrested by something in the manner of Thomas.

Thomas's whisper became so fine that Mr. Mergleson drew nearer to catch it and put up a hand to his ear. Thomas repeated the last remark. "He's just through there—on the landing—cursing and swearing—'orrible things— more like a mad turkey than a human being."

"Where's Bealby?"

"He must almost 'ave run into 'im," said Thomas after consideration.

"But now—where is he?"

Thomas pantomimed infinite perplexity.

Mr. Mergleson reflected and decided upon his line. He came up the service staircase, lifted his chin and with an air of meek officiousness went through the green door. There was no one now on the landing, there was nothing remarkable on the landing except a broken tumbler, but half-way up the grand staircase stood the Lord Chancellor. Under one arm the great jurist carried a soda water syphon and he grasped a decanter of whisky in his hand. He turned sharply at the sound of the green baize door and bent upon Mr. Mergleson the most terrible eyebrows that ever, surely! adorned a legal visage. He was very red in the face and savage-looking.

"Was it *you*," he said with a threatening gesture of the decanter, and his voice betrayed a noble indignation, "Was it *you* who slapped me behind?"

"Slapped you behind, me lord??"

"Slapped me *behind*. Don't I speak—plainly?"

"I—such a libbuty, me lord!"

"Idiot! I ask you a plain question—"

With almost inconceivable alacrity Mr. Mergleson rushed up three steps, leapt forward and caught the syphon as it slipped from his lordship's arm.

He caught it, but at a price. He overset and, clasping it in his hands, struck his lordship first with the syphon on the left shin and then butted him with a face that was still earnestly respectful in the knees. His lordship's legs were driven sideways, so that they were no longer beneath his centre of gravity. With a monosyllabic remark of a topographical nature his lordship collapsed upon Mr. Mergleson. The decanter flew out of his grasp and smashed presently with emphasis upon the landing below. The syphon, escaping from the wreckage of Mr. Mergleson and drawn no doubt by a natural affinity, rolled noisily from step to step in pursuit of the decanter....

It was a curious little procession that hurried down the great staircase of Shonts that night. First the whisky like a winged harbinger with the pedestrian syphon in pursuit. Then the great lawyer gripping the great butler by the tails of his coat and punching furiously. Then Mr. Mergleson trying wildly to be respectful—even in disaster. First the Lord Chancellor dived over Mr. Mergleson, grappling as he passed, then Mr. Mergleson, attempting explanations, was pulled backwards over the Lord Chancellor; then again the Lord Chancellor was for a giddy but vindictive moment uppermost; a second rotation and they reached the landing.

Bang! There was a deafening report—

CHAPTER II
A WEEK-END AT SHONTS

§ 1

The week-end visit is a form of entertainment peculiar to Great Britain. It is a thing that could have been possible only in a land essentially aristocratic and mellow, in which even the observance of the sabbath has become mellow. At every London terminus on a Saturday afternoon the outgoing trains have an unusually large proportion of first class carriages, and a peculiar abundance of rich-looking dressing-bags provoke the covetous eye. A discreet activity of valets and maids mingles with the stimulated alertness of the porters. One marks celebrities in gay raiment. There is an indefinable air of distinction upon platform and bookstall. Sometimes there are carriages reserved for especially privileged parties. There are greetings.

"And so *you* are coming too!"

"No, this time it is Shonts."

"The place where they found the Rubens. Who *has* it now?" ...

Through this cheerfully prosperous throng went the Lord Chancellor with his high nose, those eyebrows of his which he seemed to be able to furl or unfurl at will and his expression of tranquil self-sufficiency. He was going to Shonts for his party and not for his pleasure, but there was no reason why that should appear upon his face. He went along preoccupied, pretending to see nobody, leaving to others the disadvantage of the greeting. In his right hand he carried a small important bag of leather. Under his left arm he bore a philosophical work by Doctor MacTaggart, three illustrated papers, the *Fortnightly Review*, the day's *Times*, the *Hibbert Journal*, *Punch* and two blue books. His Lordship never quite knew the limits set to what he could carry under his arm. His man, Candler, followed therefore at a suitable distance with several papers that had already been dropped, alert to retrieve any further losses.

At the large bookstall they passed close by Mrs. Rampound Pilby who, according to her custom, was feigning to be a member of the general public and was asking the clerk about her last book. The Lord Chancellor saw Rampound Pilby hovering at hand and deftly failed to catch his eye. He loathed the Rampound Pilbys. He speculated for a moment what sort of people could possibly stand Mrs. Pilby's vast pretensions—even from Saturday to Monday. One dinner party on her right hand had glutted him for life. He chose a corner seat, took possession of both it and the seat opposite it in order to have somewhere to put his feet, left Candler to watch over and pack in his hand luggage and went high up the platform, remaining there with his back to the world—rather like a bigger more aquiline Napoleon—in order to evade the great novelist.

In this he was completely successful.

He returned however to find Candler on the verge of a personal conflict with a very fair young man in grey. He was so fair as to be almost an albino, except that his eyes were quick and brown; he was blushing the brightest pink and speaking very quickly.

"These two places," said Candler, breathless with the badness of his case, "are engaged."

"Oh ve-*very* well," said the very fair young man with his eyebrows and moustache looking very pale by contrast, "have it so. But do permit me to occupy the middle seat of the carriage. With a residuary interest in the semi-gentleman's place."

"You little know, young man, *whom* you are calling a semi-gentleman," said Candler, whose speciality was grammar.

"Here he is!" said the young gentleman.

"Which place will you have, my Lord?" asked Candler, abandoning his case altogether.

"Facing," said the Lord Chancellor slowly unfurling the eyebrows and scowling at the young man in grey.

"Then I'll have the other," said the very fair young man talking very glibly. He spoke with a quick low voice, like one who forces himself to keep going. "You see," he said, addressing the great jurist with the extreme familiarity of the courageously nervous, "I've gone into this sort of thing before. First, mind you, I have a far look for a vacant corner. I'm not the sort to spoil sport. But if there isn't a vacant corner I look for traces of a semi-gentleman. A semi-gentleman is one who has a soft cap and not an umbrella—his friend in the opposite seat has the umbrella—or he has an umbrella and not a soft cap, or a waterproof and not a bag, or a bag and not a waterproof. And a half interest in a rug. That's what I call a semi-gentleman. You see the idea. Sort of divided beggar. Nothing in any way offensive."

"Sir," said the Lord Chancellor, interrupting in a voice of concentrated passion, "I don't care a *rap* what you call a semi-gentleman. *Will* you get out of my way?"

"Just as you please," said the very fair young gentleman, and going a few paces from the carriage door he whistled for the boy with the papers. He was bearing up bravely.

"*Pink 'un?*" said the very fair young gentleman almost breathlessly. "*Black and White.* What's all these others? *Athenæum? Sporting and Dramatic?* Right O. And—Eh! What? Do I *look* the sort that buys a *Spectator?* You don't know! My dear boy, where's your *savoir faire?*"

§ 2

The Lord Chancellor was a philosopher and not easily perturbed. His severe manner was consciously assumed and never much more than skin-deep. He had already furled his eyebrows and dismissed his vis-a-vis from his mind before the train started. He turned over the *Hibbert Journal*, and read in it with a large tolerance.

Dimly on the outskirts of his consciousness the very fair young man hovered, as a trifling annoyance, as something pink and hot rustling a sheet of a discordant shade of pink, as something that got in the way of his legs and whistled softly some trivial cheerful air, just to show how little it cared. Presently, very soon, this vague trouble would pass out of his consciousness altogether....

The Lord Chancellor was no mere amateur of philosophy. His activities in that direction were a part of his public reputation. He lectured on religion and æsthetics. He was a fluent Hegelian. He spent his holidays, it was understood, in the Absolute—at any rate in Germany. He would sometimes break into philosophy at dinner tables and particularly over the desert and be more luminously incomprehensible while still apparently sober, than almost anyone. An article in the Hibbert caught and held his attention. It attempted to define a new and doubtful variety of Infinity. You know, of course, that there are many sorts and species of Infinity, and that the Absolute is just the king among Infinities as the lion is king among the Beasts....

"I say," said a voice coming out of the world of Relativity and coughing the cough of those who break a silence, "you aren't going to Shonts, are you?"

The Lord Chancellor returned slowly to earth.

"Just seen your label," said the very fair young man. "You see,—*I'm* going to Shonts."

The Lord Chancellor remained outwardly serene. He reflected for a moment. And then he fell into that snare which is more fatal to great lawyers and judges perhaps than to any other class of men, the snare of the crushing repartee. One had come into his head now,—a beauty.

"Then we shall meet there," he said in his suavest manner.

"Well—rather."

"It would be a great pity," said the Lord Chancellor with an effective blandness, using a kind of wry smile that he employed to make things humorous, "it would be a great pity, don't you think, to anticipate that pleasure."

And having smiled the retort well home with his head a little on one side, he resumed with large leisurely movements the reading of his *Hibbert Journal*.

"Got me there," said the very fair young man belatedly, looking boiled to a turn, and after a period of restlessness settled down to an impatient perusal of *Black and White*.

"There's a whole blessed week-end of course," the young man remarked presently without looking up from his paper and apparently pursuing some obscure meditations....

A vague uneasiness crept into the Lord Chancellor's mind as he continued to appear to peruse. Out of what train of thought could such a remark arise? His weakness for crushing retort had a little betrayed him....

It was, however, only when he found himself upon the platform of Chelsome, which as everyone knows is the station for Shonts, and discovered Mr. and Mrs. Rampound Pilby upon the platform, looking extraordinarily like a national monument and its custodian, that the Lord Chancellor, began to realize that he was in the grip of fate, and that the service he was doing his party by week-ending with the Laxtons was likely to be not simply joyless but disagreeable.

Well, anyhow, he had MacTaggart, and he could always work in his own room....

§ 3

By the end of dinner the Lord Chancellor was almost at the end of his large but clumsy endurance; he kept his eyebrows furled only by the most strenuous relaxation of his muscles, and within he was a sea of silent blasphemies. All sorts of little things had accumulated....

He exercised an unusual temperance with the port and old brandy his host pressed upon him, feeling that he dared not relax lest his rage had its way with him. The cigars were quite intelligent at any rate, and he smoked and listened with a faintly perceptible disdain to the conversation of the other men. At any rate Mrs. Rampound Pilby was out of the room. The talk had arisen out of a duologue that had preceded the departure of the ladies, a duologue of Timbre's, about apparitions and the reality of the future life. Sir Peter Laxton, released from the eyes of his wife, was at liberty to say he did not believe in all this stuff; it was just thought transference and fancy and all that sort of thing. His declaration did not arrest the flow of feeble instances and experiences into which such talk invariably degenerates. His Lordship remained carelessly attentive, his eyebrows unfurled but drooping, his cigar upward at an acute angle; he contributed no anecdotes, content now and then to express himself compactly by some brief sentence of pure Hegelian—much as a Mahometan might spit.

"Why! come to that, they say Shonts is haunted," said Sir Peter. "I suppose we could have a ghost here in no time if I chose to take it on. Rare place for a ghost, too."

The very fair young man of the train had got a name now and was Captain Douglas. When he was not blushing too brightly he was rather good looking. He was a distant cousin of Lady Laxton's. He impressed the Lord Chancellor as unabashed. He engaged people in conversation with a cheerful familiarity that excluded only the Lord Chancellor, and even at the Lord Chancellor he looked ever and again. He pricked up his ears at the mention of ghosts, and afterwards when the Lord Chancellor came to think things over, it seemed to him that he had caught a curious glance of the Captain's bright little brown eye.

"What sort of ghost, Sir Peter? Chains? Eh? No?"

"Nothing of that sort, it seems. I don't know much about it, I wasn't sufficiently interested. No, sort of spook that bangs about and does you a mischief. What's its name? Plundergeist?"

"Poltergeist," the Lord Chancellor supplied carelessly in the pause.

"Runs its hand over your hair in the dark. Taps your shoulder. All nonsense. But we don't tell the servants. Sort of thing I don't believe in. Easily explained,—what with panelling and secret passages and priests' holes and all that."

"Priests' holes!" Douglas was excited.

"Where they hid. Perfect rabbit warren. There's one going out from the drawing-room alcove. Quite a good room in its way. But you know,"—a note of wrath crept into Sir Peter's voice,—"they didn't treat me fairly about these priests' holes. I ought to have had a sketch and a plan of these priests' holes. When a chap is given possession of a place, he ought to be given possession. Well! I don't know where half of them are myself. That's not possession. Else we might refurnish them and do them up a bit. I guess they're pretty musty."

Captain Douglas spoke with his eye on the Lord Chancellor. "Sure there isn't a murdered priest in the place, Sir Peter?" he asked.

"Nothing of the sort," said Sir Peter. "I don't believe in these priests' holes. Half of 'em never had priests in 'em. It's all pretty tidy rot I expect—come to the bottom of it...."

The conversation did not get away from ghosts and secret passages until the men went to the drawing-room. If it seemed likely to do so Captain Douglas pulled it back. He seemed to delight in these silly particulars; the sillier they were the more he was delighted.

The Lord Chancellor was a little preoccupied by one of those irrational suspicions that will sometimes afflict the most intelligent of men. Why did Douglas want to know all the particulars about the Shonts ghosts? Why every now and then did he glance with that odd expression at one's face,—a glance half appealing and half amused. Amused! It was a strange fancy, but the Lord Chancellor could almost have sworn that the young man was laughing at him. At dinner he had had that feeling one has at times of being talked about; he had glanced along the table to discover the Captain and a rather plain woman, that idiot Timbre's wife she probably was, with their heads together looking up at him quite definitely and both manifestly pleased by something Douglas was telling her....

What was it Douglas had said in the train? Something like a threat. But the exact words had slipped the Lord Chancellor's memory....

The Lord Chancellor's preoccupation was just sufficient to make him a little unwary. He drifted into grappling distance of Mrs. Rampound Pilby. Her voice caught him like a lasso and drew him in.

"Well, and *how* is Lord Moggeridge now?" she asked.

What on earth is one to say to such an impertinence?

She was always like that. She spoke to a man of the calibre of Lord Bacon as though she was speaking to a schoolboy home for the holidays. She had an invincible air of knowing all through everybody. It gave rather confidence to her work than charm to her manner.

"Do you still go on with your philosophy?" she said.

"No," shouted the Lord Chancellor, losing all self-control for the moment and waving his eyebrows about madly, "no, I go *off* with it."

"For your vacations? Ah, Lord Moggeridge, how I envy you great lawyers your long vacations. *I*—never get a vacation. Always we poor authors are pursued by our creations, sometimes it's typescript, sometimes it's proofs. Not that I really complain of proofs. I confess to a weakness for proofs. Sometimes, alas! it's criticism. Such *undiscerning* criticism!..."

The Lord Chancellor began to think very swiftly of some tremendous lie that would enable him to escape at once without incivility from Lady Laxton's drawing-room. Then he perceived that Mrs. Rampound Pilby was asking him; "Is that *the* Captain Douglas, or his brother, who's in love with the actress woman?"

The Lord Chancellor made no answer. What he thought was "Great Silly Idiot! How should *I* know?"

"I think it must be *the* one,—the one who had to leave Portsmouth in disgrace because of the ragging scandal. He did nothing there, they say, but organize practical jokes. Some of them were quite subtle practical jokes. He's a cousin of our hostess; that perhaps accounts for his presence...."

The Lord Chancellor's comment betrayed the drift of his thoughts. "He'd better not try that sort of thing on here," he said. "I abominate—clowning."

Drawing-room did not last very long. Even Lady Laxton could not miss the manifest gloom of her principal guest, and after the good-nights and barley water and lemonade on the great landing Sir Peter led Lord Moggeridge by the arm—he hated being led by the arm—into the small but still spacious apartment that was called the study. The Lord Chancellor was now very thirsty; he was not used to abstinence of any sort; but Sir Peter's way of suggesting a drink roused such a fury of resentment in him that he refused tersely and conclusively. There was nobody else in the study but Captain Douglas, who seemed to hesitate upon the verge of some familiar address, and Lord Woodenhouse, who was thirsty, too, and held a vast tumbler of whisky and soda, with a tinkle of ice in it, on his knee in a way annoying to a parched man. The Lord Chancellor helped himself to a cigar and assumed the middle of the fireplace with an air of contentment, but he could feel the self-control running out of the heels of his boots.

Sir Peter, after a quite unsuccessful invasion of his own hearthrug—the Lord Chancellor stood like a rock—secured the big arm-chair, stuck his feet out towards his distinguished guest and resumed a talk that he had been holding with Lord Woodenhouse about firearms. Mergleson had as usual been too attentive to his master's glass, and the fine edge was off Sir Peter's deference. "I always have carried firearms," he said, "and I always shall. Used properly they are a great protection. Even in the country how are you to know who you're going to run up against—anywhere?"

"But you might shoot and hit something," said Douglas.

"Properly used, I said—properly used. Whipping out a revolver and shooting *at* a man, that's not properly used. Almost as bad as pointing it at him—which is pretty certain to make him fly straight at you. If he's got an ounce of pluck. But *I* said properly used and I *mean* properly used."

The Lord Chancellor tried to think about that article on Infinities, while appearing to listen to this fool's talk. He despised revolvers. Armed with such eyebrows as his it was natural for him to despise revolvers.

"Now, I've got some nice little barkers upstairs," said Sir Peter. "I'd almost welcome a burglar, just to try them."

"If you shoot a burglar," said Lord Woodenhouse abruptly, with a gust of that ill-temper that was frequent at Shonts towards bedtime, "when he's not attacking you, it's murder."

Sir Peter held up an offensively pacifying hand. "I know *that*," he said; "you needn't tell me *that*."

He raised his voice a little to increase his already excessive accentuations. "*I* said properly used."

A yawn took the Lord Chancellor unawares and he caught it dexterously with his hand. Then he saw Douglas hastily pull at his little blond moustache to conceal a smile,—grinning ape! What was there to smile at? The man had been smiling all the evening.

Up to something?

"Now let me *tell* you," said Sir Peter, "let me *tell* you the proper way to use a revolver. You whip it out and *instantly* let fly at the ground. You should never let anyone see a revolver ever before they hear it—see? You let fly at the ground first off, and the concussion stuns them. It doesn't stun you. *You* expect it, *they* don't. See? There you are—five shots left, master of the situation."

"I think, Sir Peter, I'll bid you good-night," said the Lord Chancellor, allowing his eye to rest for one covetous moment on the decanter, and struggling with the devil of pride.

Sir Peter made a gesture of extreme friendliness from his chair, expressive of the Lord Chancellor's freedom to do whatever he pleased at Shonts. "I may perhaps tell you a little story that happened once in Morocco."

"My eyes won't keep open any longer," said Captain Douglas suddenly, with a whirl of his knuckles into his sockets, and stood up.

Lord Woodenhouse stood up too.

"You see," said Sir Peter, standing also but sticking to his subject and his hearer. "This was when I was younger than I am now, you must understand, and I wasn't married. Just mooching about a bit, between business and pleasure. Under such circumstances one goes into parts of a foreign town where one wouldn't go if one was older and wiser...."

Captain Douglas left Sir Peter and Woodenhouse to it.

He emerged on the landing and selected one of the lighted candlesticks upon the table. "Lord!" he whispered. He grimaced in soliloquy and then perceived the Lord Chancellor regarding him with suspicion and disfavour from the ascending staircase. He attempted ease. For the first time since the train incident he addressed Lord Moggeridge.

"I gather, my lord,—don't believe in ghosts?" he said.

"No, Sir," said the Lord Chancellor, "I don't."

"They won't trouble me to-night."

"They won't trouble any of us."

"Fine old house anyhow," said Captain Douglas.

The Lord Chancellor disdained to reply. He went on his way upstairs.

§ 4

When the Lord Chancellor sat down before the thoughtful fire in the fine old panelled room assigned to him he perceived that he was too disturbed to sleep. This was going to be an infernal week-end. The worst week-end he had ever had. Mrs. Rampound Pilby maddened him; Timbre, who was a Pragmatist—which stands in the same relation to a Hegelian that a small dog does to a large cat—exasperated him; he loathed Laxton, detested Rampound Pilby and feared—as far as he was capable of fearing anything—Captain Douglas. There was no refuge, no soul in the house to whom he could turn for consolation and protection from these others. Slinker Bond could talk only of the affairs of the party, and the Lord Chancellor, being Lord Chancellor, had long since lost any interest in the affairs of the party; Woodenhouse could talk of nothing. The women were astonishingly negligible. There were practically no pretty women. There ought always to be pretty young women for a Lord Chancellor, pretty *young* women who can at least seem to listen....

And he was atrociously thirsty.

His room was supplied only with water,—stuff you use to clean your teeth—and nothing else....

No good thinking about it....

He decided that the best thing he could do to compose himself before turning in would be to sit down at the writing-table and write a few sheets of Hegelian—about that Infinity article in the Hibbert. There is indeed no better consolation for a troubled mind than the Hegelian exercises; they lift it above—everything. He took off his coat and sat down to this beautiful amusement, but he had scarcely written a page before his thirst became a torment. He kept thinking of that great tumbler Woodenhouse had held,—sparkling, golden, cool—and stimulating.

What he wanted was a good stiff whisky and a cigar, one of Laxton's cigars, the only good thing in his entertainment so far.

And then Philosophy.

Even as a student he had been a worker of the Teutonic type,—never abstemious.

He thought of ringing and demanding these comforts, and then it occurred to him that it was a little late to ring for things. Why not fetch them from the study himself?...

He opened his door and looked out upon the great staircase. It was a fine piece of work, that staircase. Low, broad, dignified....

There seemed to be nobody about. The lights were still on. He listened for a little while, and then put on his coat and went with a soft swiftness that was still quite dignified downstairs to the study, the study redolent of Sir Peter.

He made his modest collection.

Lord Moggeridge came nearer to satisfaction as he emerged from the study that night at Shonts than at any other moment during this ill-advised week-end. In his pocket were four thoroughly good cigars. In one hand he held a cut glass decanter of whisky. In the other a capacious tumbler. Under his arm, with that confidence in the unlimited portative power of his arm that nothing could shake, he had tucked the syphon. His soul rested upon the edge of tranquillity like a bird that has escaped the fowler. He was already composing his next sentence about that new variety of Infinity....

Then something struck him from behind and impelled him forward a couple of paces. It was something hairy, something in the nature, he thought afterwards, of a worn broom. And also there were two other things softer and a little higher on each side....

Then it was he made that noise like the young of some large animal.

He dropped the glass in a hasty attempt to save the syphon....

"What in the name of Heaven—?" he cried, and found himself alone.

"Captain Douglas!"

The thought leapt to his mind.

But indeed, it was not Captain Douglas. It was Bealby. Bealby in panic flight from Thomas. And how was Bealby to know that this large, richly laden man was the Lord Chancellor of England? Never before had Bealby seen anyone in evening dress except a butler, and so he supposed this was just some larger, finer kind of butler that they kept upstairs. Some larger, finer kind of butler blocking the path of escape. Bealby had taken in the situation with the rapidity of a hunted animal. The massive form blocked the door to the left....

In the playground of the village school Bealby had been preëminent for his dodging; he moved as quickly as a lizard. His little hands, his head, poised with the skill of a practised butter, came against that mighty back, and then Bealby had dodged into the study....

But it seemed to Lord Moggeridge, staggering over his broken glass and circling about defensively, that this fearful indignity could come only from Captain Douglas. Foolery.... Blup, blup.... Sham Poltergeist. Imbeciles....

He said as much, believing that this young man and possibly confederates were within hearing; he said as much—hotly. He went on to remark of an unphilosophical tendency about Captain Douglas generally, and about army officers, practical joking, Laxton's hospitalities, Shonts.... Thomas, you will remember, heard him....

Nothing came of it. No answer, not a word of apology.

At last in a great dudgeon and with a kind of wariness about his back, the Lord Chancellor, with things more spoilt for him than ever, went on his way upstairs.

When the green baize door opened behind him, he turned like a shot, and a large foolish-faced butler appeared. Lord Moggeridge, with a sceptre-like motion of the decanter, very quietly and firmly asked him a simple question and then, then the lunatic must needs leap up three stairs and dive suddenly and upsettingly at his legs.

Lord Moggeridge was paralyzed with amazement. His legs were struck from under him. He uttered one brief topographical cry.

(To Sir Peter unfortunately it sounded like "Help!")

For a few seconds the impressions that rushed upon Lord Moggeridge were too rapid for adequate examination. He had a compelling fancy to kill butlers. Things culminated in a pistol shot. And then he found himself sitting on the landing beside a disgracefully dishevelled manservant, and his host was running downstairs to them with a revolver in his hand.

On occasion Lord Moggeridge could produce a tremendous voice. He did so now. For a moment he stared panting at Sir Peter, and then emphasized by a pointing finger came the voice. Never had it been so charged with emotion.

"What does this *mean*, you, Sir?" he shouted. "What does this mean?"

It was exactly what Sir Peter had intended to say.

§ 5

Explanations are detestable things.

And anyhow it isn't right to address your host as "You, Sir."

§ 6

Throughout the evening the persuasion had grown in Lady Laxton's mind that all was not going well with the Lord Chancellor. It was impossible to believe he was enjoying himself. But she did not know how to give things a turn for the better. Clever women would have known, but she was so convinced she was not clever that she did not even try.

Thing after thing had gone wrong.

How was she to know that there were two sorts of philosophy,—quite different? She had thought philosophy was philosophy. But it seemed that there were these two sorts, if not more; a round large sort that talked about the Absolute and was scornfully superior and rather irascible, and a jabby-pointed sort that called people "Tender" or "Tough," and was generally much too familiar. To bring them together was just mixing trouble. There ought to be little books for hostesses explaining these things....

Then it was extraordinary that the Lord Chancellor, who was so tremendously large and clever, wouldn't go and talk to Mrs. Rampound Pilby, who was also so tremendously large and clever. Repeatedly Lady Laxton had tried to get them into touch with one another. Until at last the Lord Chancellor had said distinctly and deliberately, when she had suggested his going across to the eminent writer, "God forbid!" Her dream of a large clever duologue that she could afterwards recall with pleasure was altogether shattered. She thought the Lord Chancellor uncommonly hard to please. These weren't the only people for him. Why couldn't he chat party secrets with Slinker Bond or say things to Lord Woodenhouse? You could say anything you liked to Lord Woodenhouse. Or talk with Mr. Timbre. Mrs. Timbre had given him an excellent opening; she had asked, "Wasn't it a dreadful anxiety always to have the Great Seal to mind?" He had simply *grunted*.... And then why did he keep on looking so *dangerously* at Captain Douglas?...

Perhaps to-morrow things would take a turn for the better....

One can at least be hopeful. Even if one is not *clever* one can be that....

From such thoughts as these it was that this unhappy hostess was roused by a sound of smashing glass, a rumpus, and a pistol shot.

She stood up, she laid her hand on her heart, she said "*Oh!*" and gripped her dressing-table for support....

After a long time and when it seemed that it was now nothing more than a hubbub of voices, in which her husband's could be distinguished clearly, she crept out very softly upon the upper landing.

She perceived her cousin, Captain Douglas, looking extremely fair and frail and untrustworthy in a much too gorgeous kimono dressing-gown of embroidered Japanese silk. "I can assure you, my lord," he was saying in a strange high-pitched deliberate voice, "on—my—word—of—honour—as—a—soldier, that I know absolutely nothing about it."

"Sure it wasn't all imagination, my lord?" Sir Peter asked with his inevitable infelicity....

She decided to lean over the balustrading and ask very quietly and clearly:

"Lord Moggeridge, please! is anything the matter?"

§ 6

All human beings are egotists, but there is no egotism to compare with the egotism of the very young.

Bealby was so much the centre of his world that he was incapable of any interpretation of this shouting and uproar, this smashing of decanters and firing of pistol shots, except in reference to himself. He supposed it to be a Hue and Cry. He supposed that he was being hunted—hunted by a pack of great butlers hounded on by the irreparably injured Thomas. The thought of upstairs gentlefolks passed quite out of his mind. He snatched up a faked Syrian dagger that lay, in the capacity of a paper knife, on the study table, concealed himself under the chintz valance of a sofa, adjusted its rumpled skirts neatly, and awaited the issue of events.

For a time events did not issue. They remained talking noisily upon the great staircase. Bealby could not hear what was said, but most of what was said appeared to be flat contradiction.

"Perchance," whispered Bealby to himself, gathering courage, "perchance we have eluded them.... A breathing space...."

At last a woman's voice mingled with the others and seemed a little to assuage them....

Then it seemed to Bealby that they were dispersing to beat the house for him. "Good-night *again* then," said someone.

That puzzled him, but he decided it was a "blind." He remained very, very still.

He heard a clicking in the apartment—the blue parlour it was called—between the study and the dining-room. Electric light?

Then some one came into the study. Bealby's eye was as close to the ground as he could get it. He was breathless, he moved his head with an immense circumspection. The valance was translucent but not transparent, below it there was a crack of vision, a strip of carpet, the castors of chairs. Among these things he perceived feet—not ankles, it did not go up to that, but just feet. Large flattish feet. A pair. They stood still, and Bealby's hand lighted on the hilt of his dagger.

The person above the feet seemed to be surveying the room or reflecting.

"Drunk!... Old fool's either drunk or mad! That's about the truth of it," said a voice.

Mergleson! Angry, but parroty and unmistakable.

The feet went across to the table and there were faint sounds of refreshment, discreetly administered. Then a moment of profound stillness....

"Ah!" said the voice at last, a voice renewed.

Then the feet went to the passage door, halted in the doorway. There was a double click. The lights went out. Bealby was in absolute darkness.

Then a distant door closed and silence followed upon the dark....

Mr. Mergleson descended to a pantry ablaze with curiosity.

"The Lord Chancellor's going dotty," said Mr. Mergleson, replying to the inevitable question. "*That's* what's up." ...

"I tried to save the blessed syphon," said Mr. Mergleson, pursuing his narrative, "and 'e sprang on me like a leppard. I suppose 'e thought I wanted to take it away from 'im. 'E'd broke a glass already. '*Ow*,—I *don't* know. There it was, lying on the landing...."

"'Ere's where 'e bit my 'and," said Mr. Mergleson....

A curious little side-issue occurred to Thomas. "Where's young Kicker all this time?" he asked.

"Lord!" said Mr. Mergleson, "all them other things; they clean drove 'im out of my 'ed. I suppose 'e's up there, hiding somewhere...."

He paused. His eye consulted the eye of Thomas.

"'E's got behind a curtain or something," said Mr. Mergleson....

"Queer where 'e can 'ave got to," said Mr. Mergleson....

"Can't be bothered about 'im," said Mr. Mergleson.

"I expect he'll sneak down to 'is room when things are quiet," said Thomas, after reflection.

"No good going and looking for 'im now," said Mr. Mergleson. "Things upstairs,—they *got* to settle down...."

But in the small hours Mr. Mergleson awakened and thought of Bealby and wondered whether he was in bed. This became so great an uneasiness that about the hour of dawn he got up and went along the passage to Bealby's compartment. Bealby was not there and his bed had not been slept in.

That sinister sense of gathering misfortunes which comes to all of us at times in the small hours, was so strong in the mind of Mr. Mergleson that he went on and told Thomas of this disconcerting fact. Thomas woke with difficulty and rather crossly, but sat up at last, alive to the gravity of Mr. Mergleson's mood.

"If 'e's found hiding about upstairs after all this upset," said Mr. Mergleson, and left the rest of the sentence to a sympathetic imagination.

"Now it's light," said Mr. Mergleson after a slight pause, "I think we better just go round and 'ave a look for 'im. Both of us."

So Thomas clad himself provisionally, and the two man-servants went upstairs very softly and began a series of furtive sweeping movements—very much in the spirit of Lord Kitchener's historical sweeping movements in the Transvaal—through the stately old rooms in which Bealby must be lurking....

§ 8

Man is the most restless of animals. There is an incessant urgency in his nature. He never knows when he is well off. And so it was that Bealby's comparative security under the sofa became presently too irksome to be endured. He seemed to himself to stay there for ages, but as a matter of fact, he stayed there only twenty minutes. Then with eyes tempered to the darkness he first struck out an alert attentive head, then crept out and remained for the space of half a minute on all fours surveying the indistinct blacknesses about him.

Then he knelt up. Then he stood up. Then with arms extended and cautious steps he began an exploration of the apartment.

The passion for exploration grows with what it feeds upon. Presently Bealby was feeling his way into the blue parlour and then round by its shuttered and curtained windows to the dining-room. His head was now full of the idea of some shelter, more permanent, less pervious to housemaids, than that sofa. He knew enough now of domestic routines to know that upstairs in the early morning was much routed by housemaids. He found many perplexing turns and corners, and finally got into the dining-room fireplace where it was very dark and kicked against some fire-irons. That made his heart beat fast for a time. Then groping on past it, he found in the darkness what few people could have found in the day, the stud that released the panel that hid the opening of the way that led to the priest hole. He felt the thing open, and halted perplexed. In that corner there wasn't a ray of light. For a long time he was trying to think what this opening could be, and then he concluded it was some sort of back way from downstairs.... Well, anyhow it was all exploring. With an extreme gingerliness he got himself through the panel. He closed it almost completely behind him.

Careful investigation brought him to the view that he was in a narrow passage of brick or stone that came in a score of paces to a spiral staircase going both up and down. Up this he went, and presently breathed cool night air and had a glimpse of stars through a narrow slit-like window almost blocked by ivy. Then—what was very disagreeable—something scampered.

When Bealby's heart recovered he went on up again.

He came to the priest hole, a capacious cell six feet square with a bench bed and a little table and chair. It had a small door upon the stairs that was open and a niche cupboard. Here he remained for a time. Then restlessness made him explore a cramped passage, he had to crawl along it for some yards, that came presently into a curious space with wood on one side and stone on the other. Then ahead, most blessed thing! he saw light.

He went blundering toward it and then stopped appalled. From the other side of this wooden wall to the right of him had come a voice.

"Come in!" said the voice. A rich masculine voice that seemed scarcely two yards away.

Bealby became rigid. Then after a long interval he moved—as softly as he could.

The voice soliloquized.

Bealby listened intently, and then when all was still again crept forward two paces more towards the gleam. It was a peephole.

The unseen speaker was walking about. Bealby listened, and the sound of his beating heart mingled with the pad, pad, of slippered footsteps. Then with a brilliant effort his eye was at the chink. All was still again. For a time he was perplexed by what he saw, a large pink shining dome, against a deep greenish grey background. At the base of the dome was a kind of interrupted hedge, brown and leafless....

Then he realized that he was looking at the top of a head and two enormous eyebrows. The rest was hidden....

Nature surprised Bealby into a penetrating sniff.

"Now," said the occupant of the room, and suddenly he was standing up—Bealby saw a long hairy neck sticking out of a dressing-gown—and walking to the side of the room. "I won't stand it," said the great voice, "I won't stand it. Ape's foolery!"

Then the Lord Chancellor began rapping at the panelling about his apartment.

"Hollow! It all sounds hollow."

Only after a long interval did he resume his writing....

All night long that rat behind the wainscot troubled the Lord Chancellor. Whenever he spoke, whenever he moved about, it was still; whenever he composed himself to write it began to rustle and blunder. Again and again it sniffed,—an annoying kind of sniff. At last the Lord Chancellor gave up his philosophical relaxation and went to bed, turned out the lights and attempted sleep, but this only intensified his sense of an uneasy, sniffing presence close to him. When the light was out it seemed to him that this Thing, whatever it was, instantly came into the room and set the floor creaking and snapping. A Thing perpetually attempting something and perpetually thwarted....

The Lord Chancellor did not sleep a wink. The first feeble infiltration of day found him sitting up in bed, wearily wrathful.... And now surely someone was going along the passage outside!

A great desire to hurt somebody very much seized upon the Lord Chancellor. Perhaps he might hurt that dismal *farceur* upon the landing! No doubt it was Douglas sneaking back to his own room after the night's efforts.

The Lord Chancellor slipped on his dressing-gown of purple silk. Very softly indeed did he open his bedroom door and very warily peep out. He heard the soft pad of feet upon the staircase.

He crept across the broad passage to the beautiful old balustrading. Down below he saw Mergleson—Mergleson again!—in a shameful deshabille—going like a snake, like a slinking cat, like an assassin, into the door of the study. Rage filled the great man's soul. Gathering up the skirts of his dressing-gown he started in a swift yet noiseless pursuit.

He followed Mergleson through the little parlour and into the dining-room, and then he saw it all! There was a panel open, and Mergleson very cautiously going in. Of course! They had got at him through the priest hole. They had been playing on his nerves. All night they had been doing it—no doubt in relays. The whole house was in this conspiracy.

With his eyebrows spread like the wings of a fighting cock the Lord Chancellor in five vast noiseless strides had crossed the intervening space and gripped the butler by his collarless shirt as he was disappearing. It was like a hawk striking a sparrow. Mergleson felt himself clutched, glanced over his shoulder and, seeing that fierce familiar face again close to his own, pitiless, vindictive, lost all sense of human dignity and yelled like a lost soul....

§ 9

Sir Peter Laxton was awakened from an uneasy sleep by the opening of the dressing-room door that connected his room with his wife's.

He sat up astonished and stared at her white face, its pallor exaggerated by the cold light of dawn.

"Peter," she said, "I'm sure there's something more going on."

"Something more going on?"

"Something—shouting and swearing."

"You don't mean—?"

She nodded. "The Lord Chancellor," she said, in an awe-stricken whisper. "He's at it again. Downstairs in the dining-room."

Sir Peter seemed disposed at first to receive this quite passively. Then he flashed into extravagant wrath. "I'm *damned*," he cried, jumping violently out of bed, "if I'm going to stand this! Not if he was a hundred Lord Chancellors! He's turning the place into a bally lunatic asylum. *Once*—one might excuse. But to start in again.... *What's that?*"

They both stood still listening. Faintly yet quite distinctly came the agonized cry of some imperfectly educated person,—"'Elp!"

"Here! Where's my trousers?" cried Sir Peter. "He's murdering Mergleson. There isn't a moment to lose."

§ 10

Until Sir Peter returned Lady Laxton sat quite still just as he had left her on his bed, aghast.

She could not even pray.

The sun had still to rise; the room was full of that cold weak inky light, light without warmth, knowledge without faith, existence without courage, that creeps in before the day. She waited.... In such a mood women have waited for massacre....

Downstairs a raucous shouting....

She thought of her happy childhood upon the Yorkshire wolds, before the idea of week-end parties had entered her mind. The heather. The little birds. Kind things. A tear ran down her cheek....

§ 11

Then Sir Peter stood before her again, alive still, but breathless and greatly ruffled.

She put her hands to her heart. She would be brave.

"Yes," she said. "Tell me."

"He's as mad as a hatter," said Sir Peter.

She nodded for more. She knew that.

"Has he—*killed* anyone?" she whispered.

"He looked uncommonly like trying," said Sir Peter.

She nodded, her lips tightly compressed.

"Says Douglas will either have to leave the house or he does."

"But—Douglas!"

"I know, but he won't hear a word."

"But *why* Douglas?"

"I tell you he's as mad as a hatter. Got persecution mania. People tapping and bells ringing under his pillow all night—that sort of idea.... And furious. I tell you,—he frightened me. He was *awful*. He's given Mergleson a black eye. Hit him, you know. With his fist. Caught him in the passage to the priest hole—how they got there *I* don't know—and went for him like a madman."

"But what has Douglas done?"

"I know. I asked him, but he won't listen. He's just off his head.... Says Douglas has got the whole household trying to work a ghost on him. I tell you—he's off his nut."

Husband and wife looked at each other....

"Of course if Douglas didn't mind just going off to oblige me," said Sir Peter at last....

"It might calm him," he explained.... "You see, it's all so infernally awkward...."

"Is he back in his room?"

"Yes. Waiting for me to decide about Douglas. Walking up and down."

For a little while their minds remained prostrate and inactive.

"I'd been so looking forward to the lunch," she said with a joyless smile. "The county—"

She could not go on.

"You know," said Sir Peter, "one thing,—I'll see to it myself. I won't have him have a single drop of liquor more. If we have to search his room."

"What I shall say to him at breakfast," she said, "I don't know."

Sir Peter reflected. "There's no earthly reason why you should be brought into it at all. Your line is to know nothing about it. *Show* him you know nothing about it. Ask him—ask him if he's had a good night...."

CHAPTER III
THE WANDERERS

§ 1

Never had the gracious eastward face of Shonts looked more beautiful than it did on the morning of the Lord Chancellor's visit. It glowed as translucent as amber lit by flames, its two towers were pillars of pale gold. It looked over its slopes and parapets upon a great valley of mist-barred freshness through which the distant river shone like a snake of light. The south-west façade was still in the shadow, and the ivy hung from it darkly greener than the greenest green. The stained-glass windows of the old chapel reflected the sunrise as though lamps were burning inside. Along the terrace a pensive peacock trailed his sheathed splendours through the dew.

Amidst the ivy was a fuss of birds.

And presently there was pushed out from amidst the ivy at the foot of the eastward tower a little brownish buff thing, that seemed as natural there as a squirrel or a rabbit. It was a head,—a ruffled human head. It remained still for a moment contemplating the calm spaciousness of terrace and garden and countryside. Then it emerged further and rotated and surveyed the house above it. Its expression was one of alert caution. Its natural freshness and innocence were a little marred by an enormous transverse smudge, a bar-sinister of smut, and the elfin delicacy of the left ear was festooned with a cobweb—probably a genuine antique. It was the face of Bealby.

He was considering the advisability of leaving Shonts—for good.

Presently his decision was made. His hands and shoulders appeared following his head, and then a dusty but undamaged Bealby was running swiftly towards the corner of the shrubbery. He crouched lest at any moment that pursuing pack of butlers should see him and give tongue. In another moment he was hidden from the house altogether, and rustling his way through a thicket of budding rhododendra. After those dirty passages the morning air was wonderfully sweet—but just a trifle hungry.

Grazing deer saw Bealby fly across the park, stared at him for a time with great gentle unintelligent eyes, and went on feeding.

They saw him stop ever and again. He was snatching at mushrooms, that he devoured forthwith as he sped on.

On the edge of the beech-woods he paused and glanced back at Shonts.

Then his eyes rested for a moment on the clump of trees through which one saw a scrap of the head gardener's cottage, a bit of the garden wall....

A physiognomist might have detected a certain lack of self-confidence in Bealby's eyes.

But his spirit was not to be quelled. Slowly, joylessly perhaps, but with a grave determination, he raised his hand in that prehistoric gesture of the hand and face by which youth, since ever there was youth, has asserted the integrity of its soul against established and predominant things.

"*Ketch* me!" said Bealby.

§ 2

Bealby left Shonts about half-past four in the morning. He went westward because he liked the company of his shadow and was amused at first by its vast length. By half-past eight he had covered ten miles, and he was rather bored by his shadow. He had eaten nine raw mushrooms, two green apples and a quantity of unripe blackberries. None of these things seemed quite at home in him. And he had discovered himself to be wearing slippers. They were stout carpet slippers, but still they were slippers,—and the road was telling on them. At the ninth mile the left one began to give on the outer seam. He got over a stile into a path that ran through the corner of a wood, and there he met a smell of frying bacon that turned his very soul to gastric juice.

He stopped short and sniffed the air—and the air itself was sizzling.

"Oh, Krikey," said Bealby, manifestly to the Spirit of the World. "This is a bit too strong. I wasn't thinking much before."

Then he saw something bright yellow and bulky just over the hedge.

From this it was that the sound of frying came.

He went to the hedge, making no effort to conceal himself. Outside a great yellow caravan with dainty little windows stood a largish dark woman in a deerstalker hat, a short brown skirt, a large white apron and spatterdashes (among other things), frying bacon and potatoes in a frying pan. She was very red in the face, and the frying pan was spitting at her as frying pans do at a timid cook....

Quite mechanically Bealby scrambled through the hedge and drew nearer this divine smell. The woman scrutinized him for a moment, and then blinking and averting her face went on with her cookery.

Bealby came quite close to her and remained, noting the bits of potato that swam about in the pan, the jolly curling of the rashers, the dancing of the bubbles, the hymning splash and splutter of the happy fat....

(If it should ever fall to my lot to be cooked, may I be fried in potatoes and butter. May I be fried with potatoes and good butter made from the milk of the cow. God send I am spared boiling; the prison of the pot, the rattling lid, the evil darkness, the greasy water....)

"I suppose," said the lady prodding with her fork at the bacon, "I suppose you call yourself a Boy."

"Yes, miss," said Bealby.

"Have you ever fried?"

"I could, miss."

"Like this?"

"Better"

"Just lay hold of this handle—for it's scorching the skin off my face I am." She seemed to think for a moment and added, "entirely."

In silence Bealby grasped that exquisite smell by the handle, he took the fork from her hand and put his hungry eager nose over the seething mess. It wasn't only bacon; there were onions, onions giving it—an *edge*! It cut to the quick of appetite. He could have wept with the intensity of his sensations.

A voice almost as delicious as the smell came out of the caravan window behind Bealby's head.

"*Ju*-dy!" cried the voice.

"Here!—I mean,—it's here I am," said the lady in the deerstalker.

"Judy—you didn't take my stockings for your own by any chance?"

The lady in the deerstalker gave way to delighted horror. "Sssh, Mavourneen!" she cried—she was one of that large class of amiable women who are more Irish than they need be—"there's a Boy here!"

§ 3

There was indeed an almost obsequiously industrious and obliging Boy. An hour later he was no longer a Boy but *the* Boy, and three friendly women were regarding him with a merited approval.

He had done the frying, renewed a waning fire with remarkable skill and dispatch, reboiled a neglected kettle in the shortest possible time, laid almost without direction a simple meal, very exactly set out campstools and cleaned the frying pan marvellously. Hardly had they taken their portions of that appetizing savouriness, than he had whipped off with that implement, gone behind the caravan, busied himself there, and returned with the pan—

glittering bright. Himself if possible brighter. One cheek indeed shone with an animated glow.

"But wasn't there some of the bacon and stuff left?" asked the lady in the deerstalker.

"I didn't think it was wanted, Miss," said Bealby. "So I cleared it up."

He met understanding in her eye. He questioned her expression.

"Mayn't I wash up for you, miss?" he asked to relieve the tension.

He washed up, swiftly and cleanly. He had never been able to wash up to Mr. Mergleson's satisfaction before, but now he did everything Mr. Mergleson had ever told him. He asked where to put the things away and he put them away. Then he asked politely if there was anything else he could do for them. Questioned, he said he liked doing things. "You haven't," said the lady in the deerstalker, "a taste for cleaning boots?"

Bealby declared he had.

"Surely," said a voice that Bealby adored, "'tis an angel from heaven."

He had a taste for cleaning boots! This was an extraordinary thing for Bealby to say. But a great change had come to him in the last half-hour. He was violently anxious to do things, any sort of things, servile things, for a particular person. He was in love.

The owner of the beautiful voice had come out of the caravan, she had stood for a moment in the doorway before descending the steps to the ground and the soul of Bealby had bowed down before her in instant submission. Never had he seen anything so lovely. Her straight slender body was sheathed in blue; fair hair, a little tinged with red, poured gloriously back from her broad forehead, and she had the sweetest eyes in the world. One hand lifted her dress from her feet; the other rested on the lintel of the caravan door. She looked at him and smiled.

So for two years she had looked and smiled across the footlights to the Bealby in mankind. She had smiled now on her entrance out of habit. She took the effect upon Bealby as a foregone conclusion.

Then she had looked to make sure that everything was ready before she descended.

"How good it smells, Judy!" she had said.

"I've had a helper," said the woman who wore spats.

That time the blue-eyed lady had smiled at him quite definitely....

The third member of the party had appeared unobserved; the irradiations of the beautiful lady had obscured her. Bealby discovered her about. She was bareheaded; she wore a simple grey dress with a Norfolk jacket, and she had a pretty clear white profile under black hair. She answered to the name of "Winnie." The beautiful lady was Madeleine. They made little obscure jokes with each other and praised the morning ardently. "This is the best place of all," said Madeleine.

"All night," said Winnie, "not a single mosquito."

None of these three ladies made any attempt to conceal the sincerity of their hunger or their appreciation of Bealby's assistance. How good a thing is appreciation! Here he was doing, with joy and pride and an eager excellence, the very services he had done so badly under the cuffings of Mergleson and Thomas....

§ 4

And now Bealby, having been regarded with approval for some moments and discussed in tantalizing undertones, was called upon to explain himself.

"Boy," said the lady in the deerstalker, who was evidently the leader and still more evidently the spokeswoman of the party, "come here."

"Yes, miss." He put down the boot he was cleaning on the caravan step.

"In the first place, know by these presents, I am a married woman."

"Yes, miss."

"And miss is not a seemly mode of address for me."

"No, miss. I mean—" Bealby hung for a moment and by the happiest of accidents, a scrap of his instruction at Shonts came up in his mind. "No," he said, "your—ladyship."

A great light shone on the spokeswoman's face. "Not yet, my child," she said, "not yet. He hasn't done his duty by me. I am—a simple Mum."

Bealby was intelligently silent.

"Say—Yes, Mum."

"Yes, Mum," said Bealby and everybody laughed very agreeably.

"And now," said the lady, taking pleasure in her words, "know by these presents—By the bye, what is your name?"

Bealby scarcely hesitated. "Dick Mal-travers, Mum," he said and almost added, "The Dauntless Daredevil of the Diamond-fields Horse," which was the second title.

"Dick will do," said the lady who was called Judy, and added suddenly and very amusingly: "You may keep the rest."

(These were the sort of people Bealby liked. The *right* sort.)

"Well, Dick, we want to know, have you ever been in service?"

It was sudden. But Bealby was equal to it. "Only for a day or two, miss—I mean, Mum,—just to be useful."

"*Were* you useful?"

Bealby tried to think whether he had been, and could recall nothing but the face of Thomas with the fork hanging from it. "I did my best, Mum," he said impartially.

"And all that is over?"

"Yes, Mum."

"And you're at home again and out of employment?"

"Yes, Mum."

"Do you live near here?"

"No—leastways, not very far."

"With your father."

"Stepfather, Mum. I'm a Norfan."

"Well, how would you like to come with us for a few days and help with things? Seven-and-sixpence a week."

Bealby's face was eloquent.

"Would your stepfather object?"

Bealby considered. "I don't think he would," he said.

"You'd better go round and ask him."

"I—suppose—yes," he said.

"And get a few things."

"Things, Mum?"

"Collars and things. You needn't bring a great box for such a little while."

"Yes, Mum...."

He hovered rather undecidedly.

"Better run along now. Our man and horse will be coming presently. We shan't be able to wait for you long...."

Bealby assumed a sudden briskness and departed.

At the gate of the field he hesitated almost imperceptibly and then directed his face to the Sabbath stillness of the village.

Perplexity corrugated his features. The stepfather's permission presented no difficulties, but it was more difficult about the luggage.

A voice called after him.

"Yes, Mum?" he said attentive and hopeful. Perhaps—somehow—they wouldn't want luggage.

"You'll want Boots. You'll have to walk by the caravan, you know. You'll want some good stout Boots."

"All right, Mum," he said with a sorrowful break in his voice. He waited a few moments but nothing more came. He went on—very slowly. He had forgotten about the boots.

That defeated him....

It is hard to be refused admission to Paradise for the want of a hand-bag and a pair of walking-boots....

§ 5

Bealby was by no means certain that he was going back to that caravan. He wanted to do so quite painfully, but—

He'd just look a fool going back without boots and—nothing on earth would reconcile him to the idea of looking a fool in the eyes of that beautiful woman in blue.

"Dick," he whispered to himself despondently, "Daredevil Dick!" (A more miserable-looking face you never set eyes on.) "It's all up with your little schemes, Dick, my boy. You *must* get a bag—and nothing on earth will get you a bag."

He paid little heed to the village through which he wandered. He knew there were no bags there. Chance rather than any volition of his own guided him down a side path that led to the nearly dry bed of a little rivulet, and there he sat down on some weedy grass under a group of willows. It was an untidy place that needed all the sunshine of the morning to be tolerable; one of those places where stinging nettles take heart and people throw old kettles, broken gallipots, jaded gravel, grass cuttings, rusty rubbish, old boots—.

For a time Bealby's eyes rested on the objects with an entire lack of interest.

Then he was reminded of his not so very remote childhood when he had found an old boot and made it into a castle....

Presently he got up and walked across to the rubbish heap and surveyed its treasures with a quickened intelligence. He picked up a widowed boot and weighed it in his hand.

He dropped it abruptly, turned about and hurried back into the village street.

He had ideas, two ideas, one for the luggage and one for the boots.... If only he could manage it. Hope beat his great pinions in the heart of Bealby.

Sunday! The shops were shut. Yes, that was a fresh obstacle. He'd forgotten that.

The public-house stood bashfully open, the shy uninviting openness of Sunday morning before closing time, but public-houses, alas! at all hours are forbidden to little boys. And besides he wasn't likely to get what he wanted in a public-house; he wanted a shop, a general shop. And here before him was the general shop—and its door ajar! His desire carried him over the threshold. The Sabbatical shutters made the place dark and cool, and the smell of bacon and cheese and chandleries, the very spirit of grocery, calm and unhurried, was cool and Sabbatical, too, as if it sat there for the day in its best clothes. And a pleasant woman was talking over the counter to a thin and worried one who carried a bundle.

Their intercourse had a flavour of emergency, and they both stopped abruptly at the appearance of Bealby.

His desire, his craving was now so great that it had altogether subdued the natural wiriness of his appearance. He looked meek, he looked good, he was swimming in propitiation and tender with respect. He produced an effect of being much smaller. He had got nice eyes. His movements were refined and his manners perfect.

"Not doing business to-day, my boy," said the pleasant woman.

"Oh, *please* 'm," he said from his heart.

"Sunday, you know."

"Oh, *please* 'm. If you could just give me a nold sheet of paper 'm, please."

"What for?" asked the pleasant woman.

"Just to wrap something up 'm."

She reflected, and natural goodness had its way with her.

"A nice *big* bit?" said the woman.

"Please 'm."

"Would you like it brown?"

"Oh, *please* 'm."

"And you got some string??

"Only cottony stuff," said Bealby, disembowelling a trouser pocket. "Wiv knots. But I dessay I can manage."

"You'd better have a bit of good string with it, my dear," said the pleasant woman, whose generosity was now fairly on the run, "Then you can do your parcel up nice and tidy...."

§ 6

The white horse was already in the shafts of the caravan, and William, a deaf and clumsy man of uncertain age and a vast sharp nosiness, was lifting in the basket of breakfast gear and grumbling in undertones at the wickedness and unfairness of travelling on Sunday, when Bealby returned to gladden three waiting women.

"Ah!" said the inconspicuous lady, "I knew he'd come."

"Look at his poor little precious parsivel," said the actress.

Regarded as luggage it was rather pitiful; a knobby, brown paper parcel about the size—to be perfectly frank—of a tin can, two old boots and some grass, very carefully folded and tied up,—and carried gingerly.

"But—" the lady in the deerstalker began, and then paused.

"Dick," she said, as he came nearer, "where's your boots?"

"Oh please, Mum," said the dauntless one, "they was away being mended. My stepfather thought perhaps you wouldn't mind if I didn't have boots. He said perhaps I might be able to get some more boots out of my salary...."

The lady in the deerstalker looked alarmingly uncertain and Bealby controlled infinite distresses.

"Haven't you got a mother, Dick?" asked the beautiful voice suddenly. Its owner abounded in such spasmodic curiosities.

"She—last year...." Matricide is a painful business at any time. And just as you see, in spite of every effort you have made, the jolliest lark in the world slipping out of your reach. And the sweet voice so sorry for him! So sorry!

Bealby suddenly veiled his face with his elbow and gave way to honourable tears....

A simultaneous desire to make him happy, help him to forget his loss, possessed three women....

"That'll be all right, Dick," said the lady in the deerstalker, patting his shoulder. "We'll get you some boots to-morrow. And to-day you must sit up beside William and spare your feet. You'll have to go to the inns with him...."

"It's wonderful, the elasticity of youth," said the inconspicuous lady five minutes later. "To see that boy now, you'd never imagine he'd had a sorrow in the world."

"Now get up there," said the lady who was the leader. "We shall walk across the fields and join you later. You understand where you are to wait for us, William?"

She came nearer and shouted, "You understand, William?"

William nodded ambiguously. "'Ent a *Vool*," he said.

The ladies departed. "*You'll* be all right, Dick," cried the actress kindly.

He sat up where he had been put, trying to look as Orphan Dick as possible after all that had occurred.

§ 7

"Do you know the wind on the heath—have you lived the Gypsy life? Have you spoken, wanderers yourselves, with 'Romany chi and Romany chal' on the wind-swept moors at home or abroad? Have you tramped the broad highways, and, at close of day, pitched your tent near a running stream and cooked your supper by starlight over a fire of pinewood? Do you know the dreamless sleep of the wanderer at peace with himself and all the world?"

For most of us the answer to these questions of the Amateur Camping Club is in the negative.

Yet every year the call of the road, the Borrovian glamour, draws away a certain small number of the imaginative from the grosser comforts of a complex civilization, takes them out into tents and caravans and intimate communion with nature, and, incidentally, with various ingenious appliances designed to meet the needs of cooking in a breeze. It is an adventure to which high spirits and great expectations must be brought, it is an experience in proximity which few friendships survive—and altogether very great fun.

The life of breezy freedom resolves itself in practice chiefly into washing up and an anxious search for permission to camp. One learns how rich and fruitful our world can be in bystanders, and how easy it is to forget essential groceries....

The heart of the joy of it lies in its perfect detachment. There you are in the morning sunlight under the trees that overhang the road, going whither you will. Everything you need you have. Your van creaks along at your side. You are outside inns, outside houses, a home, a community, an *imperium in imperio*. At any moment you may draw out of the traffic upon the wayside grass and say, "Here—until the owner catches us at it—is home!" At any time—subject to the complaisance of William and your being able to find him—you may inspan and go onward. The world is all before you. You taste the complete yet leisurely insouciance of the snail.

And two of those three ladies had other satisfactions to supplement their pleasures. They both adored Madeleine Philips. She was not only perfectly sweet and lovely, but she was known to be so; she had that most potent charm for women, prestige. They had got her all to themselves. They could show now how false is the old idea that there is no friendship nor conversation among women. They were full of wit and pretty things for one another and snatches of song in between. And they were free too from their "menfolk." They were doing without them. Dr. Bowles, the husband of the lady in the deerstalker, was away in Ireland, and Mr. Geedge, the lord of the inconspicuous woman, was golfing at Sandwich. And Madeleine Philips, it was understood, was only too glad to shake herself free from the crowd of admirers that hovered about her like wasps about honey....

Yet after three days each one had thoughts about the need of helpfulness and more particularly about washing-up, that were better left unspoken, that were indeed conspicuously unspoken beneath their merry give and take, like a black and silent river flowing beneath a bridge of ivory. And each of them had a curious feeling in the midst of all this fresh free behaviour, as though the others were not listening sufficiently, as though something of the effect of them was being wasted. Madeleine's smiles became rarer; at times she was almost impassive, and Judy preserved nearly all her wit and verbal fireworks for the times when they passed through villages.... Mrs. Geedge was less visibly affected. She had thoughts of writing a book about it all, telling in the gayest, most provocative way, full of the quietest quaintest humour, just how jolly they had been. Menfolk would read it. This kept a little thin smile upon her lips....

As an audience William was tough stuff. He pretended deafness; he never looked. He did not want to look. He seemed always to be holding his nose in front of his face to prevent his observation—as men pray into their hats at church. But once Judy Bowles overheard a phrase or so in his private soliloquy. "Pack o' wimmin," William was saying. "Dratted petticoats. *Dang* 'em. That's what I say to 'um. *Dang* 'em!"

As a matter of fact, he just fell short of saying it to them. But his manner said it....

You begin to see how acceptable an addition was young Bealby to this company. He was not only helpful, immensely helpful, in things material, a vigorous and at first a careful washer-up, an energetic boot-polisher, a most serviceable cleaner and tidier of things, but he was also belief and support. Undisguisedly he thought the caravan the loveliest thing going, and its three mistresses the most wonderful of people. His alert eyes followed them about full of an unstinted admiration and interest; he pricked his ears when Judy opened her mouth, he handed things to Mrs. Geedge. He made no secret about Madeleine. When she spoke to him, he lost his breath, he reddened and was embarrassed....

They went across the fields saying that he was the luckiest of finds. It was fortunate his people had been so ready to spare him. Judy said boys were a race very cruelly maligned; see how *willing* he was! Mrs. Geedge said there was something elfin about Bealby's little face; Madeleine smiled at the thought of his quaint artlessness. She knew quite clearly that he'd die for her....

§ 8

There was a little pause as the ladies moved away.

Then William spat and spoke in a note of irrational bitterness.

"Brasted Voolery," said William, and then loudly and fiercely, "Cam up, y'ode Runt you."

At these words the white horse started into a convulsive irregular redistribution of its feet, the caravan strained and quivered into motion and Bealby's wanderings as a caravanner began.

For a time William spoke no more, and Bealby scarcely regarded him. The light of strange fortunes and deep enthusiasm was in Bealby's eyes....

"One Thing," said William, "they don't 'ave the Sense to lock anythink up—whatever."

Bealby's attention was recalled to the existence of his companion.

William's face was one of those faces that give one at first the impression of a solitary and very conceited nose. The other features are entirely subordinated to that salient effect. One sees them later. His eyes were small and uneven, his mouth apparently toothless, thin-lipped and crumpled, with the upper lip falling over the other in a manner suggestive of a meagre firmness mixed with appetite. When he spoke he made a faint slobbering sound. "Everyfink," he said, "behind there."

He became confidential. "I been *in* there. I larked about wiv their Fings."

"They got some choc'late," he said, lusciously. "Oo Fine!"

"All sorts of Fings."

He did not seem to expect any reply from Bealby.

"We going far before we meet 'em?" asked Bealby.

William's deafness became apparent.

His mind was preoccupied by other ideas. One wicked eye came close to Bealby's face. "We going to 'ave a bit of choc'late," he said in a wet desirous voice.

He pointed his thumb over his shoulder at the door. "*You* get it," said William with reassuring nods and the mouth much pursed and very oblique.

Bealby shook his head.

"It's in a little dror, under 'er place where she sleeps."

Bealby's head-shake became more emphatic.

"*Yus*, I tell you," said William.

"No," said Bealby.

"Choc'late, I tell you," said William, and ran the tongue of appetite round the rim of his toothless mouth.

"Don't want choc'late," said Bealby, thinking of a large lump of it.

"Go on," said William. "Nobody won't see you...."

"*Go* it!" said William....

"You're afraid," said William....

"Here, *I*'ll go," said William, losing self-control. "You just 'old these reins."

Bealby took the reins. William got up and opened the door of the caravan. Then Bealby realized his moral responsibility—and, leaving the reins, clutched William firmly by his baggy nether garments. They were elderly garments, much sat upon. "Don't be a Vool," said William struggling. "Leago my slack."

Something partially gave way, and William's head came round to deal with Bealby.

"What you mean pullin' my cloes orf me?"

"That,"—he investigated. "Take me a Nour to sew up."

"I ain't going to steal," shouted Bealby into the ear of William.

"Nobody arst you to steal—"

"Nor you neither," said Bealby.

The caravan bumped heavily against a low garden wall, skidded a little and came to rest. William sat down suddenly. The white horse, after a period of confusion with its legs, tried the flavour of some overhanging lilac branches and was content.

"Gimme those reins," said William. "You be the Brastedest Young Vool...."

"Sittin' 'ere," said William presently, "chewin' our teeth, when we might be eatin' choc'late...."

"I 'ent got no use for *you*," said William, "blowed if I 'ave...."

Then the thought of his injuries returned to him.

"I'd make you sew 'em up yourself, darned if I wount—on'y you'd go running the brasted needle into me.... Nour's work there is—by the feel of it.... Mor'n nour.... Goddobe done, too.... All I got...."

"I'll give you Sumpfin, you little Beace, 'fore I done wi' you."

"I wouldn't steal 'er choc'lates," said young Bealby, "not if I was starving."

"Eh?" shouted William.

"*Steal!*" shouted Bealby.

"I'll steal ye, 'fore I done with ye," said William. "Tearin' my cloes for me.... Oh! Cam *up*, y'old Runt. We don't want *you* to stop and lissen. Cam *up*, I tell you!"

§ 8

They found the ladies rather, it seemed, by accident than design, waiting upon a sandy common rich with purple heather and bordered by woods of fir and spruce. They had been waiting some time, and it was clear that the sight of the yellow caravan relieved an accumulated anxiety. Bealby rejoiced to see them. His soul glowed with the pride of chocolate resisted and William overcome. He resolved to distinguish himself over the preparation of the midday meal. It was a pleasant little island of green they chose for their midday pitch, a little patch of emerald turf amidst the purple, a patch already doomed to removal, as a bare oblong and a pile of rolled-up turfs witnessed. This pile and a little bank of heather and bramble promised shelter from the breeze, and down the hill a hundred yards away was a spring and a built-up pool. This spot lay perhaps fifty yards away from the high road and one reached it along a rutty track which had been made by the turf cutters. And overhead was the glorious sky of an English summer, with great clouds like sunlit, white-sailed ships, the Constable sky. The white horse was hobbled and turned out to pasture among the heather, and William was sent off to get congenial provender at the nearest public house. "William!" shouted Mrs. Bowles as he departed, shouting confidentially into his ear, "Get your clothes mended."

"Eh?" said William.

"Mend your clothes."

"Yah! 'E did that," said William viciously with a movement of self-protection, and so went.

Nobody watched him go. Almost sternly they set to work upon the luncheon preparation as William receded. "William," Mrs. Bowles remarked, as she bustled with the patent cooker, putting it up wrong way round so that afterwards it collapsed, "William—takes offence. Sometimes I think he takes offence almost too often.... Did you have any difficulty with him, Dick?"

"It wasn't anything, miss," said Bealby meekly.

Bealby was wonderful with the firelighting, and except that he cracked a plate in warming it, quite admirable as a cook. He burnt his fingers twice— and liked doing it; he ate his portion with instinctive modesty on the other side of the caravan and he washed up—as Mr. Mergleson had always instructed him to do. Mrs. Bowles showed him how to clean knives and forks by sticking them into the turf. A little to his surprise these ladies lit and smoked cigarettes. They sat about and talked perplexingly. Clever stuff. Then he had to get water from the neighbouring brook and boil the kettle for an early tea. Madeleine produced a charmingly bound little book and read in it, the other two professed themselves anxious for the view from a neighbouring hill. They produced their sensible spiked walking sticks such as one does not see in England; they seemed full of energy. "You go," Madeleine had said, "while I and Dick stay here and make tea. I've walked enough to-day...."

So Bealby, happy to the pitch of ecstacy, first explored the wonderful interior of the caravan,—there was a dresser, a stove, let-down chairs and tables and all manner of things,—and then nursed the kettle to the singing stage on the patent cooker while the beautiful lady reclined close at hand on a rug.

"Dick!" she said.

He had forgotten he was Dick.

"Dick!"

He remembered his personality with a start. "Yes, miss!" He knelt up, with a handful of twigs in his hand and regarded her.

"*Well*, Dick," she said.

He remained in flushed adoration. There was a little pause and the lady smiled at him an unaffected smile.

"What are you going to be, Dick, when you grow up?"

"I don't know, miss. I've wondered."

"What would you like to be?"

"Something abroad. Something—so that you could see things."

"A soldier?"

"Or a sailor, miss."

"A sailor sees nothing but the sea."

"I'd rather be a sailor than a common soldier, miss."

"You'd like to be an officer?"

"Yes, miss—only—"

"One of my very best friends is an officer," she said, a little irrelevantly it seemed to Bealby.

"I'd be a Norficer like a shot," said Bealby, "if I 'ad 'arf a chance, miss."

"Officers nowadays," she said, "have to be very brave, able men."

"I know, miss," said Bealby modestly....

The fire required attention for a little while....

The lady turned over on her elbow. "What do you think you are *likely* to be, Dick!" she asked.

He didn't know.

"What sort of man is your stepfather?"

Bealby looked at her. "He isn't much," he said.

"What is he?"

Bealby hadn't the slightest intention of being the son of a gardener. "'E's a law-writer."

"What! in that village."

"'E 'as to stay there for 'is 'ealth, miss," he said. "Every summer. 'Is 'ealth is very pre-precocious, miss...."

He fed his fire with a few judiciously administered twigs.

"What was your own father, Dick?"

With that she opened a secret door in Bealby's imagination. All stepchildren have those dreams. With him they were so frequent and vivid that they had long since become a kind of second truth. He coloured a little and answered with scarcely an interval for reflection. "'E passed as Maltravers," he said.

"Wasn't that his name?"

"I don't rightly know, miss. There was always something kep' from me. My mother used to say, 'Artie,' she used to say: 'there's things that some day you must know, things that concern you. Things about your farver. But poor as we are now and struggling.... Not yet.... Some day you shall know truly—*who you are.*' That was 'ow she said it, miss."

"And she died before she told you?"

He had almost forgotten that he had killed his mother that very morning. "Yes, miss," he said.

She smiled at him and something in her smile made him blush hotly. For a moment he could have believed she understood. And indeed, she did understand, and it amused her to find this boy doing—what she herself had done at times—what indeed she felt it was still in her to do. She felt that most delicate of sympathies, the sympathy of one rather over-imaginative person for another. But her next question dispelled his doubt of her though it left him red and hot. She asked it with a convincing simplicity.

"Have you any idea, Dick, have you any guess or suspicion, I mean, who it is you really are?"

"I wish I had, miss," he said. "I suppose it doesn't matter, really—but one can't help wondering...."

How often he had wondered in his lonely wanderings through that dear city of day-dreams where all the people one knows look out of windows as one passes and the roads are paved with pride! How often had he decided and changed and decided again!

§ 9

Now suddenly a realization of intrusion shattered this conversation. A third person stood over the little encampment, smiling mysteriously and waving a cleek in a slow hieratic manner through the air.

"De licious lill' corn'," said the newcomer in tones of benediction.

He met their enquiring eyes with a luxurious smile, "Licious," he said, and remained swaying insecurely and failing to express some imperfectly apprehended deep meaning by short peculiar movements of the cleek.

He was obviously a golfer astray from some adjacent course—and he had lunched.

"Mighty Join you," he said, and then very distinctly in a full large voice, "Miss Malleleine Philps." There are the penalties of a public and popular life.

"He's *drunk*," the lady whispered. "Get him to go away, Dick. I can't endure drunken men."

She stood up and Bealby stood up. He advanced in front of her, slowly with his nose in the air, extraordinarily like a small terrier smelling at a strange dog.

"I said Mighty Join you," the golfer repeated. His voice was richly excessive. He was a big heavy man with a short-cropped moustache, a great deal of neck and dewlap and a solemn expression.

"Prup. Be'r. Introzuze m'self," he remarked. He tried to indicate himself by waving his hand towards himself, but finally abandoned the attempt as impossible. "Ma' Goo' Soch'l Poshishun," he said.

Bealby had a disconcerting sense of retreating footsteps behind him. He glanced over his shoulder and saw Miss Philips standing at the foot of the steps that led up to the fastnesses of the caravan. "Dick," she cried with a sharp note of alarm in her voice, "get rid of that man."

A moment after Bealby heard the door shut and a sound of a key in its lock. He concealed his true feelings by putting his arms akimbo, sticking his legs wider apart and contemplating the task before him with his head a little on one side. He was upheld by the thought that the yellow caravan had a window looking upon him....

The newcomer seemed to consider the ceremony of introduction completed. "*I* done care for goff," he said, almost vaingloriously.

He waved his cleek to express his preference. "Natua," he said with a satisfaction that bordered on fatuity.

He prepared to come down from the little turfy crest on which he stood to the encampment.

"'Ere!" said Bealby. "This is Private."

The golfer indicated by solemn movements of the cleek that this was understood but that other considerations overrode it.

"You—You got to go!" cried Bealby in a breathless squeak. "You get out of here."

The golfer waved an arm as who should say, "You do not understand, but I forgive you," and continued to advance towards the fire. And then Bealby, at the end of his tact, commenced hostilities.

He did so because he felt he had to do something, and he did not know what else to do.

"Wan' nothin' but frenly conversation sushus custm'ry webred peel," the golfer was saying, and then a large fragment of turf hit him in the neck, burst all about him and stopped him abruptly.

He remained for some lengthy moments too astonished for words. He was not only greatly surprised, but he chose to appear even more surprised than he was. In spite of the brown-black mould upon his cheek and brow and a slight displacement of his cap, he achieved a sort of dignity. He came slowly to a focus upon Bealby, who stood by the turf pile grasping a second missile. The cleek was extended sceptre-wise.

"Replace the—Divot."

"You go orf," said Bealby. "I'll chuck it if you don't. I tell you fair."

"Replace the—DIVOT," roared the golfer again in a voice of extraordinary power.

"You—you go!" said Bealby.

"Am I t'ask you. Third time. Reshpect—Roos.... Replace the Divot."

It struck him fully in the face.

He seemed to emerge through the mould. He was blinking but still dignified. "Tha'—was intentional," he said.

He seemed to gather himself together....

Then suddenly and with a surprising nimbleness he discharged himself at Bealby. He came with astonishing swiftness. He got within a foot of him.

Well, it was for Bealby that he had learnt to dodge in the village playground. He went down under the golfer's arm and away round the end of the stack, and the golfer with his force spent in concussion remained for a time clinging to the turf pile and apparently trying to remember how he got there. Then he was reminded of recent occurrences by a shrill small voice from the other side of the stack.

"You gow away!" said the voice. "Can't you see you're annoying a lady? You gow away."

"Nowish—'noy anyone. Pease wall wirl."

But this was subterfuge. He meant to catch that boy. Suddenly and rather brilliantly he turned the flank of the turf pile and only a couple of loose turfs at the foot of the heap upset his calculations. He found himself on all fours on ground from which it was difficult to rise. But he did not lose heart. "Boy—hic—scow," he said, and became for a second rush a nimble quadruped.

Again he got quite astonishingly near to Bealby, and then in an instant was on his feet and running across the encampment after him. He succeeded in kicking over the kettle, and the patent cooker, without any injury to himself or loss of pace, and succumbed only to the sharp turn behind the end of the caravan and the steps. He hadn't somehow thought of the steps. So he went down rather heavily. But now the spirit of a fine man was roused. Regardless of the scream from inside that had followed his collapse, he was up and in pursuit almost instantly. Bealby only escaped the swiftness of his rush by jumping the shafts and going away across the front of the caravan to the turf pile again. The golfer tried to jump the shafts too, but he was not equal to that. He did in a manner jump. But it was almost as much diving as jumping. And there was something in it almost like the curvetting of a Great Horse....

When Bealby turned at the crash, the golfer was already on all fours again and trying very busily to crawl out between the shaft and the front wheel. He would have been more successful in doing this if he had not begun by putting his arm through the wheel. As it was, he was trying to do too much; he was trying to crawl out at two points at once and getting very rapidly annoyed at his inability to do so. The caravan was shifting slowly forward....

It was manifest to Bealby that getting this man to go was likely to be a much more lengthy business than he had supposed.

He surveyed the situation for a moment, and then realizing the entanglement of his opponent, he seized a camp-stool by one leg, went round by the steps and attacked the prostrate enemy from the rear with effectual but inconclusive fury. He hammered....

"Steady on, young man," said a voice, and he was seized from behind. He turned—to discover himself in the grip of a second golfer....

Another! Bealby fought in a fury of fear....

He bit an arm—rather too tweedy to feel much—and got in a couple of shinners—alas! that they were only slippered shinners!—before he was overpowered....

A cuffed, crumpled, disarmed and panting Bealby found himself watching the careful extraction of the first golfer from the front wheel. Two friends assisted that gentleman with a reproachful gentleness, and his repeated statements that he was all right seemed to reassure them greatly. Altogether there were now four golfers in the field, counting the pioneer.

"He was after this devil of a boy," said the one who held Bealby.

"Yes, but how did he get here?" asked the man who was gripping Bealby.

"Feel better now?" said the third, helping the first comer to his uncertain feet. "Let me have your cleek o, man.... You won't want your cleek...."

Across the heather, lifting their heads a little, came Mrs. Bowles and Mrs. Geedge, returning from their walk. They were wondering whoever their visitors could be.

And then like music after a dispute came Madeleine Philips, a beautiful blue-robed thing, coming slowly with a kind of wonder on her face, out of the caravan and down the steps. Instinctively everybody turned to her. The drunkard with a gesture released himself from his supporter and stood erect. His cap was replaced upon him—obliquely. His cleek had been secured.

"I heard a noise," said Madeleine, lifting her pretty chin and speaking in her sweetest tones. She looked her enquiries....

She surveyed the three sober men with a practised eye. She chose the tallest, a fair, serious-looking young man standing conveniently at the drunkard's elbow.

"Will you please take your friend away," she said, indicating the offender with her beautiful white hand.

"Simly," he said in a slightly subdued voice, "simly coring."

Everybody tried for a moment to understand him.

"Look here, old man, you've got no business here," said the fair young man. "You'd better come back to the club house."

The drunken man stuck to his statement. "Simly coring," he said a little louder.

"I *think*," said a little bright-eyed man with a very cheerful yellow vest, "I *think* he's apologizing. I *hope* so."

The drunken man nodded his head. That among other matters.

The tall young man took his arm, but he insisted on his point. "Simly coring," he said with emphasis. "If—if—done *wan'* me to cor. Notome. Nottot.... Mean' say. Nottot tat-tome. Nottotome. Orny way—sayin' not-ome. No wish 'trude. No wish 'all."

"Well, then, you see, you'd better come away."

"I *ars'* you—are you *tome?* Miss—Miss Pips." He appealed to Miss Philips.

"If you'd answer him—" said the tall young man.

"No, sir," she said with great dignity and the pretty chin higher than ever. "I am *not* at home."

"Nuthin' more t' say then," said the drunken man, and with a sudden stoicism he turned away.

"Come," he said, submitting to support.

"Simly orny arfnoon cor," he said generally and permitted himself to be led off.

"Orny frenly cor...."

For some time he was audible as he receded, explaining in a rather condescending voice the extreme social correctness of his behaviour. Just for a moment or so there was a slight tussle, due to his desire to return and leave cards....

He was afterwards seen to be distributing a small handful of visiting cards amidst the heather with his free arm, rather in the manner of a paper chase—but much more gracefully....

Then decently and in order he was taken out of sight....

§ 10

Bealby had been unostentatiously released by his captor as soon as Miss Philips appeared, and the two remaining golfers now addressed themselves to the three ladies in regret and explanation.

The man who had held Bealby was an aquiline grey-clad person with a cascade moustache and wrinkled eyes, and for some obscure reason he seemed to be amused; the little man in the yellow vest, however, was quite earnest and serious enough to make up for him. He was one of those little fresh-coloured men whose faces stick forward openly. He had open projecting eyes, an open mouth, his cheeks were frank to the pitch of ostentation, his cap was thrust back from his exceptionally open forehead. He had a chest and a stomach. There, too, he held out. He would have held out anything. His legs leant forward from the feet. It was evidently impossible for a man of his nature to be anything but clean shaved....

"Our fault entirely," he said. "Ought to have looked after him. Can't say how sorry and ashamed we are. Can't say how sorry we are he caused you any inconvenience."

"Of course," said Mrs. Bowles, "our boy-servant ought not to have pelted him."

"He didn't exactly *pelt* him, dear," said Madeleine....

"Well, anyhow our friend ought not to have been off his chain. It was our affair to look after him and we didn't...."

"You see," the open young man went on, with the air of lucid explanation, "he's our worst player. And he got round in a hundred and twenty-seven. And beat—somebody. And—it's upset him. It's not a bit of good disguising that we've been letting him drink.... We have. To begin with, we encouraged him.... We oughtn't to have let him go. But we thought a walk alone might do him good. And some of us were a bit off him. Fed up rather. You see he'd been singing, would go on singing...."

He went on to propitiations. "Anything the club can do to show how we regret.... If you would like to pitch—later on in our rough beyond the pinewoods.... You'd find it safe and secluded.... Custodian—most civil man. Get you water or anything you wanted. Especially after all that has happened...."

Bealby took no further part in these concluding politenesses. He had a curious feeling in his mind that perhaps he had not managed this affair quite so well as he might have done. He ought to have been more tactful like, more persuasive. He was a fool to have started chucking.... Well, well. He picked up the overturned kettle and went off down the hill to get water....

What had she thought of him?...

In the meantime one can at least boil kettles.

§ 11

One consequence of this little incident of the rejoicing golfer was that the three ladies were no longer content to dismiss William and Bealby at nightfall and sleep unprotected in the caravan. And this time their pitch was a lonely one with only the golf club house within call. They were inclined even to distrust the golf club. So it was decided, to his great satisfaction, that Bealby should have a certain sleeping sack Mrs. Bowles had brought with her and that he should sleep therein between the wheels.

This sleeping sack was to have been a great feature of the expedition, but when it came to the test Judy could not use it. She had not anticipated that feeling of extreme publicity the open air gives one at first. It was like having all the world in one's bedroom. Every night she had relapsed into the caravan.

Bealby did not mind what they did with him so long as it meant sleeping. He had had a long day of it. He undressed sketchily and wriggled into the nice woolly bag and lay for a moment listening to the soft bumpings that were going on overhead. *She* was there. He had the instinctive confidence of our sex in women, and here were three of them. He had a vague idea of getting out of his bag again and kissing the underside of the van that held this dear beautiful creature....

He didn't....

Such a lot of things had happened that day—and the day before. He had been going without intermission, it seemed now for endless hours. He thought of trees, roads, dew-wet grass, frying-pans, pursuing packs of gigantic butlers hopelessly at fault,—no doubt they were hunting now—chinks and crannies, tactless missiles flying, bursting, missiles it was vain to recall. He stared for a few seconds through the wheel spokes at the dancing, crackling fire of pine-cones which it had been his last duty to replenish, stared and blinked much as a little dog might do and then he had slipped away altogether into the world of dreams....

§ 12

In the morning he was extraordinarily hard to wake....

"Is it after sleeping all day ye'd be?" cried Judy Bowles, who was always at her most Irish about breakfast time.

CHAPTER IV
THE UNOBTRUSIVE PARTING

§ 1

Monday was a happy day for Bealby.

The caravan did seventeen miles and came to rest at last in a sloping field outside a cheerful little village set about a green on which was a long tent professing to be a theatre.... At the first stopping-place that possessed a general shop Mrs. Bowles bought Bealby a pair of boots. Then she had a bright idea. "Got any pocket money, Dick?" she asked.

She gave him half a crown, that is to say she gave him two shillings and sixpence, or five sixpences or thirty pennies—according as you choose to look at it—in one large undivided shining coin.

Even if he had not been in love, here surely was incentive to a generous nature to help and do distinguished services. He dashed about doing things. The little accident on Sunday had warned him to be careful of the plates, and the only flaw upon a perfect day's service was the dropping of an egg on its way to the frying pan for supper. It remained where it fell and there presently he gave it a quiet burial. There was nothing else to be done with it....

All day long at intervals Miss Philips smiled at him and made him do little services for her. And in the evening, after the custom of her great profession when it keeps holiday, she insisted on going to the play. She said it would be the loveliest fun. She went with Mrs. Bowles because Mrs. Geedge wanted to sit quietly in the caravan and write down a few little things while they were still fresh in her mind. And it wasn't in the part of Madeleine Philips not to insist that both William and Bealby must go too; she gave them each a shilling—though the prices were sixpence, threepence, two-pence and a penny—and Bealby saw his first real play.

It was called *Brothers in Blood, or the Gentleman Ranker*. There was a poster— which was only very slightly justified by the performance—of a man in khaki with a bandaged head proposing to sell his life dearly over a fallen comrade.

One went to the play through an open and damaged field gate and across trampled turf. Outside the tent were two paraffin flares illuminating the poster and a small cluster of the impecunious young. Within on grass that was worn and bleached were benches, a gathering audience, a piano played by an off-hand lady, and a drop scene displaying the Grand Canal, Venice. The Grand Canal was infested by a crowded multitude of zealous and excessive reflections of the palaces above and by peculiar crescentic black boats floating entirely out of water and having no reflections at all. The off-hand lady gave a broad impression of the wedding march in Lohengrin, and the back seats assisted by a sort of gastric vocalization called humming and by whistling between the teeth. Madeleine Philips evidently found it tremendous fun, even before the curtain rose.

And then—illusion....

The scenery was ridiculous; it waved about, the actors and actresses were surely the most pitiful of their tribe and every invention in the play impossible, but the imagination of Bealby, like the loving kindness of God, made no difficulties; it rose and met and embraced and gave life to all these things. It was a confused story in the play, everybody was more or less somebody else all the way through, and it got more confused in Bealby's mind, but it was clear from the outset that there was vile work afoot, nets spread and sweet simple people wronged. And never were sweet and simple people quite so sweet and simple. There was the wrongful brother who was weak and wicked and the rightful brother who was vindictively, almost viciously, good, and there was an ingrained villain who was a baronet, a man who wore a frock coat and a silk hat and carried gloves and a stick in every scene and upon all occasions—that sort of man. He looked askance, always. There was a dear simple girl, with a vast sweet smile, who was loved according to their natures by the wrongful and the rightful brother, and a large wicked red-clad, lip-biting woman whose passions made the crazy little stage quiver. There was a comic butler—very different stuff from old Mergleson—who wore an evening coat and plaid trousers and nearly choked Bealby. Why weren't all butlers like that? Funny. And there were constant denunciations. Always there were denunciations going on or denunciations impending. That took Bealby particularly. Never surely in all the world were bad people so steadily and thoroughly scolded and told what. Everybody hissed them; Bealby hissed them. And when they were told what, he applauded. And yet they kept on with their wickedness to the very curtain. They retired—askance to the end. Foiled but pursuing. "A time will come," they said.

There was a moment in the distresses of the heroine when Bealby dashed aside a tear. And then at last most wonderfully it all came right. The company lined up and hoped that Bealby was satisfied. Bealby wished he had more hands. His heart seemed to fill his body. Oh *prime! prime!*...

And out he came into the sympathetic night. But he was no longer a trivial Bealby; his soul was purged, he was a strong and silent man, ready to explode into generous repartee or nerve himself for high endeavour. He slipped off in the opposite direction from the caravan because he wanted to be alone for a time and *feel*. He did not want to jar upon a sphere of glorious illusion that had blown up in his mind like a bubble....

He was quite sure that he had been wronged. Not to be wronged is to forego the first privilege of goodness. He had been deeply wronged by a plot,—all those butlers were in the plot or why should they have chased him,—he was much older than he really was, it had been kept from him, and in truth he was a rightful earl. "Earl Shonts," he whispered; and indeed, why not? And Madeleine too had been wronged; she had been reduced to wander in this uncomfortable caravan; this Gipsy Queen; she had been brought to it by villains, the same villains who had wronged Bealby....

Out he went into the night, the kindly consenting summer night, where there is nothing to be seen or heard that will contradict these delicious wonderful persuasions.

He was so full of these dreams that he strayed far away along the dark country lanes and had at last the utmost difficulty in finding his way back to the caravan. And when ultimately he got back after hours and hours of heroic existence it did not even seem that they had missed him. It did not seem that he had been away half an hour.

§ 2

Tuesday was not so happy a day for Bealby as Monday.

Its shadows began when Mrs. Bowles asked him in a friendly tone when it was clean-collar day.

He was unready with his answer.

"And don't you ever use a hair brush, Dick?" she asked. "I'm sure now there's one in your parcel."

"I do use it *sometimes*, Mum," he admitted.

"And I've never detected you with a toothbrush yet. Though that perhaps is extreme. And Dick—soap? I think you'd better be letting me give you a cake of soap."

"I'd be very much obliged, Mum."

"I hardly dare hint, Dick, at a clean handkerchief. Such things are known."

"If you wouldn't mind—when I've got the breakfast things done, Mum...."

The thing worried him all through breakfast. He had not expected—personalities from Mrs. Bowles. More particularly personalities of this kind. He felt he had to think hard.

He affected modesty after he had cleared away breakfast and carried off his little bundle to a point in the stream which was masked from the encampment by willows. With him he also brought that cake of soap. He began by washing his handkerchief, which was bad policy because that left him no dry towel but his jacket. He ought, he perceived, to have secured a dish-cloth or a newspaper. (This he must remember on the next occasion.) He did over his hands and the more exposed parts of his face with soap and jacket. Then he took off and examined his collar. It certainly was pretty bad....

"Why!" cried Mrs. Bowles when he returned, "that's still the same collar."

"They all seem to've got crumpled 'm," said Bealby.

"But are they all as dirty?"

"I 'ad some blacking in my parcel," said Bealby, "and it got loose, Mum. I'll have to get another collar when we come to a shop."

It was a financial sacrifice, but it was the only way, and when they came to the shop Bealby secured a very nice collar indeed, high with pointed turn-down corners, so that it cut his neck all round, jabbed him under the chin and gave him a proud upcast carriage of the head that led to his treading upon and very completely destroying a stray plate while preparing lunch. But it was more of a man's collar, he felt, than anything he had ever worn before. And it cost sixpence halfpenny, six dee and a half.

(I should have mentioned that while washing up the breakfast things he had already broken the handle off one of the breakfast cups. Both these accidents deepened the cloud upon his day.)

And then there was the trouble of William. William having meditated upon the differences between them for a day had now invented an activity. As Bealby sat beside him behind the white horse he was suddenly and frightfully pinched. *Gee!* One wanted to yelp.

"Choc'late," said William through his teeth and very very savagely. "*Now* then."

After William had done that twice Bealby preferred to walk beside the caravan. Thereupon William whipped up the white horse and broke records and made all the crockery sing together and forced the pace until he was spoken to by Mrs. Bowles....

It was upon a Bealby thus depressed and worried that the rumour of impending "men-folk" came. It began after the party had stopped for letters at a village post office; there were not only letters but a telegram, that Mrs. Bowles read with her spats far apart and her head on one side. "Ye'd like to know about it," she said waggishly to Miss Philips, "and you just shan't."

She then went into her letters.

"You've got some news," said Mrs. Geedge.

"I have that," said Mrs. Bowles, and not a word more could they get from her....

"I'll keep my news no longer," said Mrs. Bowles, lighting her cigarette after lunch as Bealby hovered about clearing away the banana skins and suchlike vestiges of dessert. "To-morrow night as ever is, if so be we get to Winthorpe-Sutbury, there'll be Men among us."

"But Tom's not coming," said Mrs. Geedge.

"He asked Tim to tell me to tell you."

"And you've kept it these two hours, Judy."

"For your own good and peace of mind. But now the murther's out. Come they will, your Man and my Man, pretending to a pity because they can't do without us. But like the self-indulgent monsters they are, they must needs stop at some grand hotel, Redlake he calls it, the Royal, on the hill above Winthorpe-Sutbury. The Royal! The very name describes it. Can't you see the lounge, girls, with its white cane chairs? And saddlebacks! No other hotel it seems is good enough for them, and we if you please are asked to go in and have—what does the man call it—the 'comforts of decency'—and let the caravan rest for a bit."

"Tim promised me I should run wild as long as I chose," said Mrs. Geedge, looking anything but wild.

"They're after thinking we've had enough of it," said Mrs. Bowles.

"It sounds like that."

"Sure I'd go on like this for ever," said Judy. "'Tis the Man and the House and all of it that oppresses me. Vans for Women...."

"Let's not go to Winthorpe-Sutbury," said Madeleine.

(The first word of sense Bealby had heard.)

"Ah!" said Mrs. Bowles archly, "who knows but what there'll be a Man for you? Some sort of Man anyhow."

(Bealby thought that a most improper remark.)

"I want no man."

"Ah!"

"Why do you say *Ah* like that?"

"Because I mean *Ah* like that."

"Meaning?"

"Just that."

Miss Philips eyed Mrs. Bowles and Mrs. Bowles eyed Miss Philips.

"Judy," she said, "you've got something up your sleeve."

"Where it's perfectly comfortable," said Mrs. Bowles.

And then quite maddeningly, she remarked, "Will you be after washing up presently, Dick?" and looked at him with a roguish quiet over her cigarette. It was necessary to disabuse her mind at once of the idea that he had been listening. He took up the last few plates and went off to the washing place by the stream. All the rest of that conversation *had* to be lost.

Except that as he came back for the Hudson's soap he heard Miss Philips say, "Keep your old Men. I'll just console myself with Dick, my dears. Making such a Mystery!"

To which Mrs. Bowles replied darkly, "She *little* knows...."

A kind of consolation was to be got from that.... But what was it she little knew?...

§ 3

The men-folk when they came were nothing so terrific to the sight as Bealby had expected. And thank Heaven there were only two of them and each assigned. Something he perceived was said about someone else, he couldn't quite catch what, but if there was to have been someone else, at any rate there now wasn't. Professor Bowles was animated and Mr. Geedge was gracefully cold, they kissed their wives but not offensively, and there was a chattering pause while Bealby walked on beside the caravan. They were on the bare road that runs along the high ridge above Winthorpe-Sutbury, and the men had walked to meet them from some hotel or other—Bealby wasn't clear about that—by the golf links. Judy was the life and soul of the encounter, and all for asking the men what they meant by intruding upon three independent women who, sure-alive, could very well do without them. Professor Bowles took her pretty calmly, and seemed on the whole to admire her.

Professor Bowles was a compact little man wearing spectacles with alternative glasses, partly curved, partly flat; he was hairy and dressed in that sort of soft tweedy stuff that ravels out—he seemed to have been sitting among thorns—and baggy knickerbockers with straps and very thick stockings and very sensible, open air, in fact quite mountainous, boots. And yet though he was short and stout and active he had a kind of authority about him, and it was clear that for all her persuasiveness his wife merely ran over him like a creeper without making any great difference to him. "I've found," he said, "the perfect place for your encampment." She had been making suggestions. And presently he left the ladies and came hurrying after the caravan to take control.

He was evidently a very controlling person.

"Here, you get down," he said to William. "That poor beast's got enough to pull without *you*."

And when William mumbled he said, "Hey?" in such a shout that William for ever after held his peace.

"Where d'you come from, you boy, you?" he asked suddenly, and Bealby looked to Mrs. Bowles to explain.

"Great silly collar you've got," said the Professor, interrupting her reply. "Boy like this ought to wear a wool shirt. Dirty too. Take it off, boy. It's choking you. Don't you *feel* it?"

Then he went on to make trouble about the tackle William had rigged to contain the white horse.

"This harness makes me sick," said Professor Bowles. "It's worse than Italy...."

"Ah!" he cried and suddenly darted off across the turf, going inelegantly and very rapidly, with peculiar motions of the head and neck as he brought first the flat and then the curved surface of his glasses into play. Finally he dived into the turf, remained scrabbling on all fours for a moment or so, became almost still for the fraction of a minute and then got up and returned to his wife, holding in an exquisite manner something that struggled between his finger and his thumb.

"That's the third to-day," he said, triumphantly. "They swarm here. It's a migration."

Then he resumed his penetrating criticism of the caravan outfit.

"That boy," he said suddenly with his glasses oblique, "hasn't taken off his collar yet."

Bealby revealed the modest secrets of his neck and pocketed the collar....

Mr. Geedge did not appear to observe Bealby. He was a man of the super-aquiline type with a nose like a rudder, he held his face as if it was a hatchet in a procession, and walked with the dignity of a man of honour. You could see at once he was a man of honour. Inflexibly, invincibly, he was a man of honour. You felt that anywhen, in a fire, in an earthquake, in a railway accident when other people would be running about and doing things he would have remained—a man of honour. It was his pride rather than his vanity to be mistaken for Sir Edward Grey. He now walked along with Miss Philips and his wife behind the disputing Bowleses, and discoursed in deep sonorous tones about the healthiness of healthy places and the stifling feeling one had in towns when there was no air.

§ 4

The Professor was remarkably active when at last the point he had chosen for the encampment was reached. Bealby was told to "look alive" twice, and William was assigned to his genus and species; "The man's an absolute idiot," was the way the Professor put it. William just shot a glance at him over his nose. The place certainly commanded a wonderful view. It was a turfy bank protected from the north and south by bushes of yew and the beech-bordered edge of a chalk pit; it was close beside the road, a road which went steeply down the hill into Winthorpe-Sutbury, with that intrepid decision peculiar to the hill-roads of the south of England. It looked indeed as though you could throw the rinse of your teacups into the Winthorpe-Sutbury street; as if you could jump and impale yourself upon the church spire. The hills bellied out east and west and carried hangers, and then swept round to the west in a long level succession of projections, a perspective that merged at last with the general horizon of hilly bluenesses, amidst which Professor Bowles insisted upon a "sapphire glimpse" of sea. "The Channel," said Professor Bowles, as though that made it easier for them. Only Mr. Geedge refused to see even that mitigated version of the sea. There was something perhaps bluish and level, but he was evidently not going to admit it was sea until he had paddled in it and tested it in every way known to him....

"Good *Lord*!" cried the Professor. "What's the man doing now?"

William stopped the struggles and confidential discouragements he was bestowing upon the white horse and waited for a more definite reproach.

"Putting the caravan alongside to the sun! Do you think it will ever get cool again? And think of the blaze of the sunset—through the glass of that door!"

William spluttered. "If I put'n tother way—goo runnin' down t'hill like," said William.

"Imbecile!" cried the Professor. "Put something under the wheels. *Here!*" He careered about and produced great grey fragments of a perished yew tree. "Now then," he said. "Head up hill."

William did his best.

"Oh! *not* like that! Here, *you*!"

Bealby assisted with obsequious enthusiasm.

It was some time before the caravan was adjusted to the complete satisfaction of the Professor. But at last it was done, and the end door gaped at the whole prospect of the Weald with the steps hanging out idiotically like a tongue. The hind wheels were stayed up very cleverly by lumps of chalk and chunks of yew, living and dead, and certainly the effect of it was altogether taller and better. And then the preparations for the midday cooking began. The Professor was full of acute ideas about camping and cooking, and gave Bealby a lively but instructive time. There was no stream handy, but William was sent off to the hotel to fetch a garden water-cart that the Professor with infinite foresight had arranged should be ready.

The Geedges held aloof from these preparations,—they were unassuming people; Miss Philips concentrated her attention upon the Weald—it seemed to Bealby a little discontentedly—as if it was unworthy of her—and Mrs. Bowles hovered smoking cigarettes over her husband's activities, acting great amusement.

"You see it pleases me to get Himself busy," she said. "You'll end a Camper yet, Darlint, and us in the hotel."

The Professor answered nothing, but seemed to plunge deeper into practicality.

Under the urgency of Professor Bowles Bealby stumbled and broke a glass jar of marmalade over some fried potatoes, but otherwise did well as a cook's assistant. Once things were a little interrupted by the Professor going off to catch a cricket, but whether it was the right sort of cricket or not he failed to get it. And then with three loud reports—for a moment Bealby thought the mad butlers from Shonts were upon him with firearms—Captain Douglas arrived and got off his motor bicycle and left it by the roadside. His machine accounted for his delay, for those were the early days of motor bicycles. It also accounted for a black smudge under one of his bright little eyes. He was fair and flushed, dressed in oilskins and a helmet-shaped cap and great gauntlets that made him, in spite of the smudge, look strange and brave and handsome, like a Crusader—only that he was clad in oilskin and not steel, and his moustache was smaller than those Crusaders wore; and when he came across the turf to the encampment Mrs. Bowles and Mrs. Geedge both set up a cry of "A-*Ah!*" and Miss Philips turned an accusing face upon those two ladies. Bealby knelt with a bunch of knives and forks in his hand, laying the cloth for lunch, and when he saw Captain Douglas approaching Miss Philips, he perceived clearly that that lady had already forgotten her lowly adorer, and his little heart was smitten with desolation. This man was arrayed like a chivalrous god, and how was a poor Bealby, whose very collar, his one little circlet of manhood, had been reft from him, how was he to compete with this tremendousness? In that hour the ambition for mechanism, the passion for leather and oilskin, was sown in Bealby's heart.

"I told you not to come near me for a month," said Madeleine, but her face was radiant.

"These motor bicycles—very difficult to control," said Captain Douglas, and all the little golden-white hairs upon his sunlit cheek glittered in the sun.

"And besides," said Mrs. Bowles, "it's all nonsense."

The Professor was in a state of arrested administration; the three others were frankly audience to a clearly understood scene.

"You ought to be in France."

"I'm not in France."

"I sent you into exile for a month," and she held out a hand for the captain to kiss.

He kissed it.

Someday, somewhere, it was written in the book of destiny Bealby should also kiss hands. It was a lovely thing to do.

"Month! It's been years," said the captain. "Years and years."

"Then you ought to have come back before," she replied and the captain had no answer ready....

§ 5

When William arrived with the water-cart, he brought also further proofs of the Professor's organizing ability. He brought various bottles of wine, red Burgundy and sparkling hock, two bottles of cider, and peculiar and meritorious waters; he brought tinned things for *hors d'œuvre*; he brought some luscious pears. When he had a moment with Bealby behind the caravan he repeated thrice in tones of hopeless sorrow, "They'll eat um all. I *knows* they'll eat um all." And then plumbing a deeper deep of woe, "Ef they *don't* they'll count um. Ode Goggles'll bag um.... E's a *bagger*, 'e is."

It was the brightest of luncheons that was eaten that day in the sunshine and spaciousness above Winthorpe-Sutbury. Everyone was gay, and even the love-torn Bealby, who might well have sunk into depression and lethargy, was galvanized into an activity that was almost cheerful by flashes from the Professor's glasses. They talked of this and that; Bealby hadn't much time to attend, though the laughter that followed various sallies from Judy Bowles was very tantalizing, and it had come to the pears before his attention wasn't so much caught as felled by the word "Shonts."... It was as if the sky had suddenly changed to vermilion. *All these people were talking of Shonts!*...

"Went there," said Captain Douglas, "in perfect good faith. Wanted to fill up Lucy's little party. One doesn't go to Shonts nowadays for idle pleasure. And then—I get ordered out of the house, absolutely Told to Go."

(This man had been at Shonts!)

"That was on Sunday morning?" said Mrs. Geedge.

"On Sunday morning," said Mrs. Bowles suddenly, "we were almost within sight of Shonts."

(This man had been at Shonts even at the time when Bealby was there!)

"Early on Sunday morning. Told to go. I was fairly flabbergasted. What the deuce is a man to do? Where's he to go? Sunday? One doesn't go to places, Sunday morning. There I'd been sleeping like a lamb all night and suddenly in came Laxton and said, 'Look here, you know,' he said, 'you've got to oblige me and pack your bag and go. Now.' 'Why?' said I. 'Because you've driven the Lord Chancellor stark staring mad!'"

"But how?" asked the Professor, almost angrily, "how? I don't see it. Why should he ask you to go?"

"*I* don't know!" cried Captain Douglas.

"Yes, but—!" said the Professor, protesting against the unreasonableness of mankind.

"I'd had a word or two with him in the train. Nothing to speak of. About occupying two corner seats—always strikes me as a cad's trick—but on my honour I didn't rub it in. And then he got it into his head we were laughing at him at dinner—we were a bit, but only the sort of thing one says about anyone—way he works his eyebrows and all that—and then he thought I was ragging him.... I *don't* rag people. Got it so strongly he made a row that night. Said I'd made a ghost slap him on his back. Hang it!—what *can* you say to a thing like that? In my room all the time."

"You suffer for the sins of your brother," said Mrs. Bowles.

"Heavens!" cried the captain, "I never thought of that! Perhaps he mistook me...."

He reflected for a moment and continued his narrative. "Then in the night, you know, he heard noises."

"They always do," said the Professor nodding confirmation.

"Couldn't sleep."

"A sure sign," said the Professor.

"And finally he sallied out in the early morning, caught the butler in one of the secret passages—"

"How did the butler get into the secret passage?"

"Going round, I suppose. Part of his duties.... Anyhow he gave the poor beggar an awful doing—awful—*brutal*—black eye,—all that sort of thing; man much too respectful to hit back. Finally declared I'd been getting up a kind of rag,—squaring the servants to help and so forth.... Laxton, I fancy, half believed it.... Awkward thing, you know, having it said about that you ragged the Lord Chancellor. Makes a man seem a sort of mischievous idiot. Injures a man. Then going away, you see, seems a kind of admission...."

"Why did you go?"

"Lucy," said the captain compactly. "Hysterics."

"Shonts would have burst," he added, "if I hadn't gone."

Madeleine was helpful. "But you'll have to do *something* further," she said.

"What is one to *do*?" squealed the captain.

"The sooner you get the Lord Chancellor certified a lunatic," said the Professor soundly, "the better for your professional prospects."

"He went on pretty bad after I'd gone."

"You've heard"

"Two letters. I picked 'em up at Wheatley Post Office this morning. You know he hadn't done with that butler. Actually got out of his place and scruffed the poor devil at lunch. Shook him like a rat, she says. Said the man wasn't giving him anything to drink—nice story, eh? Anyhow he scruffed him until things got broken...."

"I had it all from Minnie Timbre—you know, used to be Minnie Flax." He shot a propitiating glance at Madeleine. "Used to be neighbours of ours, you know, in the old time. Half the people, she says, didn't know what was happening. Thought the butler was apoplectic and that old Moggeridge was helping him stand up. Taking off his collar. It was Laxton thought of saying it was a fit. Told everybody, she says. Had to tell 'em Something, I suppose. But she saw better and she thinks a good many others did. Laxton ran 'em both out of the room. Nice scene for Shonts, eh? Thundering awkward for poor Lucy. Not the sort of thing the county expected. Has her both ways. Can't go to a house where the Lord Chancellor goes mad. One alternative. Can't go to a house where the butler has fits. That's the other. See the dilemma?..."

"I've got a letter from Lucy, too. It's here"—he struggled—"See? Eight sheets—pencil. No Joke for a man to read that. And she writes worse than any decent self-respecting illiterate woman has a right to do. Quivers. Like writing in a train. Can't read half of it. But *she's* got something about a boy on her mind. Mad about a boy. Have I taken away a boy? They've lost a boy. Took him in my luggage, I suppose. She'd better write to the Lord Chancellor. Likely as not he met him in some odd corner and flew at him. Smashed him to atoms. Dispersed him. Anyhow they've lost a boy."

He protested to the world. "*I* can't go hunting lost boys for Lucy. I've done enough coming away as I did...."

Mrs. Bowles held out an arresting cigarette.

"What sort of boy was lost?" she asked.

"*I* don't know. Some little beast of a boy. I daresay she'd only imagined it. Whole thing been too much for her."

"Read that over again," said Mrs. Bowles, "about losing a boy. We've found one."

"That *little* chap?"

"We found that boy"—she glanced over her shoulder, but Bealby was nowhere to be seen—"on Sunday morning near Shonts. He strayed into us like a lost kitten."

"But I thought you said you knew his father, Judy," objected the Professor.

"Didn't verify," said Mrs. Bowles shortly, and then to Captain Douglas, "read over again what Lady Laxton says about him...."

§ 6

Captain Douglas struggled with the difficulties of his cousin's handwriting.

Everybody drew together over the fragments of the dessert with an eager curiosity, and helped to weigh Lady Laxton's rather dishevelled phrases....

§ 7

"We'll call the principal witness," said Mrs. Bowles at last, warming to the business. "Dick!"

"Di-ick!"

"*Dick!*"

The Professor got up and strolled round behind the caravan. Then he returned. "No boy there."

"He *heard*!" said Mrs. Bowles in a large whisper and making round wonder-eyes.

"She *says*," said Douglas, "that the chances are he's got into the secret passages...."

The Professor strolled out to the road and looked up it and then down upon the roofs of Winthorpe-Sutbury. "No," he said. "He's mizzled."

"He's only gone away for a bit," said Mrs. Geedge. "He does sometimes after lunch. He'll come back to wash up."

"He's probably taking a snooze among the yew bushes before facing the labours of washing up," said Mrs. Bowles. "He *can't* have mizzled. You see — in there — He can't by any chance have taken his luggage!"

She got up and clambered—with a little difficulty because of its piled-up position, into the caravan. "It's all right," she called out of the door. "His little parsivel is still here."

Her head disappeared again.

"I don't think he'd go away like this," said Madeleine. "After all, what is there for him to go to—even if he is Lady Laxton's missing boy...."

"I don't believe he heard a word of it," said Mrs. Geedge....

Mrs. Bowles reappeared, with a curious-looking brown paper parcel in her hand. She descended carefully. She sat down by the fire and held the parcel on her knees. She regarded it and her companions waggishly and lit a fresh cigarette. "Our link with Dick," she said, with the cigarette in her mouth.

She felt the parcel, she poised the parcel, she looked at it more and more waggishly. "I *wonder*," she said.

Her expression became so waggish that her husband knew she was committed to behaviour of the utmost ungentlemanliness. He had long ceased to attempt restraint in these moods. She put her head on one side and tore open the corner of the parcel just a little way.

"A tin can," she said in a stage whisper.

She enlarged the opening. "Blades of grass," she said.

The Professor tried to regard it humorously. "Even if you have ceased to be decent you can still be frank.... I think, now, my dear, you might just straightforwardly undo the parcel."

She did. Twelve unsympathetic eyes surveyed the evidences of Bealby's utter poverty.

"He's coming," cried Madeleine suddenly.

Judy repacked hastily, but it was a false alarm.

"I said he'd mizzled," said the Professor.

"And without washing up!" wailed Madeleine, "I couldn't have thought it of him...."

§ 8

But Bealby had not "mizzled," although he was conspicuously not in evidence about the camp. There was neither sight nor sound of him for all the time they sat about the vestiges of their meal. They talked of him and of topics arising out of him, and whether the captain should telegraph to Lady Laxton, "Boy practically found." "I'd rather just find him," said the captain, "and anyhow until we get hold of him we don't know it's her particular boy." Then they talked of washing-up and how detestable it was. And suddenly the two husbands, seeing their advantage, renewed their proposals that the caravanners should put up at the golflinks hotel, and have baths and the comforts of civilization for a night or so—and anyhow walk thither for tea. And as William had now returned—he was sitting on the turf afar off smoking a nasty-looking short clay pipe—they rose up and departed. But Captain Douglas and Miss Philips for some reason did not go off exactly with the others, but strayed apart, straying away more and more into a kind of solitude....

First the four married people and then the two lovers disappeared over the crest of the downs....

§ 9

For a time, except for its distant sentinel, the caravan seemed absolutely deserted, and then a clump of bramble against the wall of the old chalk pit became agitated and a small rueful disillusioned white-smeared little Bealby crept back into the visible universe again. His heart was very heavy.

The time had come to go.

And he did not want to go. He had loved the caravan. He had adored Madeleine.

He would go, but he would go beautifully—touchingly.

He would wash up before he went, he would make everything tidy, he would leave behind him a sense of irreparable loss....

With a mournful precision he set about this undertaking. If Mergleson could have seen, Mergleson would have been amazed....

He made everything look wonderfully tidy.

Then in the place where she had sat, lying on her rug, he found her favourite book, a small volume of Swinburne's poems very beautifully bound. Captain Douglas had given it to her.

Bealby handled it with a kind of reverence. So luxurious it was, so unlike the books in Bealby's world, so altogether of her quality.... Strange forces prompted him. For a time he hesitated. Then decision came with a rush. He selected a page, drew the stump of a pencil from his pocket, wetted it very wet and, breathing hard, began to write that traditional message, "Farewell. Remember Art Bealby."

To this he made an original addition: "I washt up before I went."

Then he remembered that so far as this caravan went he was not Art Bealby at all. He renewed the wetness of his pencil and drew black lines athwart the name of "Art Bealby" until it was quite unreadable; then across this again and pressing still deeper so that the subsequent pages re-echoed it he wrote these singular words "Ed rightful Earl Shonts." Then he was ashamed, and largely obliterated this by still more forcible strokes. Finally above it all plainly and nakedly he wrote "Dick Mal-travers...."

He put down the book with a sigh and stood up.

Everything was beautifully in order. But could he not do something yet? There came to him the idea of wreathing the entire camping place with boughs of yew. It would look lovely—and significant. He set to work. At first he toiled zealously, but yew is tough to get and soon his hands were painful. He cast about for some easier way, and saw beneath the hind wheels of the caravan great green boughs—one particularly a splendid long branch.... It seemed to him that it would be possible to withdraw this branch from the great heap of sticks and stones that stayed up the hind wheels of the caravan. It seemed to him that that was so. He was mistaken, but that was his idea.

He set to work to do it. It was rather more difficult to manage than he had supposed; there were unexpected ramifications, wider resistances. Indeed, the thing seemed rooted.

Bealby was a resolute youngster at bottom.

He warmed to his task.... He tugged harder and harder....

§ 10

How various is the quality of humanity!

About Bealby there was ever an imaginative touch; he was capable of romance, of gallantries, of devotion. William was of a grosser clay, slave of his appetites, a materialist. Such men as William drive one to believe in born inferiors, in the existence of a lower sort, in the natural inequality of men.

While Bealby was busy at his little gentle task of reparation, a task foolish perhaps and not too ably conceived, but at any rate morally gracious, William had no thought in the world but the satisfaction of those appetites that the consensus of all mankind has definitely relegated to the lower category. And which Heaven has relegated to the lower regions of our frame. He came now slinking towards the vestiges of the caravanners' picnic, and no one skilled in the interpretation of the human physiognomy could have failed to read the significance of the tongue tip that drifted over his thin oblique lips. He came so softly towards the encampment that Bealby did not note him. Partly William thought of remnants of food, but chiefly he was intent to drain the bottles. Bealby had stuck them all neatly in a row a little way up the hill. There was a cider bottle with some heel-taps of cider, William drank that; then there was nearly half a bottle of hock and William drank that, then there were the drainings of the Burgundy and Apollinaris. It was all drink to William.

And after he had drained each bottle William winked at the watching angels and licked his lips, and patted the lower centres of his being with a shameless base approval. Then fired by alcohol, robbed of his last vestiges of self-control, his thoughts turned to the delicious chocolates that were stored in a daintily beribboned box in the little drawers beneath the sleeping bunk of Miss Philips. There was a new brightness in his eye, a spot of pink in either cheek. With an expression of the lowest cunning he reconnoitred Bealby.

Bealby was busy about something at the back end of the caravan, tugging at something.

With swift stealthy movements of an entirely graceless sort, William got up into the front of the caravan.

Just for a moment he hesitated before going in. He craned his neck to look round the side at the unconscious Bealby, wrinkled the vast nose into an unpleasant grimace and then—a crouching figure of appetite—he crept inside.

Here they were! He laid his hand in the drawer, halted listening....

What was that?...

Suddenly the caravan swayed. He stumbled, and fear crept into his craven soul. The caravan lurched. It was moving.... Its hind wheels came to the ground with a crash....

He took a step doorward and was pitched sideways and thrown upon his knees.... Then he was hurled against the dresser and hit by a falling plate. A cup fell and smashed and the caravan seemed to leap and bound....

Through the little window he had a glimpse of yew bushes hurrying upward. The caravan was going down hill....

"Lummy!" said William, clutching at the bunks to hold himself upright....

"Ca-arnt be that drink!" said William, aspread and aghast....

He attempted the door.

"Crikey! Here! Hold in! My shin!" ... "'Tis thut Brasted Vool of a Boy!"

"...." said William. "....———....

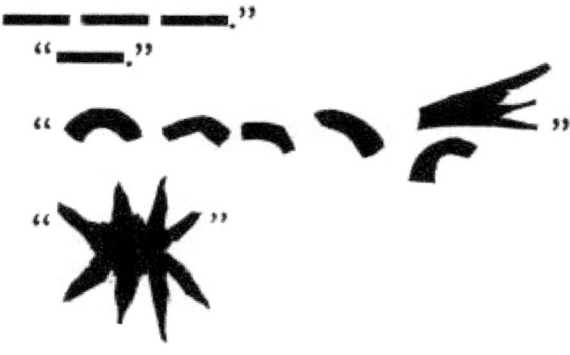

§ 11

The caravan party soon came to its decision. They would stay the night in the hotel. And so as soon as they had had some tea they decided to go back and make William bring the caravan and all the ladies' things round to the hotel. With characteristic eagerness, Professor Bowles led the way.

And so it was Professor Bowles who first saw the release of the caravan. He barked. One short sharp bark. "Whup!" he cried, and very quickly, "Whatstheboydoing?"

Then quite a different style of noise, with the mouth open "Wha—hoop!"

Then he set off running very fast down towards the caravan, waving his arms and shouting as he ran, "Yaaps! You *Idiot*. Yaaps!"

The others were less promptly active.

Down the slope they saw Bealby, a little struggling active Bealby, tugging away at a yew branch until the caravan swayed with his efforts, and then— then there was a movement as though the thing tossed its head and reared, and a smash as the heap of stuff that stayed up its hind wheels collapsed....

It plunged like a horse with a dog at its heels, it lurched sideways, and then with an air of quiet deliberation started down the grass slope to the road and Winthorpe-Sutbury....

Professor Bowles sped in pursuit like the wind, and Mrs. Bowles after a gasping moment set off after her lord, her face round and resolute. Mr. Geedge followed at a more dignified pace, making the only really sound suggestion that was offered on the occasion. "Hue! Stop it!" cried Mr. Geedge, for all the world like his great prototype at the Balkan Conference. And then like a large languid pair of scissors he began to run. Mrs. Geedge after some indefinite moments decided to see the humour of it all, and followed after her lord, in a fluttering rush, emitting careful little musical giggles as she ran, giggles that she had learnt long ago from a beloved schoolfellow. Captain Douglas and Miss Philips were some way behind the others, and the situation had already developed considerably before they grasped what was happening. Then obeying the instincts of a soldier the captain came charging to support the others, and Miss Madeleine Philips after some wasted gestures realized that nobody was looking at her, and sat down quietly on the turf until this paralyzing state of affairs should cease.

The caravan remained the centre of interest.

Without either indecent haste or any complete pause it pursued its way down the road towards the tranquil village below. Except for the rumbling of its wheels and an occasional concussion it made very little sound: once or twice there was a faint sound of breaking crockery from its interior and once the phantom of an angry yell, but that was all.

There was an effect of discovered personality about the thing. This vehicle, which had hitherto been content to play a background part, a yellow patch amidst the scenery, was now revealing an individuality. It was purposeful and touched with a suggestion of playfulness, at once kindly and human; it had its thoughtful instants, its phases of quick decision, yet never once did it altogether lose a certain mellow dignity. There was nothing servile about it; never for a moment, for example, did it betray its blind obedience to gravitation. It was rather as if it and gravitation were going hand in hand. It came out into the road, butted into the bank, swept round, meditated for a full second, and then shafts foremost headed downhill, going quietly faster and faster and swaying from bank to bank. The shafts went before it like arms held out....

It had a quality—as if it were a favourite elephant running to a beloved master from whom it had been over-long separated. Or a slightly intoxicated and altogether happy yellow guinea-pig making for some coveted food....

At a considerable distance followed Professor Bowles, a miracle of compact energy, running so fast that he seemed only to touch the ground at very rare intervals....

And then, dispersedly, in their order and according to their natures, the others....

There was fortunately very little on the road.

There was a perambulator containing twins, whose little girl guardian was so fortunate as to be high up on the bank gathering blackberries.

A ditcher, ditching.

A hawker lost in thought.

His cart, drawn by a poor little black screw of a pony and loaded with the cheap flawed crockery that is so popular among the poor.

A dog asleep in the middle of the village street.... Amidst this choice of objects the caravan displayed a whimsical humanity. It reduced the children in the perambulator to tears, but passed. It might have reduced them to a sort of red-currant jelly. It lurched heavily towards the ditcher and spared him, it chased the hawker up the bank, it whipped off a wheel from the cart of crockery (which after an interval of astonishment fell like a vast objurgation) and then it directed its course with a grim intentness towards the dog.

It just missed the dog.

He woke up not a moment too soon. He fled with a yelp of dismay.

And then the caravan careered on a dozen yards further, lost energy and—the only really undignified thing in its whole career—stood on its head in a wide wet ditch. It did this with just the slightest lapse into emphasis. *There!* It was as if it gave a grunt—and perhaps there was the faintest suggestion of William in that grunt—and then it became quite still....

For a time the caravan seemed finished and done. Its steps hung from its upper end like the tongue of a tired dog. Except for a few minute noises as though it was scratching itself inside, it was as inanimate as death itself.

But up the hill road the twins were weeping, the hawker and the ditcher were saying raucous things, the hawker's pony had backed into the ditch and was taking ill-advised steps, for which it was afterwards to be sorry, amidst his stock-in-trade, and Professor Bowles, Mrs. Bowles, Mr. Geedge, Captain Douglas and Mrs. Geedge were running—running—one heard the various patter of their feet.

And then came signs of life at the upward door of the caravan, a hand, an arm, an active investigating leg seeking a hold, a large nose, a small intent vicious eye; in fact—William.

William maddened.

Professor Bowles had reached the caravan. With a startling agility he clambered up by the wheels and step and confronted the unfortunate driver. It was an occasion for mutual sympathy rather than anger, but the Professor was hasty, efficient and unsympathetic with the lower classes, and William's was an ill-regulated temperament.

"You consummate *ass*!" began Professor Bowles....

When William heard Professor Bowles say this, incontinently he smote him in the face, and when Professor Bowles was smitten in the face he grappled instantly and very bravely and resolutely with William.

For a moment they struggled fearfully, they seemed to be endowed instantaneously with innumerable legs, and then suddenly they fell through the door of the caravan into the interior, their limbs seemed to whirl for a wonderful instant and then they were swallowed up....

The smash was tremendous. You would not have thought there was nearly so much in the caravan still left to get broken....

A healing silence....

At length smothered noises of still inadequate adjustment within....

The village population in a state of scared delight appeared at a score of points and converged upon the catastrophe. Sounds of renewed dissension between William and the Professor inside the rearing yellow bulk, promised further interests and added an element of mystery to this manifest disaster.

§ 12

As Bealby, still grasping his great branch of yew, watched these events, a sense of human futility invaded his youthful mind. For the first time he realized the gulf between intention and result. He had meant so well....

He perceived it would be impossible to explain....

The thought of even attempting to explain things to Professor Bowles was repellent to him....

He looked about him with round despairful eyes. He selected a direction which seemed to promise the maximum of concealment with the minimum of conversational possibility, and in that direction and without needless delay he set off, eager to turn over an entirely fresh page in his destiny as soon as possible....

To get away, the idea possessed all his being.

From the crest of the downs a sweet voice floated after his retreating form and never overtook him.

"Di-ick!"

§ 13

Then presently Miss Philips arose to her feet, gathered her skirts in her hand and with her delicious chin raised and an expression of countenance that was almost businesslike, descended towards the gathering audience below. She wore wide-flowing skirts and came down the hill in Artemesian strides.

It was high time that somebody looked at her.

CHAPTER V
THE SEEKING OF BEALBY

§ 1

On the same Monday evening that witnessed Bealby's first experience of the theatre, Mr. Mergleson, the house steward of Shonts, walked slowly and thoughtfully across the corner of the park between the laundry and the gardens. His face was much recovered from the accidents of his collision with the Lord Chancellor, resort to raw meat in the kitchen had checked the development of his injuries, and only a few contusions in the side of his face were more than faintly traceable. And suffering had on the whole rather ennobled than depressed his bearing. He had a black eye, but it was not, he felt, a common black eye. It came from high quarters and through no fault of Mr. Mergleson's own. He carried it well. It was a fruit of duty rather than the outcome of wanton pleasure-seeking or misdirected passion.

He found Mr. Darling in profound meditation over some peach trees against the wall. They were not doing so well as they ought to do and Mr. Darling was engaged in wondering why.

"Good evening, Mr. Darling," said Mr. Mergleson.

Mr. Darling ceased rather slowly to wonder and turned to his friend. "Good evening, Mr. Mergleson," he said. "I don't quite like the look of these here peaches, *blowed* if I do."

Mr. Mergleson glanced at the peaches, and then came to the matter that was nearest his heart.

"You 'aven't I suppose seen anything of your stepson these last two days, Mr. Darling?"

"Naturally *not*," said Mr. Darling, putting his head on one side and regarding his interlocutor. "Naturally not,—I've left that to you, Mr. Mergleson."

"Well, that's what's awkward," said Mr. Mergleson, and then, with a forced easiness, "You see, I ain't seen 'im either."

"No!"

"No. I lost sight of 'im—" Mr. Mergleson appeared to reflect—"late on Sattiday night."

"'Ow's that, Mr. Mergleson?"

Mr. Mergleson considered the difficulties of lucid explanation. "We missed 'im," said Mr. Mergleson simply, regarding the well-weeded garden path with a calculating expression and then lifting his eyes to Mr. Darling's with an air of great candour. "And we continue to miss him."

"*Well?*" said Mr. Darling. "That's rum."

"Yes," said Mr. Mergleson.

"It's decidedly rum," said Mr. Darling.

"We thought 'e might be 'iding from 'is work. Or cut off 'ome."

"You didn't send down to ask."

"We was too busy with the week-end people. On the 'ole we thought if 'e '*ad* cut 'ome, on the 'ole, 'e wasn't a very serious loss. 'E got in the way at times.... And there was one or two things 'appened—... Now that they're all gone and 'e 'asn't turned up—Well, I came down, Mr. Darling, to arst you. Where's 'e gone?"

"'E ain't come 'ere," said Mr. Darling surveying the garden.

"I 'arf expected 'e might and I 'arf expected 'e mightn't," said Mr. Mergleson with the air of one who had anticipated Mr. Darling's answer but hesitated to admit as much.

The two gentlemen paused for some seconds and regarded each other searchingly.

"Where's 'e *got* to?" said Mr. Darling.

"Well," said Mr. Mergleson, putting his hands where the tails of his short jacket would have been if it hadn't been short, and looking extraordinarily like a parrot in its more thoughtful moods, "to tell you the truth, Mr. Darling, I've 'ad a dream about 'im—and it worries me. I got a sort of ideer of 'im as being in one of them secret passages. 'Iding away. There was a guest, well, I say it with all respec' but *anyone* might 'ave 'id from 'im.... S'morning soon as the week-end 'ad cleared up and gone 'ome, me and Thomas went through them passages as well as we could. Not a trace of 'im. But I still got that ideer. 'E was a wriggling, climbing,—enterprising sort of boy."

"I've checked 'im for it once or twice," said Mr. Darling with the red light of fierce memories gleaming for a moment in his eyes.

"'E might even," said Mr. Mergleson, "well, very likely 'ave got 'imself jammed in one of them secret passages...."

"Jammed," repeated Mr. Darling.

"Well—got 'imself somewhere where 'e can't get out. I've 'eard tell there's walled-up dungeons."

"They say," said Mr. Darling, "there's underground passages to the Abbey ruins—three good mile away."

"Orkward," said Mr. Mergleson....

"Drat 'is eyes!" said Mr. Darling, scratching his head. "What does 'e mean by it?"

"We can't leave 'im there," said Mr. Mergleson.

"I knowed a young devil once what crawled up a culvert," said Mr. Darling. "'Is father 'ad to dig 'im out like a fox.... Lord! 'ow 'e walloped 'im for it."

"Mistake to 'ave a boy in so young," said Mr. Mergleson.

"It's all very awkward," said Mr. Darling, surveying every aspect of the case. "You see—. 'Is mother sets a most estrordinary value on 'im. Most estrordinary."

"I don't know whether she oughtn't to be told," said Mr. Mergleson. "I was thinking of that."

Mr. Darling was not the sort of man to meet trouble half-way. He shook his head at that. "Not yet, Mr. Mergleson. I don't think yet. Not until everything's been tried. I don't think there's any need to give her needless distress,—none whatever. If you don't mind I think I'll come up to-night—nineish say—and 'ave a talk to you and Thomas about it—a quiet talk. Best to begin with a *quiet* talk. It's a dashed rum go, and me and you we got to think it out a bit."

"That's what *I* think," said Mr. Mergleson with unconcealed relief at Mr. Darling's friendliness. "That's exactly the light, Mr. Darling, in which it appears to me. Because, you see—if 'e's all right and in the 'ouse, why doesn't 'e come for 'is vittels?"

§ 2

In the pantry that evening the question of telling someone was discussed further. It was discussed over a number of glasses of Mr. Mergleson's beer. For, following a sound tradition, Mr. Mergleson brewed at Shonts, and sometimes he brewed well and sometimes he brewed ill, and sometimes he brewed weak and sometimes he brewed strong, and there was no monotony in the cups at Shonts. This was sturdy stuff and suited Mr. Darling's mood, and ever and again with an author's natural weakness and an affectation of abstraction Mr. Mergleson took the jug out empty and brought it back foaming.

Henry, the second footman, was disposed to a forced hopefulness so as not to spoil the evening, but Thomas was sympathetic and distressed. The red-haired youth made cigarettes with a little machine, licked them and offered them to the others, saying little, as became him. Etiquette deprived him of an uninvited beer, and Mr. Mergleson's inattention completed what etiquette began.

"I can't bear to think of the poor little beggar, stuck head foremost into some cobwebby cranny, blowed if I can," said Thomas, getting help from the jug.

"He was an interesting kid," said Thomas in a tone that was frankly obituary. "He didn't like his work, one could see that, but he was lively—and I tried to help him along all I could, when I wasn't too busy myself."

"There was something sensitive about him," said Thomas.

Mr. Mergleson sat with his arms loosely thrown out over the table.

"What we got to do is to tell someone," he said, "I don't see 'ow I can put off telling 'er ladyship—after to-morrow morning. And then—'eaven 'elp us!"

"'Course *I* got to tell *my* missis," said Mr. Darling, and poured in a preoccupied way, some running over.

"We'll go through them passages again now before we go to bed," said Mr. Mergleson, "far as we can. But there's 'oles and chinks on'y a boy could get through."

"*I* got to tell the missis," said Mr. Darling. "That's what's worrying me...."

As the evening wore on there was a tendency on the part of Mr. Darling to make this the refrain of his discourse. He sought advice. "'Ow'd you tell the missis?" he asked Mr. Mergleson, and emptied a glass to control his impatience before Mr. Mergleson replied.

"I shall tell 'er ladyship, just simply, the fact. I shall say, your ladyship, here's my boy gone and we don't know where. And as she arsts me questions so shall I give particulars."

Mr. Darling reflected and then shook his head slowly.

"'Ow'd *ju* tell the missis?" he asked Thomas.

"Glad I haven't got to," said Thomas. "*Poor* little beggar."

"Yes, but 'ow *would* you tell 'er?" Mr. Darling said, varying the accent very carefully.

"I'd go to 'er and I'd pat her back and I'd say, 'bear up,' see, and when she asked what for, I'd just tell her what for—gradual like."

"You don't know the missis," said Mr. Darling. "Henry, 'ow'd *ju* tell 'er?"

"Let 'er find out," said Henry. "Wimmin do."

Mr. Darling reflected, and decided that too was unworkable.

"'Ow'd *you*?" he asked with an air of desperation of the red-haired youth.

The red-haired youth remained for a moment with his tongue extended, licking the gum of a cigarette paper, and his eyes on Mr. Darling. Then he finished the cigarette slowly, giving his mind very carefully to the question he had been honoured with. "I think," he said, in a low serious voice, "I should say, just simply, Mary—or Susan—or whatever her name is."

"Tilda," supplied Mr. Darling.

"'Tilda,' I should say. 'The Lord gave and the Lord 'ath taken away. Tilda!—'e's gone.' Somethin' like that."

The red-haired boy cleared his throat. He was rather touched by his own simple eloquence.

Mr. Darling reflected on this with profound satisfaction for some moments. Then he broke out almost querulously, "Yes, but brast him!—*where's* 'e gone?"

"Anyhow," said Mr. Darling, "I ain't going to tell 'er, not till the morning. I ain't going to lose my night's rest if I *have* lost my stepson. Nohow. Mr. Mergleson, I *must* say, I don't think I ever 'ave tasted better beer. Never. It's—it's famous beer."

He had some more....

On his way back through the moonlight to the gardens Mr. Darling was still unsettled as to the exact way of breaking things to his wife. He had come out from the house a little ruffled because of Mr. Mergleson's opposition to a rather good idea of his that he should go about the house and "holler for 'im a bit. He'd know my voice, you see. Ladyship wouldn't mind. Very likely 'sleep by now." But the moonlight dispelled his irritation.

How was he to tell his wife? He tried various methods to the listening moon.

There was for example the off-hand newsy way. "You know tha' boy yours?" Then a pause for the reply. Then, "'E's toley dis'peared."

Only there are difficulties about the word totally.

Or the distressed impersonal manner. "Dre'fle thing happen'd. Dre'fle thing. Tha' poo' lill' chap, Artie—toley dis'peared."

Totally again.

Or the personal intimate note. "Dunno wha' you'll say t'me, Tilda, when you hear what-togottasay. Thur'ly bad news. Seems they los' our Artie up there—clean los' 'im. Can't fine 'im nowhere tall."

Or the authoritative kindly. "Tilda—you go' control yourself. Go' show whad you made of. Our boy—'e's—hic—*los'.*"

Then he addressed the park at large with a sudden despair. "Don' care wha' I say, she'll blame it on to me. I *know* 'er!"

After that the enormous pathos of the situation got hold of him. "Poor lill' chap," he said. "Poor lill' fell'," and shed a few natural tears.

"Loved 'im jessis mione son."

As the circumambient night made no reply he repeated the remark in a louder, almost domineering tone....

He spent some time trying to climb the garden wall because the door did not seem to be in the usual place. (Have to enquire about that in the morning. Difficult to see everything is all right when one is so bereaved). But finally he came on the door round a corner.

He told his wife merely that he intended to have a peaceful night, and took off his boots in a defiant and intermittent manner.

The morning would be soon enough.

She looked at him pretty hard, and he looked at her ever and again, but she never made a guess at it.

Bed.

§ 3

So soon as the week-enders had dispersed and Sir Peter had gone off to London to attend to various matters affecting the peptonizing of milk and the distribution of baby soothers about the habitable globe, Lady Laxton went back to bed and remained in bed until midday on Tuesday. Nothing short of complete rest and the utmost kindness from her maid would, she felt, save her from a nervous breakdown of the most serious description. The festival had been stormy to the end. Sir Peter's ill-advised attempts to deprive Lord Moggeridge of alcohol had led to a painful struggle at lunch, and this had been followed by a still more unpleasant scene between host and guest in the afternoon. "This is an occasion for tact," Sir Peter had said and had gone off to tackle the Lord Chancellor, leaving his wife to the direst, best founded apprehensions. For Sir Peter's tact was a thing by itself, a mixture of misconception, recrimination and familiarity that was rarely well received....

She had had to explain to the Sunday dinner party that his lordship had been called away suddenly. "Something connected with the Great Seal," Lady Laxton had whispered in a discreet mysterious whisper. One or two simple hearers were left with the persuasion that the Great Seal had been taken suddenly unwell—and probably in a slightly indelicate manner. Thomas had to paint Mergleson's eye with grease-paint left over from some private theatricals. It had been a patched-up affair altogether, and before she retired to bed that night Lady Laxton had given way to her accumulated tensions and wept.

There was no reason whatever why to wind up the day Sir Peter should have stayed in her room for an hour saying what he thought of Lord Moggeridge. She felt she knew quite well enough what he thought of Lord Moggeridge, and on these occasions he always used a number of words that she did her best to believe, as a delicately brought up woman, were unfamiliar to her ears....

So on Monday, as soon as the guests had gone, she went to bed again and stayed there, trying as a good woman should to prevent herself thinking of what the neighbours could be thinking—and saying—of the whole affair, by studying a new and very circumstantial pamphlet by Bishop Fowle on social evils, turning over the moving illustrations of some recent antivivisection literature and re-reading the accounts in the morning papers of a colliery disaster in the north of England.

To such women as Lady Laxton, brought up in an atmosphere of refinement that is almost colourless, and living a life troubled only by small social conflicts and the minor violence of Sir Peter, blameless to the point of complete uneventfulness, and secure and comfortable to the point of tedium, there is something amounting to fascination in the wickedness and sufferings of more normally situated people, there is a real attraction and solace in the thought of pain and stress, and as her access to any other accounts of vice and suffering was restricted she kept herself closely in touch with the more explicit literature of the various movements for human moralization that distinguish our age, and responded eagerly and generously to such painful catastrophes as enliven it. The counterfoils of her cheque book witnessed to her gratitude for these vicarious sensations. She figured herself to herself in her day dreams as a calm and white and shining intervention checking and reproving amusements of an undesirable nature, and earning the tearful blessings of the mangled by-products of industrial enterprise.

There is a curious craving for entire reality in the feminine composition, and there were times when in spite of these feasts of particulars, she wished she could come just a little nearer to the heady dreadfulnesses of life than simply writing a cheque against it. She would have liked to have actually *seen* the votaries of evil blench and repent before her contributions, to have, herself, unstrapped and revived and pitied some doomed and chloroformed victim of the so-called "scientist," to have herself participated in the stretcher and the hospital and humanity made marvellous by enlistment under the red-cross badge. But Sir Peter's ideals of womanhood were higher than his language, and he would not let her soil her refinement with any vision of the pain and evil in the world. "Sort of woman they want up there is a Trained Nurse," he used to say when she broached the possibility of *going* to some famine or disaster. "*You* don't want to go prying, old girl...."

She suffered, she felt, from repressed heroism. If ever she was to shine in disaster that disaster, she felt, must come to her, she might not go to meet it, and so you realize how deeply it stirred her, how it brightened her and uplifted her to learn from Mr. Mergleson's halting statements that perhaps, that probably, that almost certainly, a painful and tragical thing was happening even now within the walls of Shonts, that there was urgent necessity for action—if anguish was to be witnessed before it had ended, and life saved.

She clasped her hands; she surveyed her large servitor with agonized green-grey eyes.

"Something must be done at once," she said. "Everything possible must be done. Poor little Mite!"

"Of course, my lady, 'e *may* 'ave run away!"

"Oh no!" she cried, "he hasn't run away. He hasn't run away. How can you be so *wicked*, Mergleson. Of course he hasn't run away. He's there now. And it's too dreadful."

She became suddenly very firm and masterful. The morning's colliery tragedy inspired her imagination.

"We must get pick-axes," she said. "We must organize search parties. Not a moment is to be lost, Mergleson—not a moment.... Get the men in off the roads. Get everyone you can...."

And not a moment was lost. The road men were actually at work in Shonts before their proper dinner-hour was over.

They did quite a lot of things that afternoon. Every passage attainable from the dining-room opening was explored, and where these passages gave off chinks and crannies they were opened up with a vigour which Lady

Laxton had greatly stimulated by an encouraging presence and liberal doses of whisky. Through their efforts a fine new opening was made into the library from the wall near the window, a hole big enough for a man to fall through, because one did, and a great piece of stonework was thrown down from the Queen Elizabeth tower, exposing the upper portion of the secret passage to the light of day. Lady Laxton herself and the head housemaid went round the panelling with a hammer and a chisel, and called out "Are you there?" and attempted an opening wherever it sounded hollow. The sweep was sent for to go up the old chimneys outside the present flues. Meanwhile Mr. Darling had been set with several of his men to dig for, discover, pick up and lay open the underground passage or disused drain, whichever it was, that was known to run from the corner of the laundry towards the old ice-house, and that was supposed to reach to the abbey ruins. After some bold exploratory excavations this channel was located and a report sent at once to Lady Laxton.

It was this and the new and alarming scar on the Queen Elizabeth tower that brought Mr. Beaulieu Plummer post-haste from the estate office up to the house. Mr. Beaulieu Plummer was the Marquis of Cranberry's estate agent, a man of great natural tact, and charged among other duties with the task of seeing that the Laxtons did not make away with Shonts during the period of their tenancy. He was a sound compact little man, rarely out of extreme riding breeches and gaiters, and he wore glasses, that now glittered with astonishment as he approached Lady Laxton and her band of spade workers.

At his approach Mr. Darling attempted to become invisible, but he was unable to do so.

"Lady Laxton," Mr. Beaulieu Plummer appealed, "may I ask—?"

"Oh Mr. Beaulieu Plummer, I'm so *glad* you've come. A little boy— suffocating! I can hardly *bear* it."

"Suffocating!" cried Mr. Beaulieu Plummer, "*where?*" and was in a confused manner told.

He asked a number of questions that Lady Laxton found very tiresome. But how did she *know* the boy was in the secret passage? Of course she knew; was it likely she would do all this if she didn't know? But mightn't he have run away? How could he when he was in the secret passages? But why not first scour the countryside? By which time he would be smothered and starved and dead!...

They parted with a mutual loss of esteem, and Mr. Beaulieu Plummer, looking very serious indeed, ran as fast as he could straight to the village telegraph-office. Or to be more exact, he walked until he thought himself out of sight of Lady Laxton and then he took to his heels and ran. He sat for some time in the parlour post office spoiling telegraph forms, and composing telegrams to Sir Peter Laxton and Lord Cranberry.

He got these off at last, and then drawn by an irresistible fascination went back to the park and watched from afar the signs of fresh activities on the part of Lady Laxton.

He saw men coming from the direction of the stables with large rakes. With these they dragged the ornamental waters.

Then a man with a pick-axe appeared against the skyline and crossed the roof in the direction of the clock tower, bound upon some unknown but probably highly destructive mission.

Then he saw Lady Laxton going off to the gardens. She was going to console Mrs. Darling in her trouble. This she did through nearly an hour and a half. And on the whole it seemed well to Mr. Beaulieu Plummer that so she should be occupied....

It was striking five when a telegraph boy on a bicycle came up from the village with a telegram from Sir Peter Laxton.

"Stop all proceedings absolutely," it said, "until I get to you."

Lady Laxton's lips tightened at the message. She was back from much weeping with Mrs. Darling and altogether finely strung. Here she felt was one of those supreme occasions when a woman must assert herself. "A matter of life or death," she wired in reply, and to show herself how completely she overrode such dictation as this she sent Mr. Mergleson down to the village public-house with orders to engage anyone he could find there for an evening's work on an extraordinarily liberal overtime scale.

After taking this step the spirit of Lady Laxton quailed. She went and sat in her own room and quivered. She quivered but she clenched her delicate fist.

She would go through with it, come what might, she would go on with the excavation all night if necessary, but at the same time she began a little to regret that she had not taken earlier steps to demonstrate the improbability of Bealby having simply run away. She set to work to repair this omission. She wrote off to the Superintendent of Police in the neighbouring town, to the nearest police magistrate, and then on the off chance to various of her week-end guests, including Captain Douglas. If it was true that he had organized the annoyance of the Lord Chancellor (and though she still rejected that view she did now begin to regard it as a permissible hypothesis), then he might also know something about the mystery of this boy's disappearance.

Each letter she wrote she wrote with greater fatigue and haste than its predecessor and more illegibly.

Sir Peter arrived long after dark. He cut across the corner of the park to save time, and fell into one of the trenches that Mr. Darling had opened. This added greatly to the *éclat* with which he came into the hall.

Lady Laxton withstood him for five minutes and then returned abruptly to her bedroom and locked herself in, leaving the control of the operations in his hands....

"If he's not in the house," said Sir Peter, "all this is thunderin' foolery, and if he's in the house he's dead. If he's dead he'll smell in a bit and then'll be the time to look for him. Somethin' to go upon instead of all this blind hacking the place about. No wonder they're threatenin' proceedings...."

§ 4

Upon Captain Douglas Lady Laxton's letter was destined to have a very distracting effect. Because, as he came to think it over, as he came to put her partly illegible allusions to secret passages and a missing boy side by side with his memories of Lord Moggeridge's accusations and the general mystery of his expulsion from Shonts, it became more and more evident to him that he had here something remarkably like a clue, something that might serve to lift the black suspicion of irreverence and levity from his military reputation. And he had already got to the point of suggesting to Miss Philips that he ought to follow up and secure Bealby forthwith, before ever they came over the hill crest to witness the disaster to the caravan.

Captain Douglas, it must be understood, was a young man at war within himself.

He had been very nicely brought up, firstly in a charming English home, then in a preparatory school for selected young gentlemen, then in a good set at Eton, then at Sandhurst, where the internal trouble had begun to manifest itself. Afterwards the Bistershires.

There were three main strands in the composition of Captain Douglas. In the first place, and what was peculiarly his own quality, was the keenest interest in the *why* of things and the *how* of things and the general mechanism of things. He was fond of clocks, curious about engines, eager for science; he had a quick brain and nimble hands. He read Jules Verne and liked to think about going to the stars and making flying machines and submarines—in those days when everybody knew quite certainly that such things were impossible. His brain teemed with larval ideas that only needed air and light to become active full-fledged ideas. There he excelled most of us. In the next place, but this second strand was just a strand that most young men have, he had a natural keen interest in the other half of humanity, he thought them lovely, interesting, wonderful, and they filled him with warm curiosities and set his imagination cutting the prettiest capers. And in the third place, and there again he was ordinarily human, he wanted to be liked, admired, approved, well thought of.... And so constituted he had passed through the educational influence of that English home, that preparatory school, the good set at Eton, the Sandhurst discipline, the Bistershire mess....

Now the educational influence of the English home, the preparatory school, the good set at Eton and Sandhurst in those days—though Sandhurst has altered a little since—was all to develop that third chief strand of his being to the complete suppression of the others, to make him look well and unobtrusive, dress well and unobtrusively, behave well and unobtrusively, carry himself well, play games reasonably well, do nothing else well, and in the best possible form. And the two brothers Douglas, who were really very much alike, did honestly do their best to be such plain and simple gentlemen as our country demands, taking pretentious established things seriously, and not being odd or intelligent—in spite of those insurgent strands.

But the strands were in them. Below the surface the disturbing impulses worked and at last forced their way out....

In one Captain Douglas, as Mrs. Rampound Pilby told the Lord Chancellor, the suppressed ingenuity broke out in disconcerting mystifications and practical jokes that led to a severance from Portsmouth, in the other the pent-up passions came out before the other ingredients in an uncontrollable devotion to the obvious and challenging femininity of Miss Madeleine Philips.... His training had made him proof against ordinary women, deaf as it were to their charms, but she—she had penetrated. And impulsive forces that have been pent up—go with a bang when they go....

The first strand in the composition of Captain Douglas has still to be accounted for, the sinister strain of intelligence and inventiveness and lively curiosity. On that he had kept a warier hold. So far that had not been noted against him. He had his motor bicycle, it is true, at a time when motor bicycles were on the verge of the caddish; to that extent a watchful eye might have found him suspicious; that was all that showed. I wish I could add it was all that there was, but other things—other things were going on. Nobody knew about them. But they were going on more and more.

He read books.

Not decent fiction, not official biographies about other fellows' fathers and all the old anecdotes brought up to date and so on, but books with ideas,—you know, philosophy, social philosophy, scientific stuff, all that rot. *The sort of stuff they read in mechanics' institutes.*

He thought. He could have controlled it. But he did not attempt to control it. He *tried* to think. He knew perfectly well that it wasn't good form, but a vicious attraction drew him on.

He used to sit in his bedroom-study at Sandhurst, with the door locked, and write down on a bit of paper what he really believed and why. He would cut all sorts of things to do this. He would question—things no properly trained English gentleman ever questions.

And—he experimented.

This you know was long before the French and American aviators. It was long before the coming of that emphatic lead from abroad without which no well-bred English mind permits itself to stir. In the darkest secrecy he used to make little models of cane and paper and elastic in the hope that somehow he would find out something about flying. Flying—that dream! He used to go off by himself to lonely places and climb up as high as he could and send these things fluttering earthward. He used to moon over them and muse about them. If anyone came upon him suddenly while he was doing these things, he would sit on his model, or pretend it didn't belong to him, or clap it into his pocket, whichever was most convenient, and assume the vacuous expression of a well-bred gentleman at leisure—and so far nobody had caught him. But it was a dangerous practice.

And finally, and this now is the worst and last thing to tell of his eccentricities, he was keenly interested in the science of his profession and intensely ambitious.

He thought—though it wasn't his business to think, the business of a junior officer is to obey and look a credit to his regiment—that the military science of the British army was not nearly so bright as it ought to be, and that if big trouble came there might be considerable scope for an inventive man who had done what he could to keep abreast with foreign work, and a considerable weeding out of generals whose promotion had been determined entirely by their seniority, amiability and unruffled connubial felicity. He thought that the field artillery would be found out—there was no good in making a fuss about it beforehand—that no end of neglected dodges would have to be picked up from the enemy, that the transport was feeble, and a health service—other than surgery and ambulance—an unknown idea, but he saw no remedy but experience. So he worked hard in secret; he worked almost as hard as some confounded foreigner might have done; in the belief that after the first horrid smash-up there might be a chance to do things.

Outwardly of course he was sedulously all right. But he could not quite hide the stir in his mind. It broke out upon his surface in a chattering activity of incompleted sentences which he tried to keep as decently silly as he could.

He had done his utmost hitherto to escape the observation of the powers that were. His infatuation for Madeleine Philips had at any rate distracted censorious attention from these deeper infamies....

And now here was a crisis in his life. Through some idiotic entanglement manifestly connected with this missing boy, he had got tarred by his brother's brush and was under grave suspicion for liveliness and disrespect.

The thing might be his professional ruin. And he loved the suppressed possibilities of his work beyond measure.

It was a thing to make him absent-minded even in the company of Madeleine.

§ 5

Not only were the first and second strands in the composition of Captain Douglas in conflict with all his appearances and pretensions, but they were also in conflict with one another.

He was full of that concealed resolve to do and serve and accomplish great things in the world. That was surely purpose enough to hide behind an easy-going unpretending gentlemanliness. But he was also tremendously attracted by Madeleine Philips, more particularly when she was not there.

A beautiful woman may be the inspiration of a great career. This, however, he was beginning to find was not the case with himself. He had believed it at first and written as much and said as much, and said it very variously and gracefully. But becoming more and more distinctly clear to his intelligence was the fact that the very reverse was the case. Miss Madeleine Philips was making it very manifest to Captain Douglas that she herself was a career; that a lover with any other career in view need not—as the advertisements say—apply.

And the time she took up!

The distress of being with her!

And the distress of *not* being with her!

She was such a proud and lovely and entrancing and distressing being to remember, and such a vain and difficult thing to be with.

She knew clearly that she was made for love, for she had made herself for love; and she went through life like its empress with all mankind and numerous women at her feet. And she had an ideal of the lover who should win her which was like a oleographic copy of a Laszlo portrait of Douglas greatly magnified. He was to rise rapidly to great things, he was to be a conqueror and administrator, while attending exclusively to her. And incidentally she would gather desperate homage from all other men of mark, and these attentions would be an added glory to her love for him. At first Captain Douglas had been quite prepared to satisfy all these requirements. He had met her at Shorncliffe, for her people were quite good military people, and he had worshipped his way straight to her feet. He had made the most delightfully simple and delicate love to her. He had given up his secret vice of thinking for the writing of quite surprisingly clever love-letters, and the little white paper models had ceased for a time to flutter in lonely places.

And then the thought of his career returned to him, from a new aspect, as something he might lay at her feet. And once it had returned to him it remained with him.

"Some day," he said, "and it may not be so very long, some of those scientific chaps will invent flying. Then the army will have to take it up, you know."

"I should *love*," she said, "to soar through the air."

He talked one day of going on active service. How would it affect them if he had to do so? It was a necessary part of a soldier's lot.

"But I should come too!" she said. "I should come with you."

"It might not be altogether convenient," he said, for already he had learnt that Madeleine Philips usually travelled with quite a large number of trunks and considerable impressiveness.

"Of course," she said, "it would be splendid! How could I let you go alone. You would be the great general and I should be with you always."

"Not always very comfortable," he suggested.

"Silly boy!—I shouldn't mind *that*! How little you know me! Any hardship!"

"A woman—if she isn't a nurse—"

"I should come dressed as a man. I would be your groom...."

He tried to think of her dressed as a man, but nothing on earth could get his imagination any further than a vision of her dressed as a Principal Boy. She was so delightfully and valiantly not virile; her hair would have flowed, her body would have moved, a richly fluent femininity—visible through any disguise.

§ 6

That was in the opening stage of the controversy between their careers. In those days they were both acutely in love with each other. Their friends thought the spectacle quite beautiful; they went together so well. Admirers, fluttered with the pride of participation, asked them for week-ends together; those theatrical week-ends that begin on Sunday morning and end on Monday afternoon. She confided widely.

And when at last there was something like a rupture it became the concern of a large circle of friends.

The particulars of the breach were differently stated. It would seem that looking ahead he had announced his intention of seeing the French army manœuvres just when it seemed probable that she would be out of an engagement.

"But I ought to see what they are doing," he said. "They're going to try those new dirigibles."

Then should she come?

He wanted to whisk about. It wouldn't be any fun for her. They might get landed at nightfall in any old hole. And besides people would talk— Especially as it was in France. One could do unconventional things in England one couldn't in France. Atmosphere was different.

For a time after that halting explanation she maintained a silence. Then she spoke in a voice of deep feeling. She perceived, she said, that he wanted his freedom. She would be the last person to hold a reluctant lover to her side. He might go—to *any* manœuvres. He might go if he wished round the world. He might go away from her for ever. She would not detain him, cripple him, hamper a career she had once been assured she inspired....

The unfortunate man, torn between his love and his profession, protested that he hadn't meant *that*.

Then what *had* he meant?

He realized he had meant something remarkably like it and he found great difficulty in expressing these fine distinctions....

She banished him from her presence for a month, said he might go to his manœuvres—with her blessing. As for herself, that was her own affair. Some day perhaps he might know more of the heart of a woman.... She choked back tears—very beautifully, and military science suddenly became a trivial matter. But she was firm. He wanted to go. He must go. For a month anyhow.

He went sadly....

Into this opening breach rushed friends. It was the inestimable triumph of Judy Bowles to get there first. To begin with, Madeleine confided in her, and then, availing herself of the privilege of a distant cousinship, she commanded Douglas to tea in her Knightsbridge flat and had a good straight talk with him. She liked good straight talks with honest young men about their love affairs; it was almost the only form of flirtation that the Professor, who was a fierce, tough, undiscriminating man upon the essentials of matrimony, permitted her. And there was something peculiarly gratifying about Douglas's complexion. Under her guidance he was induced to declare that he could not live without Madeleine, that her love was the heart of his life, without it he was nothing and with it he could conquer the world.... Judy permitted herself great protestations on behalf of Madeleine, and Douglas was worked up to the pitch of kissing her intervening hand. He had little silvery hairs, she saw, all over his temples. And he was such a simple perplexed dear. It was a rich deep beautiful afternoon for Judy.

And then in a very obvious way Judy, who was already deeply in love with the idea of a caravan tour and the "wind on the heath" and the "Gipsy life" and the "open road" and all the rest of it, worked this charming little love difficulty into her scheme, utilized her reluctant husband to arrange for the coming of Douglas, confided in Mrs. Geedge....

And Douglas went off with his perplexities. He gave up all thought of France, week-ended at Shonts instead, to his own grave injury, returned to London unexpectedly by a Sunday train, packed for France and started. He reached Rheims on Monday afternoon. And then the image of Madeleine, which always became more beautiful and mysterious and commanding with every mile he put between them, would not let him go on. He made unconvincing excuses to the *Daily Excess* military expert with whom he was to have seen things. "There's a woman in it, my boy, and you're a fool to go," said the *Daily Excess* man, "but of course you'll go, and I for one don't blame you—" He hurried back to London and was at Judy's trysting-place even as Judy had anticipated.

And when he saw Madeleine standing in the sunlight, pleased and proud and glorious, with a smile in her eyes and trembling on her lips, with a strand or so of her beautiful hair and a streamer or so of delightful blue fluttering in the wind about her gracious form, it seemed to him for the moment that leaving the manœuvres and coming back to England was quite a right and almost a magnificent thing to do.

§ 7

This meeting was no exception to their other meetings.

The coming to her was a crescendo of poetical desire, the sight of her a climax, and then—an accumulation of irritations. He had thought being with her would be pure delight, and as they went over the down straying after the Bowles and the Geedges towards the Redlake Hotel he already found himself rather urgently asking her to marry him and being annoyed by what he regarded as her evasiveness.

He walked along with the restrained movement of a decent Englishman; he seemed as it were to gesticulate only through his clenched teeth, and she floated beside him, in a wonderful blue dress that with a wonderful foresight she had planned for breezy uplands on the basis of Botticelli's *Primavera*. He was urging her to marry him soon; he needed her, he could not live in peace without her. It was not at all what he had come to say; he could not recollect that he had come to say anything, but now that he was with her it was the only thing he could find to say to her.

"But, my dearest boy," she said, "how are we to marry? What is to become of *your* career and *my* career?"

"I've *left* my career!" cried Captain Douglas with the first clear note of irritation in his voice.

"Oh! don't let us quarrel," she cried. "Don't let us talk of all those *distant* things. Let us be happy. Let us enjoy just this lovely day and the sunshine and the freshness and the beauty.... Because you know we are snatching these days. We have so few days together. Each—each must be a gem.... Look, dear, how the breeze sweeps through these tall dry stems that stick up everywhere—low broad ripples."

She was a perfect work of art, abolishing time and obligations.

For a time they walked in silence. Then Captain Douglas said, "All very well—beauty and all that—but a fellow likes to know where he is."

She did not answer immediately, and then she said, "I believe you are angry because you have come away from France."

"Not a bit of it," said the Captain stoutly. "I'd come away from anywhere to be with you."

"I wonder," she said.

"Well,—haven't I?"

"I wonder if you ever are with me.... Oh!—I know you *want* me. I know you desire me. But the real thing, the happiness,—love. What is anything to love—anything at all?"

In this strain they continued until their footsteps led them through the shelter of a group of beeches. And there the gallant captain sought expression in deeds. He kissed her hands, he sought her lips. She resisted softly.

"No," she said, "only if you love me with all your heart."

Then suddenly, wonderfully, conqueringly she yielded him her lips.

"Oh!" she sighed presently, "if only you understood."

And leaving speech at that enigma she kissed again....

But you see now how difficult it was under these mystically loving conditions to introduce the idea of a prompt examination and dispatch of Bealby. Already these days were consecrated....

And then you see Bealby vanished—going seaward....

Even the crash of the caravan disaster did little to change the atmosphere. In spite of a certain energetic quality in the Professor's direction of the situation—he was a little embittered because his thumb was sprained and his knee bruised rather badly and he had a slight abrasion over one ear and William had bitten his calf—the general disposition was to treat the affair hilariously. Nobody seemed really hurt except William,—the Professor was not so much hurt as annoyed,—and William's injuries though striking were all superficial, a sprained jaw and grazes and bruises and little things like that; everybody was heartened up to the idea of damages to be paid for; and neither the internal injuries to the caravan nor the hawker's estimate of his stock-in-trade proved to be as great as one might reasonably have expected. Before sunset the caravan was safely housed in the Winthorpe-Sutbury public house, William had found a congenial corner in the bar parlour, where his account of an inside view of the catastrophe and his views upon Professor Bowles were much appreciated, the hawker had made a bit extra by carting all the luggage to the Redlake Royal Hotel and the caravanners and their menfolk had loitered harmoniously back to this refuge. Madeleine had walked along the road beside Captain Douglas and his motor bicycle, which he had picked up at the now desolate encampment.

"It only remains," she said, "for that thing to get broken."

"But I may want it," he said.

"No," she said, "Heaven has poured us together and now He has smashed the vessels. At least He has smashed one of the vessels. And look!—like a great shield, there is the moon. It's the Harvest Moon, isn't it?"

"No," said the Captain, with his poetry running away with him. "It's the Lovers' Moon."

"It's like a benediction rising over our meeting."

And it was certainly far too much like a benediction for the Captain to talk about Bealby.

That night was a perfect night for lovers, a night flooded with a kindly radiance, so that the warm mystery of the centre of life seemed to lurk in every shadow and hearts throbbed instead of beating and eyes were stars. After dinner every one found wraps and slipped out into the moonlight; the Geedges vanished like moths; the Professor made no secret that Judy was transfigured for him. Night works these miracles. The only other visitors there, a brace of couples, resorted to the boats upon the little lake.

Two enormous waiters removing the coffee cups from the small tables upon the verandah heard Madeleine's beautiful voice for a little while and then it was stilled....

§ 8

The morning found Captain Douglas in a state of reaction. He was anxious to explain quite clearly to Madeleine just how necessary it was that he should go in search of Bealby forthwith. He was beginning to realize now just what a chance in the form of Bealby had slipped through his fingers. He had dropped Bealby and now the thing to do was to pick up Bealby again before he was altogether lost. Her professional life unfortunately had given Miss Philips the habit of never rising before midday, and the Captain had to pass the time as well as he could until the opportunity for his explanation came.

A fellow couldn't go off without an explanation....

He passed the time with Professor Bowles upon the golf links.

The Professor was a first-rate player and an unselfish one; he wanted all other players to be as good as himself. He would spare no pains to make them so. If he saw them committing any of the many errors into which golfers fall, he would tell them of it and tell them why it was an error and insist upon showing them just how to avoid it in future. He would point out any want of judgment, and not confine himself, as so many professional golf teachers do, merely to the stroke. After a time he found it necessary to hint to the Captain that nowadays a military man must accustom himself to self-control. The Captain kept Pishing and Tushing, and presently, it was only too evident, swearing softly; his play got jerky, his strokes were forcible without any real strength, once he missed the globe altogether and several times he sliced badly. The eyes under his light eyelashes were wicked little things.

He remembered that he had always detested golf.

And the Professor. He had always detested the Professor.

And his caddie; at least he would have always detested his caddie if he had known him long enough. His caddie was one of those maddening boys with no expression at all. It didn't matter what he did or failed to do, there was the silly idiot with his stuffed face, unmoved. Really, of course overjoyed—but apparently unmoved....

"Why did I play it that way?" the Captain repeated. "Oh! because I like to play it that way."

"*Well*," said the Professor. "It isn't a recognized way anyhow...."

Then came a moment of evil pleasures.

He'd sliced. Old Bowles had sliced. For once in a while he'd muffed something. Always teaching others and here he was slicing! Why, sometimes the Captain didn't slice!...

He'd get out of that neatly enough. Luck! He'd get the hole yet. What a bore it all was!...

Why couldn't Madeleine get up at a decent hour to see a fellow? Why must she lie in bed when she wasn't acting? If she had got up all this wouldn't have happened. The shame of it! Here he was, an able-bodied capable man in the prime of life and the morning of a day playing this blockhead's game—!

Yes—blockhead's game!

"You play the like," said the Professor.

"*Rather*," said the Captain and addressed himself to his stroke.

"That's not your ball," said the Professor.

"Similar position," said the Captain.

"You know, you might *win* this hole," said the Professor.

"Who cares?" said the Captain under his breath and putted extravagantly.

"That saves me," said the Professor, and went down from a distance of twelve yards.

The Captain, full of an irrational resentment, did his best to halve the hole and failed.

"You ought to put in a week at nothing but putting," said the Professor. "It would save you at least a stroke a hole. I've noticed that on almost every green, if I haven't beaten you before I pull up in the putting."

The Captain pretended not to hear and said a lot of rococo things inside himself.

It was Madeleine who had got him in for this game. A beautiful healthy girl ought to get up in the mornings. Mornings and beautiful healthy girls are all the same thing really. She ought to be *dewy*—positively dewy.... There she must be lying, warm and beautiful in bed—like Catherine the Great or somebody of that sort. No. It wasn't right. All very luxurious and so on but not *right*. She ought to have understood that he was bound to fall a prey to the Professor if she didn't get up. Golf! Here he was, neglecting his career; hanging about on these *beastly* links, all the sound men away there in France— it didn't do to think of it!—and he was playing this retired tradesman's consolation!

(Beastly the Professor's legs looked from behind. The uglier a man's legs are the better he plays golf. It's almost a law.)

That's what it was, a retired tradesman's consolation. A decent British soldier has no more business to be playing golf than he has to be dressing dolls. It's a game at once worthless and exasperating. If a man isn't perfectly fit he cannot play golf, and when he is perfectly fit he ought to be doing a man's work in the world. If ever anything deserved the name of vice, if ever anything was pure, unforgivable dissipation, surely golf was that thing....

And meanwhile that boy was getting more and more start. Anyone with a ha'porth of sense would have been up at five and after that brat—might have had him bagged and safe and back to lunch. *Ass* one was at times!

"You're here, sir," said the caddie.

The captain perceived he was in a nasty place, open green ahead but with some tumbled country near at hand and to the left, a rusty old gravel pit, furze at the sides, water at the bottom. Nasty attractive hole of a place. Sort of thing one gets into. He must pull himself together for this. After all, having undertaken to play a game one must play the game. If he hit the infernal thing, that is to say the ball, if he hit the ball so that if it didn't go straight it would go to the right rather—clear of the hedge it wouldn't be so bad to the right. Difficult to manage. Best thing was to think hard of the green ahead, a long way ahead,—with just the slightest deflection to the right. Now then,— heels well down, club up, a good swing, keep your eye on the ball, keep your eye on the ball, keep your eye on the ball just where you mean to hit it—far below there and a little to the right—and *don't* worry....

Rap.

"In the pond I *think*, sir."

"The water would have splashed if it had gone in the pond," said the Professor. "It must be over there in the wet sand. You hit it pretty hard, I thought."

Search. The caddie looked as though he didn't care whether he found it or not. *He* ought to be interested. It was his profession, not just his game.

But nowadays everybody had this horrid disposition towards slacking. A Tired generation we are. The world is too much with us. Too much to think about, too much to do, Madeleines, army manœuvres, angry lawyers, lost boys—let alone such exhausting foolery as this game....

"*Got* it, sir!" said the caddie.

"Where?"

"Here, sir! Up in the bush, sir!"

It was resting in the branches of a bush two yards above the slippery bank.

"I doubt if you can play it," said the Professor, "but it will be interesting to try."

The Captain scrutinized the position. "I can play it," he said.

"You'll slip, I'm afraid," said the Professor.

They were both right. Captain Douglas drove his feet into the steep slope of rusty sand below the bush, held his iron a little short and wiped the ball up and over and as he found afterwards out of the rough. All eyes followed the ball except his. The Professor made sounds of friendly encouragement. But the Captain was going—going. He was on all fours, he scrabbled handfuls of prickly gorse, of wet sand. His feet, his ankles, his calves slid into the pond. How much more? No. He'd reached the bottom. He proceeded to get out again as well as he could. Not so easy. The bottom of the pond sucked at him....

When at last he rejoined the other three his hands were sandy red, his knees were sandy red, his feet were of clay, but his face was like the face of a little child. Like the face of a little fair child after it has been boiled red in its bath and then dusted over with white powder. His ears were the colour of roses, Lancaster roses. And his eyes too had something of the angry wonder of a little child distressed....

"I was afraid you'd slip into the pond," said the Professor.

"I didn't," said the Captain.

"!"

"I just got in to see how deep it was and cool my feet—I hate warm feet."

He lost that hole but he felt a better golfer now, his anger he thought was warming him up so that he would presently begin to make strokes by instinct, and do remarkable things unawares. After all there is something in the phrase "getting one's blood up." If only the Professor wouldn't dally so with his ball and let one's blood get down again. Tap!—the Professor's ball went soaring.

Now for it. The Captain addressed himself to his task, altered his plans rather hastily, smote and topped the ball.

The least one could expect was a sympathetic silence. But the Professor thought fit to improve the occasion.

"You'll never drive," said the Professor; "you'll never drive with that *irritable* jerk in the middle of the stroke. You might just as well smack the ball without raising your club. If you think—"

The Captain lost his self-control altogether.

"Look here," he said, "if *you* think that *I* care a single rap about how I hit the ball, if you think that I really want to win and do well at this beastly, silly, elderly, childish game—."

He paused on the verge of ungentlemanly language.

"If a thing's worth doing at all," said the Professor after a pause for reflection, "it's worth doing well."

"Then it isn't worth doing at all. As this hole gives you the game—if you don't mind—"

The Captain's hot moods were so rapid that already he was acutely ashamed of himself.

"O *certainly*, if you wish it," said the Professor.

With a gesture the Professor indicated the altered situation to the respectful caddies and the two gentlemen turned their faces towards the hotel.

For a time they walked side by side in silence, the caddies following with hushed expressions.

"Splendid weather for the French manœuvres," said the Captain presently in an off-hand tone, "that is to say if they are getting this weather."

"At present there are a series of high pressure systems over the whole of Europe north of the Alps," said the Professor. "It is as near set fair as Europe can be."

"Fine weather for tramps and wanderers," said the Captain after a further interval.

"There's a drawback to everything," said the Professor. "But it's very lovely weather."

§ 9

They got back to the hotel about half-past eleven and the Captain went and had an unpleasant time with one of the tyres of his motor bicycle which had got down in the night. In replacing the tyre he pinched the top of one of his fingers rather badly. Then he got the ordnance map of the district and sat at a green table in the open air in front of the hotel windows and speculated on the probable flight of Bealby. He had been last seen going south by east. That way lay the sea, and all boy fugitives go naturally for the sea.

He tried to throw himself into the fugitive's mind and work out just exactly the course Bealby *must* take to the sea.

For a time he found this quite an absorbing occupation.

Bealby probably had no money or very little money. Therefore he would have to beg or steal. He wouldn't go to the workhouse because he wouldn't know about the workhouse, respectable poor people never know anything about the workhouse, and the chances were he would be both too honest and too timid to steal. He'd beg. He'd beg at front doors because of dogs and things, and he'd probably go along a high road. He'd be more likely to beg from houses than from passers-by, because a door is at first glance less formidable than a pedestrian and more accustomed to being addressed. And he'd try isolated cottages rather than the village street doors, an isolated wayside cottage is so much more confidential. He'd ask for food—not money. All that seemed pretty sound.

Now this road on the map—into it he was bound to fall and along it he would go begging. No other?... No.

In the fine weather he'd sleep out. And he'd go—ten, twelve, fourteen—thirteen, thirteen miles a day.

So now, he ought to be about here. And to-night,—here.

To-morrow at the same pace,—here.

But suppose he got a lift!...

He'd only get a slow lift if he got one at all. It wouldn't make much difference in the calculation....

So if to-morrow one started and went on to these cross roads marked *Inn*, just about twenty-six miles it must be by the scale, and beat round it one ought to get something in the way of tidings of Mr. Bealby. Was there any reason why Bealby shouldn't go on south by east and seaward?...

None.

And now there remained nothing to do but to explain all this clearly to Madeleine. And why didn't she come down? Why didn't she come down?

But when one got Bealby what would one do with him?

Wring the truth out of him—half by threats and half by persuasion. Suppose after all he hadn't any connexion with the upsetting of Lord Moggeridge? He had. Suppose he hadn't. He had. He had. He had.

And when one had the truth?

Whisk the boy right up to London and confront the Lord Chancellor with the facts. But suppose he wouldn't be confronted with the facts. He was a touchy old sinner....

For a time Captain Douglas balked at this difficulty. Then suddenly there came into his head the tall figure, the long moustaches of that kindly popular figure, his adopted uncle Lord Chickney. Suppose he took the boy straight to Uncle Chickney, told him the whole story. Even the Lord Chancellor would scarcely refuse ten minutes to General Lord Chickney....

The clearer the plans of Captain Douglas grew the more anxious he became to put them before Madeleine—clearly and convincingly....

Because first he had to catch his boy....

Presently, as Captain Douglas fretted at the continued eclipse of Madeleine, his thumb went into his waistcoat pocket and found a piece of paper. He drew it out and looked at it. It was a little piece of stiff note-paper cut into the shape of a curved V rather after the fashion of a soaring bird. It must have been there for months. He looked at it. His care-wrinkled brow relaxed. He glanced over his shoulder at the house and then held this little scrap high over his head and let go. It descended with a slanting flight curving round to the left and then came about and swept down to the ground to the right.... Now why did it go like that? As if it changed its mind. He tried it again. Same result.... Suppose the curvature of the wings was a little greater? Would it make a more acute or a less acute angle? He did not know.... Try it.

He felt in his pocket for a piece of paper, found Lady Laxton's letter, produced a stout pair of nail scissors in a sheath from a waistcoat pocket, selected a good clear sheet, and set himself to cut out his improved V....

As he did so his eyes were on V number one, on the ground. It would be interesting to see if this thing turned about to the left again. If in fact it would go on zig-zagging. It ought, he felt, to do so. But to test that one ought to release it from some higher point so as to give it a longer flight. Stand on the chair?...

Not in front of the whole rotten hotel. And there was a beastly looking man in a green apron coming out of the house,—the sort of man who looks at you. He might come up and watch; these fellows are equal to anything of that sort. Captain Douglas replaced his scissors and scraps in his pockets, leaned back with an affectation of boredom, got up, lit a cigarette—sort of thing the man in the green apron would think all right—and strolled off towards a clump of beech trees, beyond which were bushes and a depression. There perhaps one might be free from observation. Just try these things for a bit. That point about the angle was a curious one; it made one feel one's ignorance not to know that....

§ 10

The ideal King has a careworn look, he rules, he has to do things, but the ideal Queen is radiant happiness, tall and sweetly dignified, simply she has to be things. And when at last towards midday Queen Madeleine dispelled the clouds of the morning and came shining back into the world that waited outside her door, she was full of thankfulness for herself and for the empire that was given her. She knew she was a delicious and wonderful thing, she knew she was well done, her hands, the soft folds of her dress as she held it up, the sweep of her hair from her forehead pleased her, she lifted her chin but not too high for the almost unenvious homage in the eyes of the housemaid on the staircase. Her descent was well timed for the lunch gathering of the hotel guests; there was "*Ah!*—here she comes at last!" and there was her own particular court out upon the verandah before the entrance, Geedge and the Professor and Mrs. Bowles—and Mrs. Geedge coming across the lawn,—and the lover?

She came on down and out into the sunshine. She betrayed no surprise. The others met her with flattering greetings that she returned smilingly. But the lover—?

He was not there!

It was as if the curtain had gone up on almost empty stalls.

He ought to have been worked up and waiting tremendously. He ought to have spent the morning in writing a poem to her or in writing a delightful poetical love letter she could carry away and read or in wandering alone and thinking about her. He ought to be feeling now like the end of a vigil. He ought to be standing now, a little in the background and with that pleasant flush of his upon his face and that shy, subdued, reluctant look that was so infinitely more flattering than any boldness of admiration. And then she would go towards him, for she was a giving type, and hold out both hands to him, and he, as though he couldn't help it, in spite of all his British reserve, would take one and hesitate—which made it all the more marked—and kiss it....

Instead of which he was just not there....

No visible disappointment dashed her bravery. She knew that at the slightest flicker Judy and Mrs. Geedge would guess and that anyhow the men would guess nothing. "I've rested," she said, "I've rested delightfully. What have you all been doing?"

Judy told of great conversations, Mr. Geedge had been looking for trout in the stream, Mrs. Geedge with a thin little smile said she had been making a few notes and—she added the word with deliberation—"observations," and Professor Bowles said he had had a round of golf with the Captain. "And he lost?" asked Madeleine.

"He's careless in his drive and impatient at the greens," said the Professor modestly.

"And then?"

"He vanished," said the Professor, recognizing the true orientation of her interest.

There was a little pause and Mrs. Geedge said, "You know—" and stopped short.

Interrogative looks focussed upon her.

"It's so odd," she said.

Curiosity increased.

"I suppose one ought not to say," said Mrs. Geedge, "and yet—why shouldn't one?"

"Exactly," said Professor Bowles, and every one drew a little nearer to Mrs. Geedge.

"One can't help being amused," she said. "It was so—extraordinary."

"Is it something about the Captain?" asked Madeleine.

"Yes. You see,—he didn't see me."

"Is he—is he writing poetry?" Madeleine was much entertained and relieved at the thought. That would account for everything. The poor dear! He hadn't been able to find some rhyme!

But one gathered from the mysterious airs of Mrs. Geedge that he was not writing poetry. "You see," she said, "I was lying out there among the bushes, just jotting down a few little things,—and he came by. And he went down into the hollow out of sight.... And what do you think he is doing? You'd never guess? He's been at it for twenty minutes."

They didn't guess.

"He's playing with little bits of paper—Oh! like a kitten plays with dead leaves. He throws them up—and they flutter to the ground—and then he pounces on them."

"But—" said Madeleine. And then very brightly, "let's go and see!"

She was amazed. She couldn't understand. She hid it under a light playfulness, that threatened to become distraught. Even when presently, after a very careful stalking of the dell under the guidance of Mrs. Geedge, with the others in support, she came in sight of him, she still found him incredible. There was her lover, her devoted lover, standing on the top bar of a fence, his legs wide apart and his body balanced with difficulty, and in his fingers poised high was a little scrap of paper. This was the man who should have been waiting in the hall with feverish anxiety. His fingers released the little model and down it went drifting....

He seemed to be thinking of nothing else in the world. She might never have been born!...

Some noise, some rustle, caught his ear. He turned his head quickly, guiltily, and saw her and her companions.

And then he crowned her astonishment. No lovelight leapt to his eyes; he uttered no cry of joy. Instead he clutched wildly at the air, shouted, "Oh damn!" and came down with a complicated inelegance on all fours upon the ground.

He was angry with her—angry; she could see that he was extremely angry.

§ 11

So it was that the incompatibilities of man and woman arose again in the just recovering love dream of Madeleine Philips. But now the discord was far more evident than it had been at the first breach.

Suddenly her dear lover, her flatterer, her worshipper, had become a strange averted man. He scrabbled up two of his paper scraps before he came towards her, still with no lovelight in his eyes. He kissed her hand as if it was a matter of course and said almost immediately: "I've been hoping for you all the endless morning. I've had to amuse myself as best I can." His tone was resentful. He spoke as if he had a claim upon her—upon her attentions. As if it wasn't entirely upon his side that obligations lay.

She resolved that shouldn't deter her from being charming.

And all through the lunch she was as charming as she could be, and under such treatment that rebellious ruffled quality vanished from his manner, vanished so completely that she could wonder if it had really been evident at any time. The alert servitor returned.

She was only too pleased to forget the disappointment of her descent and forgive him, and it was with a puzzled incredulity that she presently saw his "difficult" expression returning. It was an odd little knitting of the brows, a faint absentmindedness, a filming of the brightness of his worship. He was just perceptibly indifferent to the charmed and charming things she was saying.

It seemed best to her to open the question herself. "Is there something on your mind, Dot?"

"Dot" was his old school nickname.

"Well, no—not exactly on my mind. But—. It's a bother of course. There's that confounded boy...."

"Were you trying some sort of divination about him? With those pieces of paper?"

"No. That was different. That was—just something else. But you see that boy—. Probably clear up the whole of the Moggeridge bother—and you know it *is* a bother. Might turn out beastly awkward...."

It was extraordinarily difficult to express. He wanted so much to stay with her and he wanted so much to go.

But all reason, all that was expressible, all that found vent in words and definite suggestions, was on the side of an immediate pursuit of Bealby. So that it seemed to her he wanted and intended to go much more definitely than he actually did.

That divergence of purpose flawed a beautiful afternoon, cast chill shadows of silence over their talk, arrested endearments. She was irritated. About six o'clock she urged him to go; she did not mind, anyhow she had things to see to, letters to write, and she left him with an effect of leaving him for ever. He went and overhauled his motor bicycle thoroughly and then an aching dread of separation from her arrested him.

Dinner, the late June sunset and the moon seemed to bring them together again. Almost harmoniously he was able to suggest that he should get up very early the next morning, pursue and capture Bealby and return for lunch.

"You'd get up at dawn!" she cried. "But how perfectly Splendid the midsummer dawn must be."

Then she had an inspiration. "Dot!" she cried, "I will get up at dawn also and come with you.... Yes, but as you say he cannot be more than thirteen miles away we'd catch him warm in his little bed somewhere. And the freshness! The dewy freshness!"

And she laughed her beautiful laugh and said it would be "Such *Fun*!" entering as she supposed into his secret desires and making the most perfect of reconciliations. They were to have tea first, which she would prepare with the caravan lamp and kettle. Mrs. Geedge would hand it over to her.

She broke into song. "A Hunting we will go-ooh," she sang. "A Hunting we will go...."

But she could not conquer the churlish underside of the Captain's nature even by such efforts. She threw a glamour of vigour and fun over the adventure, but some cold streak in his composition was insisting all the time that as a boy hunt the attempt failed. Various little delays in her preparations prevented a start before half-past seven, he let that weigh with him, and when sometimes she clapped her hands and ran—and she ran like a deer, and sometimes she sang, he said something about going at an even pace.

At a quarter past one Mrs. Geedge observed them returning. They were walking abreast and about six feet apart, they bore themselves grimly, after the manner of those who have delivered ultimata, and they conversed no more....

In the afternoon Madeleine kept her own room, exhausted, and Captain Douglas sought opportunities of speaking to her in vain. His face expressed distress and perplexity, with momentary lapses into wrathful resolution, and he evaded Judy and her leading questions and talked about the weather with Geedge. He declined a proposal of the Professor's to go round the links, with especial reference to his neglected putting. "You ought to, you know," said the Professor.

About half-past three, and without any publication of his intention, Captain Douglas departed upon his motor bicycle....

Madeleine did not reappear until dinner-time, and then she was clad in lace and gaiety that impressed the naturally very good observation of Mrs. Geedge as unreal.

§ 12

The Captain, a confusion of motives that was as it were a mind returning to chaos, started. He had seen tears in her eyes. Just for one instant, but certainly they were tears. Tears of vexation. Or sorrow? (Which is the worse thing for a lover to arouse, grief or resentment?) But this boy must be caught, because if he was not caught a perpetually developing story of imbecile practical joking upon eminent and influential persons would eat like a cancer into the Captain's career. And if his career was spoilt what sort of thing would he be as a lover? Not to mention that he might never get a chance then to try flying for military purposes.... So anyhow, anyhow, this boy must be caught. But quickly, for women's hearts are tender, they will not stand exposure to hardship. There is a kind of unreasonableness natural to goddesses. Unhappily this was an expedition needing wariness, deliberation, and one brought to it a feverish hurry to get back. There must be self-control. There must be patience. Such occasions try the soldierly quality of a man....

It added nothing to the Captain's self-control that after he had travelled ten miles he found he had forgotten his quite indispensable map and had to return for it. Then he was seized again with doubts about his inductions and went over them again, sitting by the roadside. (There must be patience.) ... He went on at a pace of thirty-five miles an hour to the inn he had marked upon his map as Bealby's limit for the second evening. It was a beastly little inn, it stewed tea for the Captain atrociously and it knew nothing of Bealby. In the adjacent cottages also they had never heard of Bealby. Captain Douglas revised his deductions for the third time and came to the conclusion that he had not made a proper allowance for Wednesday afternoon. Then there was all Thursday, and the longer, lengthening part of Friday. He might have done thirty miles or more already. And he might have crossed this corner—inconspicuously.

Suppose he hadn't after all come along this road!

He had a momentary vision of Madeleine with eyes brightly tearful. "You left me for a Wild Goose Chase," he fancied her saying....

One must stick to one's job. A soldier more particularly must stick to his job. Consider Balaclava....

He decided to go on along this road and try the incidental cottages that his reasoning led him to suppose were the most likely places at which Bealby would ask for food. It was a business demanding patience and politeness.

So a number of cottagers, for the greater part they were elderly women past the fiercer rush and hurry of life, grandmothers and ancient dames or wives at leisure with their children away at the Council schools, had a caller that afternoon. Cottages are such lonely places in the daytime that even district visitors and canvassers are godsends and only tramps ill received. Captain Douglas ranked high in the scale of visitors. There was something about him, his fairness, a certain handsomeness, his quick colour, his active speech, which interested women at all times, and now an indefinable flow of romantic excitement conveyed itself to his interlocutors. He encountered the utmost civility everywhere; doors at first tentatively ajar opened wider at the sight of him and there was a kindly disposition to enter into his troubles lengthily and deliberately. People listened attentively to his demands, and before they testified to Bealby's sustained absence from their perception they would for the most part ask numerous questions in return. They wanted to hear the Captain's story, the reason for his research, the relationship between himself and the boy, they wanted to feel something of the sentiment of the thing. After that was the season for negative facts. Perhaps when everything was stated they might be able to conjure up what he wanted. He was asked in to have tea twice, for he looked not only pink and dusty, but dry, and one old lady said that years ago she had lost just such a boy as Bealby seemed to be—"Ah! not in the way *you* have lost him"—and she wept, poor old dear! and was only comforted after she had told the Captain three touching but extremely lengthy and detailed anecdotes of Bealby's vanished prototype.

(Fellow cannot rush away, you know; still all this sort of thing, accumulating, means a confounded lot of delay.)

And then there was a deaf old man.... A very, very tiresome deaf old man who said at first he *had* seen Bealby....

After all the old fellow was deaf....

The sunset found the Captain on a breezy common forty miles away from the Redlake Royal Hotel and by this time he knew that fugitive boys cannot be trusted to follow the lines even of the soundest inductions. This business meant a search.

Should he pelt back to Redlake and start again more thoroughly on the morrow?

A moment of temptation.

If he did he knew she wouldn't let him go.

No!

NO!

He must make a sweeping movement through the country to the left, trying up and down the roads that, roughly speaking, radiated from Redlake between the twenty-fifth and the thirty-fifth milestone....

It was night and high moonlight when at last the Captain reached Crayminster, that little old town decayed to a village, in the Crays valley. He was hungry, dispirited, quite unsuccessful, and here he resolved to eat and rest for the night.

He would have a meal, for by this time he was ravenous, and then go and talk in the bar or the tap about Bealby.

Until he had eaten he felt he could not endure the sound of his own voice repeating what had already become a tiresome stereotyped formula; "You haven't I suppose seen or heard anything during the last two days of a small boy—little chap of about thirteen—wandering about? He's a sturdy resolute little fellow with a high colour, short wiry hair, rather dark...."

The White Hart at Crayminster, after some negotiations, produced mutton cutlets and Australian hock. As he sat at his meal in the small ambiguous respectable dining-room of the inn—adorned with framed and glazed beer advertisements, crinkled paper fringes and insincere sporting prints—he became aware of a murmurous confabulation going on in the bar parlour. It must certainly he felt be the bar parlour....

He could not hear distinctly, and yet it seemed to him that the conversational style of Crayminster was abnormally rich in expletive. And the tone was odd. It had a steadfast quality of commination.

He brushed off a crumb from his jacket, lit a cigarette and stepped across the passage to put his hopeless questions.

The talk ceased abruptly at his appearance.

It was one of those deep-toned bar parlours that are so infinitely more pleasant to the eye than the tawdry decorations of the genteel accommodation. It was brown with a trimming of green paper hops and it had a mirror and glass shelves sustaining bottles and tankards. Six or seven individuals were sitting about the room. They had a numerous effect. There was a man in very light floury tweeds, with a floury bloom on his face and hair and an anxious depressed expression. He was clearly a baker. He sat forward as though he nursed something precious under the table. Next him was a respectable-looking, regular-featured fair man with a large head, and a ruddy-faced butcher-like individual smoked a clay pipe by the side of the fireplace. A further individual with an alert intrusive look might have been a grocer's assistant associating above himself.

"Evening," said the Captain.

"Evening," said the man with the large hand guardedly.

The Captain came to the hearthrug with an affectation of ease.

"I suppose," he began, "that you haven't any of you seen anything of a small boy, wandering about. He's a little chap about thirteen. Sturdy, resolute-looking little fellow with a high colour, short wiry hair, rather dark...."

He stopped short, arrested by the excited movements of the butcher's pipe and by the changed expressions of the rest of the company.

"We—we seen 'im," the man with the big head managed to say at last.

"We seen 'im all right," said a voice out of the darkness beyond the range of the lamp.

The baker with the melancholy expression interjected, "I don't care if I don't ever see 'im again."

"Ah!" said the Captain, astonished to find himself suddenly beyond hoping on a hot fresh scent. "Now all that's very interesting. Where did you see him?"

"Thunderin' vicious little varmint," said the butcher. "Owdacious."

"Mr. Benshaw," said the voice from the shadows, "'E's arter 'im now with a shot gun loaded up wi' oats. 'E'll pepper 'im if 'e gets 'im, Bill will, you bet your 'at. And serve 'im jolly well right *tew*."

"I doubt," said the baker, "I doubt if I'll ever get my stummik—not thoroughly proper again. It's a Blow I've 'ad. 'E give me a Blow. Oh! Mr. 'Orrocks, *could* I trouble you for another thimbleful of brandy? Just a thimbleful neat. It eases the ache...."

CHAPTER VI
BEALBY AND THE TRAMP

§ 1

Bealby was loth to leave the caravan party even when by his own gross negligence it had ceased to be a caravan party. He made off regretfully along the crest of the hills through bushes of yew and box until the clamour of the disaster was no longer in his ears. Then he halted for a time and stood sorrowing and listening and then turned up by a fence along the border of a plantation and so came into a little overhung road.

His ideas of his immediate future were vague in the extreme. He was a receptive expectation. Since his departure from the gardener's cottage circumstances had handed him on. They had been interesting but unstable circumstances. He supposed they would still hand him on. So far as he had any definite view about his intentions it was that he was running away to sea. And that he was getting hungry.

It was also, he presently discovered, getting dark very gently and steadily. And the overhung road after some tortuosities expired suddenly upon the bosom of a great grey empty common with distant mysterious hedges.

It seemed high time to Bealby that something happened of a comforting nature.

Always hitherto something or someone had come to his help when the world grew dark and cold, and given him supper and put him or sent him to bed. Even when he had passed a night in the interstices of Shonts he had known there was a bed at quite a little distance under the stairs. If only that loud Voice hadn't shouted curses whenever he moved he would have gone to it. But as he went across this common in the gloaming it became apparent that this amiable routine was to be broken. For the first time he realized the world could be a homeless world.

And it had become very still.

Disagreeably still, and full of ambiguous shadows.

That common was not only an unsheltered place, he felt, but an unfriendly place, and he hurried to a gate at the further end. He kept glancing to the right and to the left. It would be pleasanter when he had got through that gate and shut it after him.

In England there are no grey wolves.

Yet at times one thinks of wolves, grey wolves, the colour of twilight and running noiselessly, almost noiselessly, at the side of their prey for quite a long time before they close in on it.

In England, I say, there are no grey wolves.

Wolves were extinguished in the reign of Edward the Third; it was in the histories, and since then no free wolf has trod the soil of England; only menagerie captives.

Of course there may be *escaped* wolves!

Now the gate!—sharp through it and slam it behind you, and a little brisk run and so into this plantation that slopes down hill. This is a sort of path; vague, but it must be a path. Let us hope it is a path.

What was that among the trees?

It stopped, surely it stopped, as Bealby stopped. Pump, pump—. Of course! that was one's heart.

Nothing there! Just fancy. Wolves live in the open; they do not come into woods like this. And besides, there are no wolves. And if one shouts—even if it is but a phantom voice one produces, they go away. They are cowardly things—really. Such as there aren't.

And there is the power of the human eye.

Which is why they stalk you and watch you and evade you when you look and creep and creep and creep behind you!

Turn sharply.

Nothing.

How this stuff rustled under the feet! In woods at twilight, with innumerable things darting from trees and eyes watching you everywhere, it would be pleasanter if one could walk without making quite such a row. Presently, surely, Bealby told himself, he would come out on a high road and meet other people and say "good-night" as they passed. Jolly other people they would be, answering, "Good-night." He was now going at a moistening trot. It was getting darker and he stumbled against things.

When you tumble down wolves leap. Not of course that there *are* any wolves.

It was stupid to keep thinking of wolves in this way. Think of something else. Think of things beginning with a B. Beautiful things, boys, beads, butterflies, bears. The mind stuck at bears. *Are there such things as long grey bears?* Ugh! Almost endless, noiseless bears?...

It grew darker until at last the trees were black. The night was swallowing up the flying Bealby and he had a preposterous persuasion that it had teeth and would begin at the back of his legs....

§ 2

"Hi!" cried Bealby weakly, hailing the glow of the fire out of the darkness of the woods above.

The man by the fire peered at the sound; he had been listening to the stumbling footsteps for some time, and he answered nothing.

In another minute Bealby had struggled through the hedge into the visible world and stood regarding the man by the fire. The phantom wolves had fled beyond Sirius. But Bealby's face was pale still from the terrors of the pursuit and altogether he looked a smallish sort of small boy.

"Lost?" said the man by the fire.

"Couldn't find my way," said Bealby.

"Anyone with you?"

"No."

The man reflected. "Tired?"

"Bit."

"Come and sit down by the fire and rest yourself.

"I won't 'urt you," he added as Bealby hesitated.

So far in his limited experience Bealby had never seen a human countenance lit from behind by a flickering red flame. The effect he found remarkable rather than pleasing. It gave this stranger the most active and unstable countenance Bealby had ever seen. The nose seemed to be in active oscillation between pug and Roman, the eyes jumped out of black caves and then went back into them, the more permanent features appeared to be a vast triangle of neck and chin. The tramp would have impressed Bealby as altogether inhuman if it had not been for the smell of cooking he diffused. There were onions in it and turnips and pepper—mouth-watering constituents, testimonials to virtue. He was making a stew in an old can that he had slung on a cross stick over a brisk fire of twigs that he was constantly replenishing.

"I won't 'urt you, darn you," he repeated. "Come and sit down on these leaves here for a bit and tell me all abart it."

Bealby did as he was desired. "I got lost," he said, feeling too exhausted to tell a good story.

The tramp, examined more closely, became less pyrotechnic. He had a large loose mouth, a confused massive nose, much long fair hair, a broad chin with a promising beard and spots—a lot of spots. His eyes looked out of deep sockets and they were sharp little eyes. He was a lean man. His hands were large and long and they kept on with the feeding of the fire as he sat and talked to Bealby. Once or twice he leant forward and smelt the pot judiciously, but all the time the little eyes watched Bealby very closely.

"Lose yer collar?" said the tramp.

Bealby felt for his collar. "I took it orf," he said.

"Come far?"

"Over there," said Bealby.

"Where?"

"Over there."

"What place?"

"Don't know the name of it."

"Then it ain't your 'ome?"

"No."

"You've run away," said the man.

"Pr'aps I 'ave," said Bealby.

"Pr'aps you 'ave! Why pr'aps? You *'ave!* What's the good of telling lies abart it? When'd you start?"

"Monday," said Bealby.

The tramp reflected. "Had abart enough of it?"

"Dunno," said Bealby truthfully.

"Like some soup?"

"Yes."

"'Ow much?"

"I could do with a lot," said Bealby.

"Ah yah! I didn't mean that. I meant, 'ow much for some? 'Ow much will you pay for a nice, nice 'arf can of soup? I ain't a darn charity. See?"

"Tuppence," said Bealby.

The tramp shook his head slowly from side to side and took out the battered iron spoon he was using to stir the stuff and tasted the soup lusciously. It was—jolly good soup and there were potatoes in it.

"Thrippence," said Bealby.

"'Ow much you got?" asked the tramp.

Bealby hesitated perceptibly. "Sixpence," he said weakly.

"It's sixpence," said the tramp. "Pay up."

"'Ow big a can?" asked Bealby.

The tramp felt about in the darkness behind him and produced an empty can with a jagged mouth that had once contained, the label witnessed—I quote, I do not justify—*'Deep Sea Salmon.'* "That," he said, "and this chunk of bread.... Right enough?"

"You *will* do it?" said Bealby.

"Do I look a swindle?" cried the tramp, and suddenly a lump of the abundant hair fell over one eye in a singularly threatening manner. Bealby handed over the sixpence without further discussion. "I'll treat you fairly, you see," said the tramp, after he had spat on and pocketed the sixpence, and he did as much. He decided that the soup was ready to be served and he served it with care. Bealby began at once. "There's a nextry onion," said the tramp, throwing one over. "It didn't cost me much and I gives it you for nothin'. That's all right, eh? Here's 'ealth!"

Bealby consumed his soup and bread meekly with one eye upon his host. He would, he decided, eat all he could and then sit a little while, and then get this tramp to tell him the way to—anywhere else. And the tramp wiped soup out of his can with gobbets of bread very earnestly and meditated sagely on Bealby.

"You better pal in with me, matey, for a bit," he said at last. "You can't go nowhere else—not to-night."

"Couldn't I walk perhaps to a town or sumpthing?"

"These woods ain't safe."

"'Ow d'you mean?"

"Ever 'eard tell of a gurrillia?—sort of big black monkey thing."

"Yes," said Bealby faintly.

"There's been one loose abart 'ere—oh week or more. Fact. And if you wasn't a grown up man quite and going along in the dark, well—'e might say something *to* you.... Of course 'e wouldn't do nothing where there was a fire or a man—but a little chap like you. I wouldn't like to let you do it, 'strewth I wouldn't. It's risky. Course I don't want to *keep* you. There it is. You go if you like. But I'd rather you didn't. 'Onest."

"Where'd he come from?" asked Bealby.

"M'nagery," said the tramp.

"'E very near bit through the fist of a chap that tried to stop 'im," said the tramp.

Bealby after weighing tramp and gorilla very carefully in his mind decided he wouldn't and drew closer to the fire—but not too close—and the conversation deepened.

§ 3

It was a long and rambling conversation and the tramp displayed himself at times as quite an amiable person. It was a discourse varied by interrogations, and as a thread of departure and return it dealt with the life of the road and with life at large and—life, and with matters of 'must' and 'may.'

Sometimes and more particularly at first Bealby felt as though a ferocious beast lurked in the tramp and peeped out through the fallen hank of hair and might leap out upon him, and sometimes he felt the tramp was large and fine and gay and amusing, more particularly when he lifted his voice and his bristling chin. And ever and again the talker became a nasty creature and a disgusting creature, and his red-lit face was an ugly creeping approach that made Bealby recoil. And then again he was strong and wise. So the unstable needle of a boy's moral compass spins.

The tramp used strange terms. He spoke of the 'deputy' and the 'doss-house,' of the 'spike' and 'padding the hoof,' of 'screevers' and 'tarts' and 'copper's narks.' To these words Bealby attached such meanings as he could, and so the things of which the tramp talked floated unsurely into his mind and again and again he had to readjust and revise his interpretations. And through these dim and fluctuating veils a new side of life dawned upon his consciousness, a side that was strange and lawless and dirty—in every way dirty—and dreadful and—attractive. That was the queer thing about it, that attraction. It had humour. For all its squalor and repulsiveness it was lit by defiance and laughter, bitter laughter perhaps, but laughter. It had a gaiety that Mr. Mergleson for example did not possess, it had a penetration, like the penetrating quality of onions or acids or asafœtida, that made the memory of Mr. Darling insipid.

The tramp assumed from the outset that Bealby had 'done something' and run away, and some mysterious etiquette prevented his asking directly what was the nature of his offence. But he made a number of insidious soundings. And he assumed that Bealby was taking to the life of the road and that, until good cause to the contrary appeared, they were to remain together. "It's a tough life," he said, "but it has its points, and you got a toughish look about you."

He talked of roads and the quality of roads and countryside. This was a good countryside; it wasn't overdone and there was no great hostility to wanderers and sleeping out. Some roads—the London to Brighton for example, if a chap struck a match, somebody came running. But here unless you went pulling the haystacks about too much they left you alone. And they weren't such dead nuts on their pheasants, and one had a chance of an empty cowshed. "If I've spotted a shed or anything with a roof to it I stay out," said the tramp, "even if it's raining cats and dogs. Otherwise it's the doss-'ouse or the 'spike.' It's the rain is the worst thing—getting wet. You haven't been wet yet, not if you only started Monday. Wet—with a chilly wind to drive it. Gaw! I been blown out of a holly hedge. You *would* think there'd be protection in a holly hedge...."

"Spike's the last thing," said the tramp. "I'd rather go bare-gutted to a doss-'ouse anywhen. Gaw!—you've not 'ad your first taste of the spike yet."

But it wasn't heaven in the doss-houses. He spoke of several of the landladies in strange but it would seem unflattering terms. "And there's always such a blamed lot of washing going on in a doss-'ouse. Always washing they are! One chap's washing 'is socks and another's washing 'is shirt. Making a steam drying it. Disgustin'. Carn't see what they want with it all. Barnd to git dirty again...."

He discoursed of spikes, that is to say of work-houses, and of masters. "And then," he said, with revolting yet alluring adjectives, "there's the bath."

"That's the worst side of it," said the tramp.... "'Owever, it doesn't always rain, and if it doesn't rain, well, you can keep yourself dry."

He came back to the pleasanter aspects of the nomadic life. He was all for the outdoor style. "Ain't we comfortable 'ere?" he asked. He sketched out the simple larcenies that had contributed and given zest to the evening's meal. But it seemed there were also doss-houses that had the agreeable side. "Never been in one!" he said. "But where you been sleeping since Monday?"

Bealby described the caravan in phrases that seemed suddenly thin and anæmic to his ears.

"You hit it lucky," said the tramp. "If a chap's a kid he strikes all sorts of luck of that sort. Now ef *I* come up against three ladies travellin' in a van—think they'd arst me in? Not it!"

He dwelt with manifest envy on the situation and the possibilities of the situation for some time. "You ain't dangerous," he said; "that's where you get in...."

He consoled himself by anecdotes of remarkable good fortunes of a kindred description. Apparently he sometimes travelled in the company of a lady named Izzy Berners—"a fair scorcher, been a regular, slap-up circus actress." And there was also "good old Susan." It was a little difficult for Bealby to see the point of some of these flashes by a tendency on the part of the tramp while his thoughts turned on these matters to adopt a staccato style of speech, punctuated by brief, darkly significant guffaws. There grew in the mind of Bealby a vision of the doss-house as a large crowded place, lit by a great central fire, with much cooking afoot and much jawing and disputing going on, and then "me and Izzy sailed in...."

The fire sank, the darkness of the woods seemed to creep nearer. The moonlight pierced the trees only in long beams that seemed to point steadfastly at unseen things, it made patches of ashen light that looked like watching faces. Under the tramp's direction Bealby skirmished round and got sticks and fed the fire until the darkness and thoughts of a possible gorilla were driven back for some yards and the tramp pronounced the blaze a "fair treat." He had made a kind of bed of leaves which he now invited Bealby to extend and share, and lying feet to the fire he continued his discourse.

He talked of stealing and cheating by various endearing names; he made these enterprises seem adventurous and facetious; there was it seemed a peculiar sort of happy find one came upon called a "flat," that it was not only entertaining but obligatory to swindle. He made fraud seem so smart and bright at times that Bealby found it difficult to keep a firm grasp on the fact that it was—fraud....

Bealby lay upon the leaves close up to the prone body of the tramp, and his mind and his standards became confused. The tramp's body was a dark but protecting ridge on one side of him; he could not see the fire beyond his toes but its flickerings were reflected by the tree stems about them, and made perplexing sudden movements that at times caught his attention and made him raise his head to watch them.... Against the terrors of the night the tramp had become humanity, the species, the moral basis. His voice was full of consolation; his topics made one forget the watchful silent circumambient. Bealby's first distrusts faded. He began to think the tramp a fine, brotherly, generous fellow. He was also growing accustomed to a faint something—shall I call it an olfactory bar—that had hitherto kept them apart. The monologue ceased to devote itself to the elucidation of Bealby; the tramp was lying on his back with his fingers interlaced beneath his head and talking not so much to his companion as to the stars and the universe at large. His theme was no longer the wandering life simply but the wandering life as he had led it, and the spiritedness with which he had led it and the real and admirable quality of himself. It was that soliloquy of consolation which is the secret preservative of innumerable lives.

He wanted to make it perfectly clear that he was a tramp by choice. He also wanted to make it clear that he was a tramp and no better because of the wicked folly of those he had trusted and the evil devices of enemies. In the world that contained those figures of spirit; Isopel Berners and Susan, there was also it seemed a bad and spiritless person, the tramp's wife, who had done him many passive injuries. It was clear she did not appreciate her blessings. She had been much to blame. "Anybody's opinion is better than 'er 'usband's," said the tramp. "Always 'as been." Bealby had a sudden memory of Mr. Darling saying exactly the same thing of his mother. "She's the sort," said the tramp, "what would rather go to a meetin' than a music 'all. She'd rather drop a shilling down a crack than spend it on anything decent. If there was a choice of jobs going she'd ask which 'ad the lowest pay and the longest hours and she'd choose *that*. She'd feel safer. She was born scared. When there wasn't anything else to do she'd stop at 'ome and scrub the floors. Gaw! it made a chap want to put the darn' pail over 'er 'ed, so's she'd get enough of it...."

"I don't hold with all this crawling through life and saying *Please*," said the tramp. "I say it's *my* world just as much as it's *your* world. You may have your 'orses and carriages, your 'ouses and country places and all that and you may think Gawd sent me to run abart and work for you; but *I* don't. See?"

Bealby saw.

"I seek my satisfactions just as you seek your satisfactions, and if you want to get me to work you've jolly well got to make me. I don't choose to work. I choose to keep on my own and a bit loose and take my chance where I find it. You got to take your chances in this world. Sometimes they come bad and sometimes they come good. And very often you can't tell which it is when they 'ave come...."

Then he fell questioning Bealby again and then he talked of the immediate future. He was beating for the seaside. "Always something doing," he said. "You got to keep your eye on for cops; those seaside benches, they're 'ot on tramps—give you a month for begging soon as look at you—but there's flats dropping sixpences thick as flies on a sore 'orse. You want a there for all sorts of jobs. You're just the chap for it, matey. Saw it soon's ever I set eyes on you...."

He made projects....

Finally he became more personal and very flattering.

"Now you and me," he said, suddenly shifting himself quite close to Bealby, "we're going to be downright pals. I've took a liking to you. Me and you are going to pal together. See?"

He breathed into Bealby's face, and laid a hand on his knee and squeezed it, and Bealby, on the whole, felt honoured by his protection....

§ 4

In the unsympathetic light of a bright and pushful morning the tramp was shorn of much of his overnight glamour. It became manifest that he was not merely offensively unshaven, but extravagantly dirty. It was not ordinary rural dirt. During the last few days he must have had dealings of an intimate nature with coal. He was taciturn and irritable, he declared that this sleeping out would be the death of him and the breakfast was only too manifestly wanting in the comforts of a refined home. He seemed a little less embittered after breakfast, he became even faintly genial, but he remained unpleasing. A distaste for the tramp arose in Bealby's mind and as he walked on behind his guide and friend, he revolved schemes of unobtrusive detachment.

Far be it from me to accuse Bealby of ingratitude. But it is true that that same disinclination which made him a disloyal assistant to Mr. Mergleson was now affecting his comradeship with the tramp. And he was deceitful. He allowed the tramp to build projects in the confidence of his continued adhesion, he did not warn him of the defection he meditated. But on the other hand Bealby had acquired from his mother an effective horror of stealing. And one must admit, since the tramp admitted it, that the man stole.

And another little matter had at the same time estranged Bealby from the tramp and linked the two of them together. The attentive reader will know that Bealby had exactly two shillings and twopence-halfpenny when he came down out of the woods to the fireside. He had Mrs. Bowles' half-crown and the balance of Madeleine Philips' theatre shilling, minus sixpence halfpenny for a collar and sixpence he had given the tramp for the soup overnight. But all this balance was now in the pocket of the tramp. Money talks and the tramp had heard it. He had not taken it away from Bealby, but he had obtained it in this manner: "We two are pals," he said, "and one of us had better be Treasurer. That's Me. I know the ropes better. So hand over what you got there, matey."

And after he had pointed out that a refusal might lead to Bealby's evisceration the transfer occurred. Bealby was searched, kindly but firmly....

It seemed to the tramp that this trouble had now blown over completely.

Little did he suspect the rebellious and treacherous thoughts that seethed in the head of his companion. Little did he suppose that his personal appearance, his manners, his ethical flavour—nay, even his physical flavour—were being judged in a spirit entirely unamiable. It seemed to him that he had obtained youthful and subservient companionship, companionship that would be equally agreeable and useful; he had adopted a course that he imagined would cement the ties between them; he reckoned not with ingratitude. "If anyone arsts you who I am, call me uncle," he said. He walked along, a little in advance, sticking his toes out right and left in a peculiar wide pace that characterized his walk, and revolving schemes for the happiness and profit of the day. To begin with—great draughts of beer. Then tobacco. Later perhaps a little bread and cheese for Bealby. "You can't come in 'ere," he said at the first public house. "You're under age, me boy. It ain't my doing, matey; it's 'Erbert Samuel. You blame 'im. 'E don't objec' to you going to work for any other Mr. Samuel there may 'appen to be abart or anything of that sort, that's good for you, that is; but 'e's most particular you shouldn't go into a public 'ouse. So you just wait abart outside 'ere. *I'll* 'ave my eye on you."

"You going to spend my money?" asked Bealby.

"I'm going to ration the party," said the tramp.

"You—you got no right to spend my money," said Bealby.

"I—'Ang it!—I'll get you some acid drops," said the tramp in tones of remonstrance. "I tell you, blame you,—it's 'Erbert Samuel.' I can't 'elp it! I can't fight against the lor."

"You haven't any right to spend my money," said Bealby.

"*Downt* cut up crusty. 'Ow can *I* 'elp it?"

"I'll tell a policeman. You gimme back my money and lemme go."

The tramp considered the social atmosphere. It did not contain a policeman. It contained nothing but a peaceful kindly corner public house, a sleeping dog and the back of an elderly man digging.

The tramp approached Bealby in a confidential manner. "'Oo's going to believe you?" he said. "And besides, 'ow did you come by it?

"Moreover, *I* ain't going to spend *your* money. I got money of my own. *'Ere!* See?" And suddenly before the dazzled eyes of Bealby he held and instantly withdrew three shillings and two coppers that seemed familiar. He had had a shilling of his own....

Bealby waited outside....

The tramp emerged in a highly genial mood, with acid drops, and a short clay pipe going strong. "'Ere," he said to Bealby with just the faintest flavour of magnificence over the teeth-held pipe and handed over not only the acid drops but a virgin short clay. "Fill," he said, proffering the tobacco. "It's yours jus' much as it's mine. Be'r not let 'Erbert Samuel see you, though; that's all. 'E's got a lor abart it."

Bealby held his pipe in his clenched hand. He had already smoked—once. He remembered it quite vividly still, although it had happened six months ago. Yet he hated not using that tobacco. "No," he said, "I'll smoke later."

The tramp replaced the screw of red Virginia in his pocket with the air of one who has done the gentlemanly thing....

They went on their way, an ill-assorted couple.

All day Bealby chafed at the tie and saw the security in the tramp's pocket vanish. They lunched on bread and cheese and then the tramp had a good sustaining drink of beer for both of them and after that they came to a common where it seemed agreeable to repose. And after a due meed of repose in a secluded hollow among the gorse the tramp produced a pack of exceedingly greasy cards and taught Bealby to play Euchre. Apparently the tramp had no distinctive pockets in his tail coat, the whole lining was one capacious pocket. Various knobs and bulges indicated his cooking tin, his feeding tin, a turnip and other unknown properties. At first they played for love and then they played for the balance in the tramp's pocket. And by the time Bealby had learnt Euchre thoroughly, that balance belonged to the tramp. But he was very generous about it and said they would go on sharing just as they had done. And then he became confidential. He scratched about in the bagginess of his garment and drew out a little dark blade of stuff, like a flint implement, regarded it gravely for a moment and held it out to Bealby. "Guess what this is."

Bealby gave it up.

"Smell it."

It smelt very nasty. One familiar smell indeed there was with a paradoxical sanitary quality that he did not quite identify, but that was a mere basis for a complex reek of acquisitions. "What is it?" said Bealby.

"*Soap!*"

"But what's it for?"

"I thought you'd arst that.... What's soap usually for?"

"Washing," said Bealby guessing wildly.

The tramp shook his head. "Making a foam," he corrected. "That's what I has my fits with. See? I shoves a bit in my mouth and down I goes and I rolls about. Making a sort of moaning sound. Why, I been given brandy often—neat brandy.... It isn't always a cert—nothing's absolutely a cert. I've 'ad some let-downs.... Once I was bit by a nasty little dog—that brought me to pretty quick—and once I 'ad an old gentleman go through my pockets. 'Poor chap!' 'e ses, 'very likely 'e's destitoot, let's see if 'e's *got* anything.'... I'd got all sorts of things, I didn't want *'im* prying about. But I didn't come to sharp enough to stop 'im. Got me into trouble that did...."

"It's an old lay," said the tramp, "but it's astonishing 'ow it'll go in a quiet village. Sort of amuses 'em. Or dropping suddenly in front of a bicycle party. Lot of them old tricks are the best tricks, and there ain't many of 'em Billy Bridget don't know. That's where you're lucky to 'ave met me, matey. Billy Bridget's a 'ard man to starve. And I know the ropes. I know what you *can* do and what you can't do. And I got a feeling for a policeman—same as some people 'ave for cats. I'd know if one was 'idden in the room...."

He expanded into anecdotes and the story of various encounters in which he shone. It was amusing and it took Bealby on his weak side. Wasn't he the Champion Dodger of the Chelsome playground?

The tide of talk ebbed. "Well," said the tramp, "time we was up and doing...."

They went along shady lanes and across an open park and they skirted a breezy common from which they could see the sea. And among other things that the tramp said was this, "Time we began to forage a bit."

He turned his large observant nose to the right of him and the left.

§ 5

Throughout the afternoon the tramp discoursed upon the rights and wrongs of property, in a way that Bealby found very novel and unsettling. The tramp seemed to have his ideas about owning and stealing arranged quite differently from those of Bealby. Never before had Bealby thought it possible to have them arranged in any other than the way he knew. But the tramp contrived to make most possession seem unrighteous and honesty a code devised by those who have for those who haven't. "They've just got 'old of it," he said. "They want to keep it to themselves.... Do I look as though I'd stole much of anybody's? It isn't me got 'old of this land and sticking up my notice boards to keep everybody off. It isn't me spends my days and nights scheming 'ow I can get 'old of more and more of the stuff...."

"I don't *envy* it 'em," said the tramp. "Some 'as one taste and some another. But when it comes to making all this fuss because a chap who *isn't* a schemer 'elps 'imself to a mäthful,—well, it's Rot....

"It's them makes the rules of the game and nobody ever arst me to play it. I don't blame 'em, mind you. Me and you might very well do the same. But brast me if I see where the sense of *my* keeping the rules comes in. This world ought to be a share out, Gawd meant it to be a share out. And me and you—we been done out of our share. That justifies us."

"It isn't right to steal," said Bealby.

"It isn't right to steal—certainly. It isn't right—but it's universal. Here's a chap here over this fence, ask 'im where 'e got 'is land. Stealing! What you call stealing, matey, *I* call restitootion. You ain't probably never even 'eard of socialism."

"I've 'eard of socialists right enough. Don't believe in Gawd and 'aven't no morality."

"Don't you believe it. Why!—'Arf the socialists are parsons. What I'm saying *is* socialism—practically. *I'm* a socialist. I know all abart socialism. There isn't nothing you can tell me abart socialism. Why!—for three weeks I was one of these here Anti-Socialist speakers. Paid for it. And I tell you there ain't such a thing as property left; it's all a blooming old pinch. Lords, commons, judges, all of them, they're just a crew of brasted old fences and the lawyers getting in the stuff. Then you talk to me of stealing! *Stealing!*"

The tramp's contempt and his intense way of saying 'stealing' were very unsettling to a sensitive mind.

They bought some tea and grease in a village shop and the tramp made tea in his old tin with great dexterity and then they gnawed bread on which two ounces of margarine had been generously distributed. "Live like fighting cocks, we do," said the tramp wiping out his simple cuisine with the dragged-out end of his shirt sleeve. "And if I'm not very much mistaken we'll sleep to-night on a nice bit of hay...."

But these anticipations were upset by a sudden temptation, and instead of a starry summer comfort the two were destined to spend a night of suffering and remorse.

A green lane lured them off the road, and after some windings led them past a field of wire-netted enclosures containing a number of perfect and conceited-looking hens close beside a little cottage, a vegetable garden and some new elaborate outhouses. It was manifestly a poultry farm, and something about it gave the tramp the conviction that it had been left, that nobody was at home.

These realizations are instinctive, they leap to the mind. He knew it, and an ambition to know further what was in the cottage came with the knowledge. But it seemed to him desirable that the work of exploration should be done by Bealby. He had thought of dogs, and it seemed to him that Bealby might be unembarrassed by that idea. So he put the thing to Bealby. "Let's have a look round ere," he said. "You go in and see what's abart...."

There was some difference of opinion. "I don't ask you to take anything," said the tramp.... "Nobody won't catch you.... I tell you nobody won't catch you.... I tell you there ain't nobody here to catch you.... Just for the fun of seeing in. I'll go up by them outhouses. And I'll see nobody comes.... Ain't afraid to go up a garden path, are you?... I tell you, I don't want you to steal.... You ain't got much guts to funk a thing like that.... I'll be abät too.... Thought you'd be the very chap for a bit of scarting.... Thought Boy Scarts was all the go nowadays.... Well, if you ain't afraid you'd do it.... Well, why didn't you say you'd do it at the beginning?..."

Bealby went through the hedge and up a grass track between poultry runs, made a cautious inspection of the outhouses and then approached the cottage. Everything was still. He thought it more plausible to go to the door than peep into the window. He rapped. Then after an interval of stillness he lifted the latch, opened the door and peered into the room. It was a pleasantly furnished room, and before the empty summer fireplace a very old white man was sitting in a chintz-covered arm-chair, lost it would seem in painful thought. He had a peculiar grey shrunken look, his eyes were closed, a bony hand with the shiny texture of alabaster gripped the chair arm.... There was something about him that held Bealby quite still for a moment.

And this old gentleman behaved very oddly.

His body seemed to crumple into his chair, his hands slipped down from the arms, his head nodded forwards and his mouth and eyes seemed to open together. And he made a snoring sound....

For a moment Bealby remained rigidly agape and then a violent desire to rejoin the tramp carried him back through the hen runs....

He tried to describe what he had seen.

"Asleep with his mouth open," said the tramp. "Well, that ain't anything so wonderful! You *got* anything? That's what I want to know.... Did anyone ever see such a boy? 'Ere! I'll go...."

"You keep a look out here," said the tramp.

But there was something about that old man in there, something so strange and alien to Bealby, that he could not remain alone in the falling twilight. He followed the cautious advances of the tramp towards the house. From the corner by the outhouses he saw the tramp go and peer in at the open door. He remained for some time peering, his head hidden from Bealby....

Then he went in....

Bealby had an extraordinary desire that somebody else would come. His soul cried out for help against some vaguely apprehended terror. And in the very moment of his wish came its fulfilment. He saw advancing up the garden path a tall woman in a blue serge dress, hatless and hurrying and carrying a little package—it was medicine—in her hand. And with her came a big black dog. At the sight of Bealby the dog came forward barking and Bealby after a moment's hesitation turned and fled.

The dog was quick. But Bealby was quicker. He went up the netting of a hen run and gave the dog no more than an ineffectual snap at his heels. And then dashing from the cottage door came the tramp. Under one arm was a brass-bound workbox and in the other was a candlestick and some smaller articles. He did not instantly grasp the situation of his treed companion, he was too anxious to escape the tall woman, and then with a yelp of dismay he discovered himself between woman and dog. All too late he sought to emulate Bealby. The workbox slipped from under his arm, the rest of his plunder fell from him, for an uneasy moment he was clinging to the side of the swaying hen run and then it had caved in and the dog had got him.

The dog bit, desisted and then finding itself confronted by two men retreated. Bealby and the tramp rolled and scrambled over the other side of the collapsed netting into a parallel track and were halfway to the hedge before the dog,—but this time in a less vehement fashion,—resumed his attack.

He did not close with them again and at the hedge he halted altogether and remained hacking the gloaming with his rage.

The woman it seemed had gone into the house, leaving the tramp's scattered loot upon the field of battle.

"This means mizzle," said the tramp, leading the way at a trot.

Bealby saw no other course but to follow.

He had a feeling as though the world had turned against him. He did not dare to think what he was nevertheless thinking of the events of these crowded ten minutes. He felt he had touched something dreadful; that the twilight was full of accusations.... He feared and hated the tramp now, but he perceived something had linked them as they had not been linked before. Whatever it was they shared it.

§ 6

They fled through the night; it seemed to Bealby for interminable hours. At last when they were worn out and footsore they crept through a gate and found an uncomfortable cowering place in the corner of a field.

As they went they talked but little, but the tramp kept up a constant muttering to himself. He was troubled by the thought of hydrophobia.

"I know I'll 'ave it," he said, "I know I'll get it."

Bealby after a time ceased to listen to his companion. His mind was preoccupied. He could think of nothing but that very white man in the chair and the strange manner of his movement.

"Was 'e awake when you saw 'im?" he asked at last.

"Awake—who?"

"That old man."

For a moment or so the tramp said nothing. "'E wasn't awake, you young silly," he said at last.

"But—wasn't he?"

"Why!—don't you know! 'E'd croaked,—popped off the 'ooks—very moment you saw 'im."

For a moment Bealby's voice failed him.

Then he said quite faintly, "You mean—he'd —. Was dead?"

"Didn't you know?" said the tramp. "Gaw! What a kid you are!"

In that manner it was Bealby first saw a dead man. Never before had he seen anyone dead. And after that for all the night the old white man pursued him, with strange slowly-opening eyes, and a head on one side and his mouth suddenly and absurdly agape....

All night long that white figure presided over seas of dark dismay. It seemed always to be there, and yet Bealby thought of a score of other painful things. For the first time in his life he asked himself, "Where am I going? What am I drifting to?" The world beneath the old man's dominance was a world of prisons.

Bealby believed he was a burglar and behind the darkness he imagined the outraged law already seeking him. And the terrors of his associate reinforced his own.

He tried to think what he should do in the morning. He dreaded the dawn profoundly. But he could not collect his thoughts because of the tramp's incessant lapses into grumbling lamentation. Bealby knew he had to get away from the tramp, but now he was too weary and alarmed to think of running away as a possible expedient. And besides there was the matter of his money. And beyond the range of the tramp's voice there were darknesses which to-night at least might hold inconceivable forms of lurking evil. But could he not appeal to the law to save him? Repent? Was there not something called turning King's Evidence?

The moon was no comfort that night. Across it there passed with incredible slowness a number of jagged little black clouds, blacker than any clouds Bealby had ever seen before. They were like velvet palls, lined with snowy fur. There was no end to them. And one at last most horribly gaped slowly and opened a mouth....

§ 7

At intervals there would be uncomfortable movements and the voice of the tramp came out of the darkness beside Bealby lamenting his approaching fate and discoursing—sometimes with violent expressions—on watch-dogs.

"I know I shall 'ave 'idrophobia," said the tramp. "I've always 'ad a disposition to 'idrophobia. Always a dread of water—and now it's got me.

"Think of it!—keeping a beast to set at a 'uman being. Where's the brotherhood of it? Where's the law and the humanity? Getting a animal to set at a brother man. And a poisoned animal, a animal with death in his teeth. And a 'orrible death too. Where's the sense and brotherhood?

"Gaw! when I felt 'is teeth coming through my träsers—!

"Dogs oughtn't to be allowed. They're a noosance in the towns and a danger in the country. They oughtn't to be allowed anywhere—not till every blessed 'uman being 'as got three square meals a day. Then if you like, keep a dog. And see 'e's a clean dog....

"Gaw! if I'd been a bit quicker up that 'en roost—!

"I ought to 'ave landed 'im a kick.

"It's a man's duty to 'urt a dog. When 'e sees a dog 'e ought to 'urt 'im. It's a natural 'atred. If dogs were what they ought to be, if dogs understood 'ow they're situated, there wouldn't be a dog go for a man ever.

"And if one did they'd shoot 'im....

"After this if ever I get a chance to land a dog a oner with a stone I'll land 'im one. I been too sorft with dogs...."

Towards dawn Bealby slept uneasily, to be awakened by the loud snorting curiosity of three lively young horses. He sat up in a blinding sunshine and saw the tramp looking very filthy and contorted, sleeping with his mouth wide open and an expression of dismay and despair on his face.

§ 8

Bealby took his chance to steal away next morning while the tramp was engaged in artificial epilepsy.

"I feel like fits this morning," said the tramp. "I could do it well. I want a bit of human kindness again. After that brasted dog.

"I expect soon I'll 'ave the foam all right withat any soap."

They marked down a little cottage before which a benevolent-looking spectacled old gentleman in a large straw hat and a thin alpaca jacket was engaged in budding roses. Then they retired to prepare. The tramp handed over to Bealby various compromising possessions, which might embarrass an afflicted person under the searching hands of charity. There was for example the piece of soap after he had taken sufficient for his immediate needs, there was ninepence in money, there were the pack of cards with which they had played Euchre, a key or so and some wires, much assorted string, three tins, a large piece of bread, the end of a composite candle, a box of sulphur matches, list slippers, a pair of gloves, a clasp knife, sundry grey rags. They all seemed to have the distinctive flavour of the tramp....

"If you do a bunk with these," said the tramp. "By Gawd——."

He drew his finger across his throat.

(King's Evidence.)

Bealby from a safe distance watched the beginnings of the fit and it impressed him as a thoroughly nasty kind of fit. He saw the elderly gentleman hurry out of the cottage and stand for a moment looking over his little green garden gate, surveying the sufferings of the tramp with an expression of intense yet discreet commiseration. Then suddenly he was struck by an idea; he darted in among his rose bushes and reappeared with a big watering-can and an enormous syringe. Still keeping the gate between himself and the sufferer he loaded his syringe very carefully and deliberately....

Bealby would have liked to have seen more but he felt his moment had come. Another instant and it might be gone again. Very softly he dropped from the gate on which he was sitting and made off like a running partridge along the hedge of the field.

Just for a moment did he halt—at a strange sharp yelp that came from the direction of the little cottage. Then his purpose of flight resumed its control of him.

He would strike across country for two or three miles, then make for the nearest police station and give himself up. (Loud voices. Was that the tramp murdering the benevolent old gentleman in the straw hat or was it the benevolent old gentleman in the straw hat murdering the tramp? No time to question. Onward, Onward!) The tramp's cans rattled in his pocket. He drew one out, hesitated a moment and flung it away and then sent its two companions after it....

He found his police station upon the road between Someport and Crayminster, a little peaceful rural station, a mere sunny cottage with a blue and white label and a notice board covered with belated bills about the stealing of pheasants' eggs. And another bill—.

It was headed MISSING and the next most conspicuous words were £5 REWARD and the next ARTHUR BEALBY.

He was fascinated. So swift, so terribly swift is the law. Already they knew of his burglary, of his callous participation in the robbing of a dead man. Already the sleuths were upon his trail. So surely did his conscience strike to this conclusion that even the carelessly worded offer of a reward that followed his description conveyed no different intimation to his mind. "To whomsoever will bring him back to Lady Laxton, at Shonts near Chelsmore," so it ran.

"And out of pocket expenses."

And even as Bealby read this terrible document, the door of the police station opened and a very big pink young policeman came out and stood regarding the world in a friendly, self-approving manner. He had innocent, happy, blue eyes; thus far he had had much to do with order and little with crime; and his rosebud mouth would have fallen open, had not discipline already closed it and set upon it the beginnings of a resolute expression that accorded ill with the rest of his open freshness. And when he had surveyed the sky and the distant hills and the little rose bushes that occupied the leisure of the force, his eyes fell upon Bealby....

Indecision has ruined more men than wickedness. And when one has slept rough and eaten nothing and one is conscious of a marred unclean appearance, it is hard to face one's situations. What Bealby had intended to do was to go right up to a policeman and say to him, simply and frankly: "I want to turn King's Evidence, please. I was in that burglary where there was a dead old man and a workbox and a woman and a dog. I was led astray by a bad character and I did not mean to do it. And really it was him that did it and not me."

But now his tongue clove to the roof of his mouth, he felt he could not speak, could not go through with it. His heart had gone down into his feet. Perhaps he had caught the tramp's constitutional aversion to the police. He affected not to see the observant figure in the doorway. He assumed a slack careless bearing like one who reads by chance idly. He lifted his eyebrows to express unconcern. He pursed his mouth to whistle but no whistle came. He stuck his hands into his pockets, pulled up his feet as one pulls up plants by the roots and strolled away.

He quickened his stroll as he supposed by imperceptible degrees. He glanced back and saw that the young policeman had come out of the station and was reading the notice. And as the young policeman read he looked ever and again at Bealby like one who checks off items.

Bealby quickened his pace and then, doing his best to suggest by the movements of his back a more boyish levity quite unconnected with the law, he broke into a trot.

Then presently he dropped back into a walking pace, pretended to see something in the hedge, stopped and took a sidelong look at the young policeman.

He was coming along with earnest strides; every movement of his suggested a stealthy hurry!

Bealby trotted and then becoming almost frank about it ran. He took to his heels.

From the first it was not really an urgent chase; it was a stalking rather than a hunt, because the young policeman was too young and shy and lacking in confidence really to run after a boy without any definite warrant for doing so. When anyone came along he would drop into a smart walk and pretend not to be looking at Bealby but just going somewhere briskly. And after two miles of it he desisted, and stood for a time watching a heap of mangold wurzel directly and the disappearance of Bealby obliquely, and then when Bealby was quite out of sight he turned back thoughtfully towards his proper place.

On the whole he considered he was well out of it. He might have made a fool of himself....

And yet,—five pounds reward!

CHAPTER VII
THE BATTLE OF CRAYMINSTER

§ 1

Bealby was beginning to realize that running away from one's situation and setting up for oneself is not so easy and simple a thing as it had appeared during those first days with the caravan. Three things he perceived had arisen to pursue him, two that followed in the daylight, the law and the tramp, and a third that came back at twilight, the terror of the darkness. And within there was a hollow faintness, for the afternoon was far advanced and he was extremely hungry. He had dozed away the early afternoon in the weedy corner of a wood. But for his hunger I think he would have avoided Crayminster.

Within a mile of that place he had come upon the 'Missing' notice again stuck to the end of a barn. He had passed it askance, and then with a sudden inspiration returned and tore it down. Somehow with the daylight his idea of turning King's Evidence against the tramp had weakened. He no longer felt sure.

Mustn't one wait and be asked first to turn King's Evidence?

Suppose they said he had merely confessed....

The Crayminster street had a picturesque nutritious look. Half-way down it was the White Hart with cyclist club signs on its walls and geraniums over a white porch, and beyond a house being built and already at the roofing pitch. To the right was a baker's shop diffusing a delicious suggestion of buns and cake and to the left a little comfortable sweetstuff window and a glimpse of tables and a board: 'Teas.' Tea! He resolved to break into his ninepence boldly and generously. Very likely they would boil him an egg for a penny or so. Yet on the other hand if he just had three or four buns, soft new buns. He hovered towards the baker's shop and stopped short. That bill was in the window!

He wheeled about sharply and went into the sweetstuff shop and found a table with a white cloth and a motherly little woman in a large cap. Tea? He could have an egg and some thick bread and butter and a cup of tea for fivepence. He sat down respectfully to await her preparations.

But he was uneasy.

He knew quite well that she would ask him questions. For that he was prepared. He said he was walking from his home in London to Someport to save the fare. "But you're so dirty!" said the motherly little woman. "I sent my luggage by post, ma'm, and I lost my way and didn't get it. And I don't much mind, ma'm, if you don't. Not washing...."

All that he thought he did quite neatly. But he wished there was not that bill in the baker's window opposite and he wished he hadn't quite such a hunted feeling. A faint claustrophobia affected him. He felt the shop might be a trap. He would be glad to get into the open again. Was there a way out behind if for example a policeman blocked the door? He hovered to the entrance while his egg was boiling and then when he saw a large fat baker surveying the world with an afternoon placidity upon his face, he went back and sat by the table. He wondered if the baker had noted him.

He had finished his egg; he was drinking his tea with appreciative noises, when he discovered that the baker *had* noted him. Bealby's eyes, at first inanely open above the tilting tea cup, were suddenly riveted on something that was going on in the baker's window. From where he sat he could see that detestable bill, and then slowly, feeling about for it, he beheld a hand and a floury sleeve. The bill was drawn up and vanished and then behind a glass shelf of fancy bread and a glass shelf of buns something pink and indistinct began to move jerkily.... It was a human face and it was trying to peer into the little refreshment shop that sheltered Bealby....

Bealby's soul went faint.

He had one inadequate idea. "Might I go out," he said, "by your back way?"

"There isn't a back way," said the motherly little woman. "There's a yard—."

"If I might," said Bealby, and was out in it.

No way at all! High walls on every side. He was back like a shot in the shop, and now the baker was half-way across the road. "Fivepence," said Bealby and gave the little old woman sixpence. "Here," she cried, "take your penny!"

He did not wait. He darted out of the door.

The baker was all over the way of escape. He extended arms that seemed abnormally long and with a weak cry Bealby found himself trapped. Trapped, but not hopelessly. He knew how to do it. He had done it in milder forms before, but now he did it with all his being. Under the diaphragm of the baker smote Bealby's hard little head, and instantly he was away running up the quiet sunny street. Man when he assumed the erect attitude made a hostage of his belly. It is a proverb among the pastoral Berbers of the Atlas mountains that the man who extends his arms in front of an angry ram is a fool.

It seemed probable to Bealby that he would get away up the street. The baker was engaged in elaborately falling backward, making the most of sitting down in the road, and the wind had been knocked out of him so that he could not shout. He emitted "Stop him!" in large whispers. Away ahead there were only three builder's men sitting under the wall beyond the White Hart, consuming tea out of their tea cans. But the boy who was trimming the top of the tall privet hedge outside the doctor's saw the assault of the baker and incontinently uttered the shout that the baker could not. Also he fell off his steps with great alacrity and started in pursuit of Bealby. A young man from anywhere—perhaps the grocer's shop—also started for Bealby. But the workmen were slow to rise to the occasion. Bealby could have got past them. And then, abruptly at the foot of the street ahead the tramp came into view, a battered disconcerting figure. His straw-coloured hat which had recently been wetted and dried in the sun was a swaying mop. The sight of Bealby seemed to rouse him from some disagreeable meditations. He grasped the situation with a terrible quickness. Regardless of the wisdom of the pastoral Berbers he extended his arms and stood prepared to intercept.

Bealby thought at the rate of a hundred thoughts to the minute. He darted sideways and was up the ladder and among the beams and rafters of the unfinished roof before the pursuit had more than begun. "Here, come off that," cried the foreman builder, only now joining in the hunt with any sincerity. He came across the road while Bealby regarded him wickedly from the rafters above. Then as the good man made to ascend Bealby got him neatly on the hat, it was a bowler hat, with a tile. This checked the advance. There was a disposition to draw a little off and look up at Bealby. One of the younger builders from the opposite sidewalk got him very neatly in the ribs with a stone. But two other shots went wide and Bealby shifted to a more covered position behind the chimney stack.

From here, however, he had a much less effective command of the ladder, and he perceived that his tenure of the new house was not likely to be a long one.

Below, men parleyed. "Who *is* 'e?" asked the foreman builder. "Where'd 'e come from?" "'E's a brasted little thief," said the tramp. "'E's one of the wust characters on the road." The baker was recovering his voice now. "There's a reward out for 'im," he said, "and 'e butted me in the stummick."

"'Ow much reward?" asked the foreman builder.

"Five pound for the man who catches him."

"'Ere!" cried the foreman builder in an arresting voice to the tramp. "Just stand away from that ladder...."

Whatever else Bealby might or might not be, one thing was very clear about him and that was that he was a fugitive. And the instinct of humanity is to pursue fugitives. Man is a hunting animal, enquiry into the justice of a case is an altogether later accretion to his complex nature, and that is why, whatever you are or whatever you do, you should never let people get you on the run. There is a joy in the mere fact of hunting, the sight of a scarlet coat and a hound will brighten a whole village, and now Crayminster was rousing itself like a sleeper who wakes to sunshine and gay music. People were looking out of windows and coming out of shops, a policeman appeared and heard the baker's simple story, a brisk hatless young man in a white apron and with a pencil behind his ear became prominent. Bealby, peeping over the ridge of the roof, looked a thoroughly dirty and unpleasant little creature to all these people. The only spark of human sympathy for him below was in the heart of the little old woman in the cap who had given him his breakfast. She surveyed the roof of the new house from the door of her shop, she hoped Bealby wouldn't hurt himself up there, and she held his penny change clutched in her hand in her apron pocket with a vague idea that perhaps presently if he ran past she could very quickly give it him.

§ 2

Considerable delay in delivering the assault on the house was caused by the foreman's insistence that he alone should ascend the ladder to capture Bealby. He was one of those regular-featured men with large heads who seem to have inflexible backbones, he was large and fair and full with a sweetish chest voice and in all his movements authoritative and deliberate. Whenever he made to ascend he discovered that people were straying into his building, and he had to stop and direct his men how to order them off. Inside his large head he was trying to arrange everybody to cut off Bealby's line of retreat without risking that anybody but himself should capture the fugitive. It was none too easy and it knitted his brows. Meanwhile Bealby was able to reconnoitre the adjacent properties and to conceive plans for a possible line of escape. He also got a few tiles handy against when the rush up the ladder came. At the same time two of the younger workmen were investigating the possibility of getting at him from inside the house. There was still no staircase, but there were ways of clambering. They had heard about the reward and they knew that they must do this before the foreman realized their purpose, and this a little retarded them. In their pockets they had a number of stones, ammunition in reserve, if it came again to throwing.

Bealby was no longer fatigued nor depressed; anxiety for the future was lost in the excitement of the present, and his heart told him that, come what might, getting on to the roof was an extraordinarily good dodge.

And if only he could bring off a certain jump he had in mind, there were other dodges—....

In the village street an informal assembly of leading citizens, a little recovered now from their first nervousness about flying tiles, discussed the problem of Bealby. There was Mumby, the draper and vegetarian, with the bass voice and the big black beard. He advocated the fire engine. He was one of the volunteer fire brigade and never so happy as when he was wearing his helmet. He had come out of his shop at the shouting. Schocks the butcher, and his boy were also in the street. Schocks's yard, with its heap of manure and fodder, bounded the new house on the left. Rymell the vet emerged from the billiard room of the White Hart, and with his head a little on one side was watching Bealby and replying attentively to the baker, who was asking him a number of questions that struck him as irrelevant. All the White Hart people were in the street.

"I suppose, Mr. Rymell," said the baker, "there's a mort of dangerous things in a man's belly round about 'is Stummick?"

"Tiles," said Mr. Rymell. "Loose bricks. It wouldn't do if he started dropping those."

"I was saying, Mr. Rymell," said the baker, after a pause for digestion, "is a man likely to be injured badly by a Blaw in his stummick?"

Mr. Rymell stared at him for a moment with unresponsive eyes. "More likely to get you in the head," he said, and then, "Here! What's that fool of a carpenter going to do?"

The tramp was hovering on the outskirts of the group of besiegers, vindictive but dispirited. He had been brought to from his fit and given a shilling by the old gentleman, but he was dreadfully wet between his shirt— he wore a shirt, under three waistcoats and a coat—and his skin, because the old gentleman's method of revival had been to syringe him suddenly with cold water. It had made him weep with astonishment and misery. Now he saw no advantage in claiming Bealby publicly. His part, he felt, was rather a waiting one. What he had to say to Bealby could be best said without the assistance of a third person. And he wanted to understand more of this talk about a reward. If there was a reward out for Bealby—

"That's not a bad dodge!" said Rymell, changing his opinion of the foreman suddenly as that individual began his ascent of the ladder with a bricklayer's hod carried shield-wise above his head. He went up with difficulty and slowly because of the extreme care he took to keep his head protected. But no tiles came. Bealby had discovered a more dangerous attack developing inside the house and was already in retreat down the other side of the building.

He did a leap that might have hurt him badly, taking off from the corner of the house and jumping a good twelve feet on to a big heap of straw in the butcher's yard. He came down on all fours and felt a little jarred for an instant, and then he was up again and had scrambled up by a heap of manure to the top of the butcher's wall. He was over that and into Maccullum's yard next door before anyone in the front of the new house had realized that he was in flight. Then one of the two workmen who had been coming up inside the house saw him from the oblong opening that was some day to be the upstairs bedroom window, and gave tongue.

It was thirty seconds later, and after Bealby had vanished from the butcher's wall that the foreman, still clinging to his hod, appeared over the ridge of the roof. At the workman's shout the policeman, who with the preventive disposition of his profession, had hitherto been stopping anyone from coming into the unfinished house, turned about and ran out into its brick and plaster and timber-littered backyard, whereupon the crowd in the street realizing that the quarry had gone away and no longer restrained, came pouring partly through the house and partly round through the butcher's gate into his yard.

Bealby had had a check.

He had relied upon the tarred felt roof of the mushroom shed of Maccullum the tailor and breeches-maker to get him to the wall that gave upon Mr. Benshaw's strawberry fields and he had not seen from his roof above the ramshackle glazed outhouse which Maccullum called his workroom and in which four industrious tailors were working in an easy dishabille. The roof of the shed was the merest tarred touchwood, it had perished as felt long ago, it collapsed under Bealby, he went down into a confusion of mushrooms and mushroom-bed, he blundered out trailing mushrooms and spawn and rich matter, he had a nine-foot wall to negotiate and only escaped by a hair's-breadth from the clutch of a little red-slippered man who came dashing out from the workroom. But by a happy use of the top of the dustbin he did just get away over the wall in time, and the red-slippered tailor, who was not good at walls, was left struggling to imitate an ascent that had looked easy enough until he came to try it.

For a moment the little tailor struggled alone and then both Maccullum's little domain and the butcher's yard next door and the little patch of space behind the new house, were violently injected with a crowd of active people, all confusedly on the Bealby trail. Someone, he never knew who, gave the little tailor a leg-up and then his red slippers twinkled over the wall and he was leading the hunt into the market gardens of Mr. Benshaw. A collarless colleague in list slippers and conspicuous braces followed. The policeman, after he had completed the wreck of Mr. Maccullum's mushroom shed, came next, and then Mr. Maccullum, with no sense of times and seasons, anxious to have a discussion at once upon the question of this damage. Mr. Maccullum was out of breath and he never got further with this projected conversation than "Here!" This he repeated several times as opportunity seemed to offer. The remaining tailors got to the top of the wall more sedately with the help of the Maccullum kitchen steps and dropped; Mr. Schocks followed, breathing hard, and then a fresh jet of humanity came squirting into the gardens through a gap in the fence at the back of the building site. This was led by the young workman who had first seen Bealby go away. Hard behind him came Rymell, the vet, the grocer's assistant, the doctor's page-boy and, less briskly, the baker. Then the tramp. Then Mumby and Schocks's boy. Then a number of other people. The seeking of Bealby had assumed the dimensions of a Hue and Cry.

The foreman with the large head and the upright back was still on the new roof; he was greatly distressed at the turn things had taken and shouted his claims to a major share in the capture of Bealby, mixed with his opinions of Bealby and a good deal of mere swearing, to a sunny but unsympathetic sky....

§ 3

Mr. Benshaw was a small holder, a sturdy English yeoman of the new school. He was an Anti-Socialist, a self-helper, an independent-spirited man. He had a steadily growing banking account and a plain but sterile wife, and he was dark in complexion and so erect in his bearing as to seem a little to lean forward. Usually he wore a sort of grey gamekeeper's suit with brown gaiters (except on Sundays when the coat was black), he was addicted to bowler hats that accorded ill with his large grave grey-coloured face, and he was altogether a very sound strong man. His bowler hats did but accentuate that. He had no time for vanities, even the vanity of dressing consistently. He went into the nearest shop and just bought the cheapest hat he could, and so he got hats designed for the youthful and giddy, hats with flighty crowns and flippant bows and amorous brims that undulated attractively to set off flushed and foolish young faces. It made his unrelenting face look rather like the Puritans under the Stuart monarchy.

He was a horticulturist rather than a farmer. He had begun his career in cheap lodgings with a field of early potatoes and cabbages, supplemented by employment, but with increased prosperity his area of cultivation had extended and his methods intensified. He now grew considerable quantities of strawberries, raspberries, celery, seakale, asparagus, early peas, late peas, and onions, and consumed more stable manure than any other cultivator within ten miles of Crayminster. He was beginning to send cut flowers to London. He had half an acre of glass and he was rapidly extending it. He had built himself a cottage on lines of austere economy, and a bony-looking dwelling house for some of his men. He also owned a number of useful sheds of which tar and corrugated iron were conspicuous features. His home was furnished with the utmost respectability, and notably joyless even in a countryside where gaiety is regarded as an impossible quality in furniture. He was already in a small local way a mortgagee. Good fortune had not turned the head of Mr. Benshaw nor robbed him of the feeling that he was a particularly deserving person, entitled to a preferential treatment from a country which in his plain unsparing way he felt that he enriched.

In many ways he thought that the country was careless of his needs. And in none more careless than in the laws relating to trespass. Across his dominions ran three footpaths, and one of these led to the public elementary school. That he should have to maintain this latter—and if he did not keep it in good order the children spread out and made parallel tracks among his cultivations—seemed to him a thing almost intolerably unjust. He mended it with cinders, acetylene refuse, which he believed and hoped to be thoroughly bad for boots, and a peculiarly slimy chalky clay, and he put on a board at each end "Keep to the footpaths, Trespassers will be prosecuted, by Order," which he painted himself to save expense when he was confined indoors by the influenza. Still more unjust it would be, he felt, for him to spend money upon effective fencing, and he could find no fencing cheap enough and ugly enough and painful enough and impossible enough to express his feelings in the matter. Every day the children streamed to and fro, marking how his fruits ripened and his produce became more esculent. And other people pursued these tracks; many, Mr. Benshaw was convinced, went to and fro through his orderly crops who had no business whatever, no honest business, to pass that way. Either, he concluded, they did it to annoy him, or they did it to injure him. This continual invasion aroused in Mr. Benshaw all that stern anger against unrighteousness latent in our race which more than any other single force has made America and the Empire what they are to-day. Once already he had been robbed—a raid upon his raspberries—and he felt convinced that at any time he might be robbed again. He had made representations to the local authority to get the footpath closed, but in vain. They defended themselves with the paltry excuse that the children would then have to go nearly a mile round to the school.

It was not only the tyranny of these footpaths that offended Mr. Benshaw's highly developed sense of Individual Liberty. All round his rather straggling dominions his neighbours displayed an ungenerous indisposition to maintain their fences to his satisfaction. In one or two places, in abandonment of his clear rights in the matter, he had, at his own expense, supplemented these lax defences with light barbed wire defences. But it was not a very satisfactory sort of barbed wire. He wanted barbed wire with extra spurs like a fighting cock; he wanted barbed wire that would start out after nightfall and attack passers-by. This boundary trouble was universal; in a way it was worse than the footpaths which after all only affected the Cage Fields where his strawberries grew. Except for the yard and garden walls of Maccullum and Schocks and that side, there was not really a satisfactory foot of enclosure all round Mr. Benshaw. On the one side rats and people's dogs and scratching cats came in, on the other side rabbits. The rabbits were intolerable and recently there had been a rise of nearly thirty per cent in the price of wire netting.

Mr. Benshaw wanted to hurt rabbits; he did not want simply to kill them, he wanted so to kill them as to put the fear of death into the burrows. He wanted to kill them so that scared little furry survivors with their tails as white as ghosts would go lolloping home and say, "I say, you chaps, we'd better shift out of this. We're up against a Strong Determined Man...."

I have made this lengthy statement of Mr. Benshaw's economic and moral difficulties in order that the reader should understand the peculiar tension that already existed upon this side of Crayminster. It has been necessary to do so now because in a few seconds there will be no further opportunity for such preparations.

There had been trouble, I may add very hastily, about the shooting of Mr. Benshaw's gun; a shower of small shot had fallen out of the twilight upon the umbrella and basket of old Mrs. Frobisher. And only a week ago an unsympathetic bench after a hearing of over an hour and in the face of overwhelming evidence had refused to convict little Lucy Mumby, aged eleven, of stealing fruit from Mr. Benshaw's fields. She had been caught red-handed....

At the very moment that Bealby was butting the baker in the stomach, Mr. Benshaw was just emerging from his austere cottage after a wholesome but inexpensive high tea in which he had finished up two left-over cold sausages, and he was considering very deeply the financial side of a furious black fence that he had at last decided should pen in the school children from further depredations. It should be of splintery tarred deal, and high, with well-pointed tops studded with sharp nails, and he believed that by making the path only two feet wide, a real saving of ground for cultivation might be made and a very considerable discomfort for the public arranged, to compensate for his initial expense. The thought of a narrow lane which would in winter be characterized by an excessive slimness and from which there would be no lateral escape was pleasing to a mind by no means absolutely restricted to considerations of pounds, shillings and pence. In his hand after his custom he carried a hoe, on the handle of which feet were marked, so that it was available not only for destroying the casual weed but also for purposes of measurement. With this he now checked his estimate and found that here he would reclaim as much as three feet of trodden waste, here a full two.

Absorbed in these calculations, he heeded little the growth of a certain clamour from the backs of the houses bordering on the High Street. It did not appear to concern him and Mr. Benshaw made it almost ostentatiously his rule to mind his own business. His eyes remained fixed on the lumpy, dusty, sunbaked track, that with an intelligent foresight he saw already transformed into a deterrent slough of despond for the young....

Then quite suddenly the shouting took on a new note. He glanced over his shoulder almost involuntarily and discovered that after all this uproar was his business. Amazingly his business. His mouth assumed a Cromwellian fierceness. His grip tightened on his hoe. That anyone should dare! But it was impossible!

His dominions were being invaded with a peculiar boldness and violence.

Ahead of everyone else and running with wild wavings of the arms across his strawberries was a small and very dirty little boy. He impressed Mr. Benshaw merely as a pioneer. Some thirty yards behind him was a little collarless, short-sleeved man in red slippers running with great effrontery and behind him another still more denuded lunatic, also in list slippers and with braces—braces of inconceivable levity. And then Wiggs, the policeman, hotly followed by Mr. Maccullum. Then more distraught tailors and Schocks the butcher. But a louder shout heralded the main attack, and Mr. Benshaw turned his eyes—already they were slightly blood-shot eyes—to the right, and saw, pouring through the broken hedge, a disorderly crowd, Rymell whom he had counted his friend, the grocer's assistant, the doctor's boy, some strangers—Mumby!

At the sight of Mumby, Mr. Benshaw leapt at a conclusion. He saw it all. The whole place was rising against him; they were asserting some infernal new right-of-way. Mumby—Mumby had got them to do it. All the fruits of fifteen years of toil, all the care and accumulation of Mr. Benshaw's prime, were to be trampled and torn to please a draper's spite!...

Sturdy yeoman as Mr. Benshaw was he resolved instantly to fight for his liberties. One moment he paused to blow the powerful police whistle he carried in his pocket and then rushed forward in the direction of the hated Mumby, the leader of trespassers, the parent and abetter and defender of the criminal Lucy. He took the hurrying panting man almost unawares, and with one wild sweep of the hoe felled him to the earth. Then he staggered about and smote again, but not quite in time to get the head of Mr. Rymell.

This whistle he carried was part of a systematic campaign he had developed against trespassers and fruit stealers. He and each of his assistants carried one, and at the first shrill note—it was his rule—everyone seized on every weapon that was handy and ran to pursue and capture. All his assistants were extraordinarily prompt in responding to these alarms, which were often the only break in long days of strenuous and strenuously directed toil. So now with an astonishing promptitude and animated faces men appeared from sheds and greenhouses and distant patches of culture, hastening to the assistance of their dour employer.

It says much for the amiable relations that existed between employers and employed in those days before Syndicalism became the creed of the younger workers that they did hurry to his assistance.

But many rapid things were to happen before they came into action. For first a strange excitement seized upon the tramp. A fantastic delusive sense of social rehabilitation took possession of his soul. Here he was pitted against a formidable hoe-wielding man, who for some inscrutable reason was resolved to cover the retreat of Bealby. And all the world, it seemed, was with the tramp and against this hoe-wielder. All the tremendous forces of human society, against which the tramp had struggled for so many years, whose power he knew and feared as only the outlaw can, had suddenly come into line with him. Across the strawberries to the right there was even a policeman hastening to join the majority, a policeman closely followed by a tradesman of the blackest, most respectable quality. The tramp had a vision of himself as a respectable man heroically leading respectable people against outcasts. He dashed the lank hair from his eyes, waved his arms laterally, and then with a loud strange cry flung himself towards Mr. Benshaw. Two pairs of superimposed coat-tails flapped behind him. And then the hoe whistled through the air and the tramp fell to the ground like a sack.

But now Schocks's boy had grasped his opportunity. He had been working discreetly round behind Mr. Benshaw, and as the hoe smote he leapt upon that hero's back and seized him about the neck with both arms and bore him staggering to the ground, and Rymell, equally quick, and used to the tackling of formidable creatures, had snatched and twisted away the hoe and grappled Mr. Benshaw almost before he was down. The first of Mr. Benshaw's helpers to reach the fray found the issue decided, his master held down conclusively and a growing circle trampling down a wide area of strawberry plants about the panting group....

Mr. Mumby, more frightened than hurt, was already sitting up, but the tramp with a glowing wound upon his cheekbone and an expression of astonishment in his face, lay low and pawed the earth.

"What d'you mean," gasped Mr. Rymell, "hitting people about with that hoe?"

"What d'you mean," groaned Mr. Benshaw, "running across my strawberries?"

"We were going after that boy."

"Pounds and pounds' worth of damage. Mischief and wickedness.... Mumby!"

Mr. Rymell, suddenly realizing the true values of the situation, released Mr. Benshaw's hands and knelt up. "Look here, Mr. Benshaw," he said, "you seem to be under the impression we are trespassing."

Mr. Benshaw, struggling into a sitting position was understood to enquire with some heat what Mr. Rymell called it. Schocks's boy picked up the hat with the erotic brim and handed it to the horticulturist silently and respectfully.

"We were not trespassing," said Mr. Rymell. "We were following up that boy. *He* was trespassing, if you like.... By the bye,—where *is* the boy? Has anyone caught him?"

At the question, attention which had been focussed upon Mr. Benshaw and his hoe, came round. Across the field in the direction of the sunlit half acre of glass the little tailor was visible standing gingerly and picking up his red slippers for the third time—they would come off in that loose good soil, everybody else had left the trail to concentrate on Mr. Benshaw—and Bealby—. Bealby was out of sight. He had escaped, clean got away.

"What boy?" asked Mr. Benshaw.

"Ferocious little beast who's fought us like a rat. Been committing all sorts of crimes about the country. Five pounds reward for him."

"Fruit stealing?" asked Mr. Benshaw.

"Yes," said Mr. Rymell, chancing it.

Mr. Benshaw reflected slowly. His eyes surveyed his trampled crops. "Gooo *Lord*!" he cried. "Look at those strawberries!" His voice gathered violence. "And that lout there!" he said. "Why!—he's lying on them! That's the brute who went for me!"

"You got him a pretty tidy one side the head!" said Maccullum.

The tramp rolled over on some fresh strawberries and groaned pitifully.

"He's hurt," said Mr. Mumby.

The tramp flopped and lay still.

"Get some water!" said Rymell, standing up.

At the word water, the tramp started convulsively, rolled over and sat up with a dazed expression.

"No water," he said weakly. "No more water," and then catching Mr. Benshaw's eye he got rather quickly to his feet.

Everybody who wasn't already standing was getting up, and everyone now was rather carefully getting himself off any strawberry plant he had chanced to find himself smashing in the excitement of the occasion.

"That's the man that started in on me," said Mr. Benshaw. "What's he doing here? Who is he?"

"Who are *you*, my man? What business have you to be careering over this field?" asked Mr. Rymell.

"I was only 'elping," said the tramp.

"Nice help," said Mr. Benshaw.

"I thought that boy was a thief or something."

"And so you made a rush at me."

"I didn't exactly—sir—I thought you was 'elping 'im."

"You be off, anyhow," said Mr. Benshaw. "Whatever you thought."

"Yes, you be off!" said Mr. Rymell.

"That's the way, my man," said Mr. Benshaw. "We haven't any jobs for you. The sooner we have you out of it the better for everyone. Get right on to the path and keep it." And with a desolating sense of exclusion the tramp withdrew. "There's pounds and pounds' worth of damage here," said Mr. Benshaw. "This job'll cost me a pretty penny. Look at them berries there. Why, they ain't fit for jam! And all done by one confounded boy." An evil light came into Mr. Benshaw's eyes. "You leave him to me and my chaps. If he's gone up among those sheds there—we'll settle with him. Anyhow there's no reason why my fruit should be trampled worse than it has been. Fruit stealer, you say, he is?"

"They live on the country this time of year," said Mr. Mumby.

"And catch them doing a day's work picking!" said Mr. Benshaw. "I know the sort."

"There's a reward of five pounds for 'im already," said the baker....

§ 4

You perceive how humanitarian motives may sometimes defeat their own end, and how little Lady Laxton's well-intentioned handbills were serving to rescue Bealby. Instead, they were turning him into a scared and hunted animal. In spite of its manifest impossibility he was convinced that the reward and this pursuit had to do with his burglary of the poultry farm, and that his capture would be but the preliminary to prison, trial and sentence. His one remaining idea was to get away. But his escape across the market gardens had left him so blown and spent, that he was obliged to hide up for a time in this perilous neighbourhood, before going on. He saw a disused-looking shed in the lowest corner of the gardens behind the greenhouses, and by doubling sharply along a hedge he got to it unseen. It was not disused—nothing in Mr. Benshaw's possession ever was absolutely disused, but it was filled with horticultural lumber, with old calcium carbide tins, with broken wheelbarrows and damaged ladders awaiting repair, with some ragged wheeling planks and surplus rolls of roofing felt. At the back were some unhinged shed doors leaning against the wall, and between them Bealby tucked himself neatly and became still, glad of any respite from the chase.

He would wait for twilight and then get away across the meadows at the back and then go—He didn't know whither. And now he had no confidence in the wild world any more. A qualm of home-sickness for the compact little gardener's cottage at Shonts, came to Bealby. Why, as a matter of fact, wasn't he there now?

He ought to have tried more at Shonts.

He ought to have minded what they told him and not have taken up a toasting fork against Thomas. Then he wouldn't now have been a hunted burglar with a reward of five pounds on his head and nothing in his pocket but threepence and a pack of greasy playing cards, a box of sulphur matches and various objectionable sundries, none of which were properly his own.

If only he could have his time over again!

Such wholesome reflections occupied his thoughts until the onset of the dusk stirred him to departure. He crept out of his hiding-place and stretched his limbs which had got very stiff, and was on the point of reconnoitring from the door of the shed when he became aware of stealthy footsteps outside.

With the quickness of an animal he shot back into his hiding-place. The footsteps had halted. For a long time it seemed the unseen waited, listening. Had he heard Bealby?

Then someone fumbled with the door of the shed; it opened, and there was a long pause of cautious inspection.

Then the unknown had shuffled into the shed and sat down on a heap of matting.

"*Gaw!*" said a voice.

The tramp's!

"If ever I struck a left-handed Mascot it was that boy," said the tramp. "The little *swine!*"

For the better part of two minutes he went on from this mild beginning to a descriptive elaboration of Bealby. For the first time in his life Bealby learnt how unfavourable was the impression he might leave on a fellow creature's mind.

"Took even my matches!" cried the tramp, and tried this statement over with variations.

"First that old fool with his syringe!" The tramp's voice rose in angry protest. "Here's a chap dying epilepsy on your doorstep and all you can do is to squirt cold water at him! Cold water! Why you might *kill* a man doing that! And then say you'd thought'd bring 'im ränd! Bring 'im ränd! You be jolly glad I didn't stash your silly face in. You [misbegotten] old fool! What's a shilling for wetting a man to 'is skin. Wet through I was. Running inside my shirt,—dripping.... And then the blooming boy clears!

"*I* don't know what boys are coming to!" cried the tramp. "These board schools it is. Gets 'old of everything 'e can and bunks! Gaw! if I get my 'ands on 'im, I'll show 'im. I'll—"

For some time the tramp revelled in the details, for the most part crudely surgical, of his vengeance upon Bealby....

"Then there's that dog bite. 'Ow do I know 'ow that's going to turn ät? If I get 'idrophobia, blowed if I don't *bite* some of 'em. 'Idrophobia. Screaming and foaming. Nice death for a man—my time o' life! Bark I shall. Bark and bite.

"And this is your world," said the tramp. "This is the world you put people into and expect 'em to be 'appy....

"I'd like to bite that dough-faced fool with the silly 'at. I'd enjoy biting *'im*. I'd spit it out but I'd bite it right enough. Wiping abät with 'is 'O. *Gaw!* Get off my ground! Be orf with you. Slash. 'E ought to be shut up.

"Where's the justice of it?" shouted the tramp. "Where's the right and the sense of it? What 'ave *I* done that I should always get the under side? Why should *I* be stuck on the under side of everything? There's worse men than me in all sorts of positions.... Judges there are. 'Orrible Kerecters. Ministers and people. I've read abät 'em in the papers....

"It's we tramps are the scapegoats. Somebody's got to suffer so as the police can show a face. Gaw! Some of these days I'll do something. I'll do something. You'll drive me too far with it, I tell you—"

He stopped suddenly and listened. Bealby had creaked.

"Gaw! What can one do?" said the tramp after a long interval.

And then complaining more gently, the tramp began to feel about to make his simple preparations for the night.

"'Unt me out of this, I expect," said the tramp. "And many sleeping in feather beds that ain't fit to 'old a candle to me. Not a hordinary farthing candle...."

§ 5

The subsequent hour or so was an interval of tedious tension for Bealby.

After vast spaces of time he was suddenly aware of three vertical threads of light. He stared at them with mysterious awe, until he realized that they were just the moonshine streaming through the cracks of the shed.

The tramp tossed and muttered in his sleep.

Footsteps?

Yes—Footsteps.

Then voices.

They were coming along by the edge of the field, and coming and talking very discreetly.

"Ugh!" said the tramp, and then softly, "what's that?" Then he too became noiselessly attentive.

Bealby could hear his own heart beating.

The men were now close outside the shed. "He wouldn't go in there," said Mr. Benshaw's voice. "He wouldn't dare. Anyhow we'll go up by the glass first. I'll let him have the whole barrelful of oats if I get a glimpse of him. If he'd gone away they'd have caught him in the road...."

The footsteps receded. There came a cautious rustling on the part of the tramp and then his feet padded softly to the door of the shed. He struggled to open it and then with a jerk got it open a few inches; a great bar of moonlight leapt and lay still across the floor of the shed. Bealby advanced his head cautiously until he could see the black obscure indications of the tramp's back as he peeped out.

"*Now*," whispered the tramp and opened the door wider. Then he ducked his head down and darted out of sight, leaving the door open behind him.

Bealby questioned whether he should follow. He came out a few steps and then went back at a shout from away up the garden. "There he goes," shouted a voice, "in the shadow of the hedge."

"Look out, Jim!"—*Bang*—and a yelp.

"Stand away! I've got another barrel!"

Bang.

Then silence for a time, and then the footsteps coming back.

"That ought to teach him," said Mr. Benshaw. "First time, I got him fair, and I think I peppered him a bit the second. Couldn't see very well, but I heard him yell. He won't forget that in a hurry. Not him. There's nothing like oats for fruit stealers. Jim, just shut that door, will you? That's where he was hiding...."

It seemed a vast time to Bealby before he ventured out into the summer moonlight, and a very pitiful and outcast little Bealby he felt himself to be.

He was beginning to realize what it means to go beyond the narrow securities of human society. He had no friends, no friends at all....

He caught at and arrested a sob of self-pity.

Perhaps after all it was not so late as Bealby had supposed. There were still lights in some of the houses and he had the privilege of seeing Mr. Benshaw going to bed with pensive deliberation. Mr. Benshaw wore a flannel night-shirt and said quite a lengthy prayer before extinguishing his candle. Then suddenly Bealby turned nervously and made off through the hedge. A dog had barked.

At first there were nearly a dozen lighted windows in Crayminster. They went out one by one. He hung for a long time with a passionate earnestness on the sole surviving one, but that too went at last. He could have wept when at last it winked out. He came down into the marshy flats by the river, but he did not like the way in which the water sucked and swirled in the vague moonlight; also he suddenly discovered a great white horse standing quite still in the misty grass not thirty yards away; so he went up to and crossed the high road and wandered up the hillside towards the allotments, which attracted him by reason of the sociability of the numerous tool sheds. In a hedge near at hand a young rabbit squealed sharply and was stilled. Why?

Then something like a short snake scrabbled by very fast through the grass.

Then he thought he saw the tramp stalking him noiselessly behind some currant bushes. That went on for some time, but came to nothing.

Then nothing pursued him, nothing at all. The gap, the void, came after him. The bodiless, the faceless, the formless; these are evil hunters in the night....

What a cold still *watching* thing moonlight can be!...

He thought he would like to get his back against something solid, and found near one of the sheds a little heap of litter. He sat down against good tarred boards, assured at least that whatever came must come in front. Whatever he did, he was resolved, he would not shut his eyes.

That would be fatal....

He awoke in broad daylight amidst a cheerful uproar of birds.

§ 6

And then again flight and pursuit were resumed.

As Bealby went up the hill away from Crayminster he saw a man standing over a spade and watching his retreat and when he looked back again presently this man was following. It was Lady Laxton's five pound reward had done the thing for him.

He was half minded to surrender and have done with it, but jail he knew was a dreadful thing of stone and darkness. He would make one last effort. So he beat along the edge of a plantation and then crossed it and forced his way through some gorse and came upon a sunken road, that crossed the hill in a gorse-lined cutting. He struggled down the steep bank. At its foot, regardless of him, unaware of him, a man sat beside a motor bicycle with his fists gripped tight and his head downcast, swearing. A county map was crumpled in his hand. "Damn!" he cried, and flung the map to the ground and kicked it and put his foot on it.

Bealby slipped, came down the bank with a run and found himself in the road within a couple of yards of the blond features and angry eyes of Captain Douglas. When he saw the Captain and perceived himself recognized, he flopped down—a done and finished Bealby....

§ 7

He had arrived just in time to interrupt the Captain in a wild and reprehensible fit of passion.

The Captain imagined it was a secret fit of passion. He thought he was quite alone and that no one could hear him or see him. So he had let himself shout and stamp, to work off the nervous tensions that tormented him beyond endurance.

In the direst sense of the words the Captain was in love with Madeleine. He was in love quite beyond the bounds set by refined and decorous people to this dangerous passion. The primordial savage that lurks in so many of us was uppermost in him. He was not in love with her prettily or delicately, he was in love with her violently and vehemently. He wanted to be with her, he wanted to be close to her, he wanted to possess her and nobody else to approach her. He was so inflamed now that no other interest in life had any importance except as it aided or interfered with this desire. He had forced himself in spite of this fever in his blood to leave her to pursue Bealby, and now he was regretting this firmness furiously. He had expected to catch Bealby overnight and bring him back to the hotel in triumph. But Bealby had been elusive. There she was, away there, hurt and indignant—neglected!

"A laggard in love," cried the Captain, "a dastard in war! God!—I run away from everything. First I leave the manœuvres, then her. Unstable as water thou shalt not prevail. Water! What does the confounded boy matter? What does he matter?

"And there she is. Alone! She'll flirt—naturally she'll flirt. Don't I deserve it? Haven't I asked for it? Just the one little time we might have had together! I fling it in her face. You fool, you laggard, you dastard! And here's this map!"

A breathing moment.

"How the *devil*," cried the Captain, "am I to find the little beast on this map?

"And twice he's been within reach of my hand!

"No decision!" cried the Captain. "No instant grip! What good is a soldier without it? What good is any man who will not leap at opportunity? I ought to have chased out last night after that fool and his oats. Then I might have had a chance!

"Chuck it! Chuck the whole thing! Go back to her. Kneel to her, kiss her, compel her!

"And what sort of reception am I likely to get?"

He crumpled the flapping map in his fist.

And then suddenly out of nowhere Bealby came rolling down to his feet, a dishevelled and earthy Bealby. But Bealby.

"Good Lord!" cried the Captain, starting to his feet and holding the map like a sword sheath.

"What do you want?"

For a second Bealby was a silent spectacle of misery.

"Oooh! I want my *breckfuss*," he burst out at last, reduced to tears.

"Are you young Bealby?" asked the Captain, seizing him by the shoulder.

"They're after me," cried Bealby. "If they catch me they'll put me in prison. Where they don't give you anything. It wasn't me did it—and I 'aven't had anything to eat—not since yesterday."

The Captain came rapidly to a decision. There should be no more faltering. He saw his way clear before him. He would act—like a whistling sword. "Here! jump up behind," he said ... "hold on tight to me...."

§ 8

For a time there was a more than Napoleonic swiftness in the Captain's movements. When Bealby's pursuer came up to the hedge that looks down into the sunken road, there was no Bealby, no Captain, nothing but a torn and dishevelled county map, an almost imperceptible odour of petrol and a faint sound—like a distant mowing machine—and the motor bicycle was a mile away on the road to Beckinstone. Eight miles, eight rather sickening miles, Bealby did to Beckinstone in eleven minutes, and there in a little coffee house he was given breakfast with eggs and bacon and marmalade (Prime!), and his spirit was restored to him while the Captain raided a bicycle and repairing shop and negotiated the hire of an experienced but fairly comfortable wickerwork trailer. And so, to London through the morning sunshine, leaving tramps, pursuers, policemen, handbills, bakers, market gardeners, terrors of the darkness and everything upon the road behind—and further behind and remote and insignificant—and so to the vanishing point.

Some few words of explanation the Captain had vouchsafed, and that was all.

"Don't be afraid about it," he said. "Don't be in the least bit afraid. You tell them about it, just simply and truthfully, exactly what you did, exactly how you got into it and out of it and all about it."

"You're going to take me up to a Magistrate, sir?"

"I'm going to take you up to the Lord Chancellor himself."

"And then they won't do anything?"

"Nothing at all, Bealby; you trust me. All you've got to do is to tell the simple truth...."

It was pretty rough going in the trailer, but very exciting. If you gripped the sides very hard, and sat quite tight, nothing very much happened and also there was a strap across your chest. And you went past everything. There wasn't a thing on the road the Captain didn't pass, lowing deeply with his great horn when they seemed likely to block his passage. And as for the burglary and everything, it would all be settled....

The Captain also found that ride to London exhilarating. At least he was no longer hanging about; he was getting to something. He would be able to go back to her—and all his being now yearned to go back to her—with things achieved, with successes to show. He'd found the boy. He would go straight to dear old uncle Chickney, and uncle Chickney would put things right with Moggeridge, the boy would bear his testimony, Moggeridge would be convinced and all would be well again. He might be back with Madeleine that evening. He would go back to her, and she would see the wisdom and energy of all he had done, and she would lift that dear chin of hers and smile that dear smile of hers and hold out her hand to be kissed and the lights and reflections would play on that strong soft neck of hers....

They buzzed along stretches of common and stretches of straight-edged meadowland, by woods and orchards, by pleasant inns and slumbering villages and the gates and lodges of country houses.

These latter grew more numerous, and presently they skirted a town, and then more road, more villages and at last signs of a nearness to London, more frequent houses, more frequent inns, hoardings and advertisements, an asphalted sidewalk, lamps, a gasworks, laundries, a stretch of suburban villadom, a suburban railway station, a suburbanized old town, an omnibus, the head of a tramline, a stretch of public common thick with noticeboards, a broad pavement, something-or-other parade, with a row of shops....

London.

CHAPTER VIII
HOW BEALBY EXPLAINED

§ 1

Lord Chickney was only slightly older than Lord Moggeridge, but he had not worn nearly so well. His hearing was not good, though he would never admit it, and the loss of several teeth greatly affected his articulation. One might generalize and say that neither physically nor mentally do soldiers wear so well as lawyers. The army ages men sooner than the law and philosophy; it exposes them more freely to germs, which undermine and destroy, and it shelters them more completely from thought, which stimulates and preserves. A lawyer must keep his law highly polished and up-to-date or he hears of it within a fortnight, a general never realizes he is out of training and behind the times until disaster is accomplished. Since the magnificent retreat from Bondy-Satina in eighty-seven and his five weeks defence of Barrowgast (with the subsequent operations) the abilities of Lord Chickney had never been exercised seriously at all. But there was a certain simplicity of manner and a tall drooping grizzled old-veteran picturesqueness about him that kept him distinguished; he was easy to recognize on public occasions on account of his long moustaches, and so he got pointed out when greater men were ignored. The autograph collectors adored him. Every morning he would spend half an hour writing autographs, and the habit was so strong in him that on Sundays, when there was no London post and autograph writing would have been wrong anyhow, he filled the time in copying out the epistle and gospel for the day. And he liked to be well in the foreground of public affairs—if possible wearing his decorations. After the autographs he would work, sometimes for hours, for various patriotic societies and more particularly for those which would impose compulsory training upon every man, woman and child in the country. He even belonged to a society for drilling the butchers' ponies and training big dogs as scouts. He did not understand how a country could be happy unless every city was fortified and every citizen wore side-arms, and the slightest error in his dietary led to the most hideous nightmares of the Channel Tunnel or reduced estimates and a land enslaved. He wrote and toiled for these societies, but he could not speak for them on account of his teeth. For he had one peculiar weakness; he had faced death in many forms but he had never faced a dentist. The thought of dentists gave him just the same sick horror as the thought of invasion.

He was a man of blameless private life, a widower and childless. In later years he had come to believe that he had once been very deeply in love with his cousin, Susan, who had married a rather careless husband named Douglas; both she and Douglas were dead now, but he maintained a touching affection for her two lively rather than satisfying sons. He called them his nephews, and by the continuous attrition of affection he had become their recognized uncle. He was glad when they came to him in their scrapes, and he liked to be seen about with them in public places. They regarded him with considerable confidence and respect and an affection that they sometimes blamed themselves for as not quite warm enough for his merits. But there is a kind of injustice about affection.

He was really gratified when he got a wire from the less discreditable of these two bright young relations, saying, "Sorely in need of your advice. Hope to bring difficulties to you to-day at twelve."

He concluded very naturally that the boy had come to some crisis in his unfortunate entanglement with Madeleine Philips, and he was flattered by the trustfulness that brought the matter to him. He resolved to be delicate but wily, honourable, strictly honourable, but steadily, patiently separative. He paced his spacious study with his usual morning's work neglected, and rehearsed little sentences in his mind that might be effective in the approaching interview. There would probably be emotion. He would pat the lad on his shoulder and be himself a little emotional. "I understand, my boy," he would say, "I understand.

"Don't forget, my boy, that I've been a young man too."

He would be emotional, he would be sympathetic, but also he must be a man of the world. "Sort of thing that won't do, you know, my boy; sort of thing that people will *not* stand.... A soldier's wife has to be a soldier's wife and nothing else.... Your business is to serve the king, not—not some celebrity. Lovely, no doubt. I don't deny the charm of her—but on the hoardings, my boy.... Now don't you think—don't you *think*?—there's some nice pure girl somewhere, sweet as violets, new as the dawn, and ready to be *yours*; a girl, I mean, a maiden fancy free, not—how shall I put it?—a woman of the world. Wonderful, I admit—but seasoned. Public. My dear, dear boy, I knew your mother when she was a girl, a sweet pure girl—a thing of dewy freshness. Ah! Well I remember her! All these years, my boy—Nothing. It's difficult...."

Tears stood in his brave old blue eyes as he elaborated such phrases. He went up and down mumbling them through the defective teeth and the long moustache and waving an eloquent hand.

§ 2

When Lord Chickney's thoughts had once started in any direction it was difficult to turn them aside. No doubt that concealed and repudiated deafness helped his natural perplexity of mind. Truth comes to some of us as a still small voice, but Lord Chickney needed shouting and prods. And Douglas did not get to him until he was finishing lunch. Moreover, it was the weakness of Captain Douglas to talk in jerky fragments and undertones, rather than clearly and fully in the American fashion. "Tell me all about it, my boy," said Lord Chickney. "Tell me all about it. Don't apologize for your clothes. I understand. Motor bicycle and just come up. But have you had any lunch, Eric?"

"Alan, uncle,—not Eric. My brother is Eric."

"Well, I called him Alan. Tell me all about it. Tell me what has happened. What are you thinking of doing? Just put the positions before me. To tell you the truth I've been worrying over this business for some time."

"Didn't know you'd heard of it, uncle. He can't have talked about it already. Anyhow,—you see all the awkwardness of the situation. They say the old chap's a thundering spiteful old devil when he's roused—and there's no doubt he was roused.... Tremendously...."

Lord Chickney was not listening very attentively. Indeed he was also talking. "Not clear to me there was another man in it," he was saying. "That makes it more complicated, my boy, makes the row acuter. Old fellow, eh? Who?"

They came to a pause at the same moment.

"You speak so indistinctly," complained Lord Chickney. "*Who* did you say?"

"I thought you understood. Lord Moggeridge."

"Lord—! Lord Moggeridge! My dear Boy! But how?"

"I thought you understood, uncle."

"He doesn't want to marry her! Tut! Never! Why, the man must be sixty if he's a day...."

Captain Douglas regarded his distinguished uncle for a moment with distressed eyes. Then he came nearer, raised his voice and spoke more deliberately.

"I don't know whether you quite understand, uncle. I am talking about this affair at Shonts last week-end."

"My dear boy, there's no need for you to shout. If only you don't mumble and clip your words—and turn head over heels with your ideas. Just tell me about it plainly. Who is Shonts? One of those Liberal peers? I seem to have heard the name...."

"Shonts, uncle, is the house the Laxtons have; you know,—Lucy."

"Little Lucy! I remember her. Curls all down her back. Married the milkman. But how does *she* come in, Alan? The story's getting—complicated. But that's the worst of these infernal affairs,—they always do get complicated. Tangled skeins—

'Oh what a tangled web we weave,

When first we venture to deceive.'

"And now, like a sensible man, you want to get out of it."

Captain Douglas was bright pink with the effort to control himself and keep perfectly plain and straightforward. His hair had become like tow and little beads of perspiration stood upon his forehead.

"I spent last week-end at Shonts," he said. "Lord Moggeridge, also there, week-ending. Got it into his head that I was pulling his leg."

"Naturally, my boy, if he goes philandering. At his time of life. What else can he expect?"

"It wasn't philandering."

"Fine distinctions. Fine distinctions. Go on—anyhow."

"He got it into his head that I was playing practical jokes upon him. Confused me with Eric. It led to a rather first-class row. I had to get out of the house. Nothing else to do. He brought all sorts of accusations—"

Captain Douglas stopped short. His uncle was no longer attending to him. They had drifted to the window of the study and the general was staring with an excitement and intelligence that grew visibly at the spectacle of Bealby and the trailer outside. For Bealby had been left in the trailer, and he was sitting as good as gold waiting for the next step in his vindication from the dark charge of burglary. He was very travel-worn and the trailer was time-worn as well as travel-worn, and both contrasted with the efficient neatness and newness of the motor bicycle in front. The contrast had attracted the attention of a tall policeman who was standing in a state of elucidatory meditation regarding Bealby. Bealby was not regarding the policeman. He had the utmost confidence in Captain Douglas, he felt sure that he would presently be purged of all the horror of that dead old man and of the brief unpremeditated plunge into crime, but still for the present at any rate he did not feel equal to staring a policeman out of countenance....

From the window the policeman very largely obscured Bealby....

Whenever hearts are simple there lurks romance. Age cannot wither nor custom stale her infinite diversity. Suddenly out of your low kindly diplomacies, your sane man-of-the-world intentions, leaps the imagination like a rocket, flying from such safe securities bang into the sky. So it happened to the old general. He became deaf to everything but the appearances before him. The world was jewelled with dazzling and delightful possibilities. His face was lit by a glow of genuine romantic excitement. He grasped his nephew's arm. He pointed. His grizzled cheeks flushed.

"That isn't," he asked with something verging upon admiration in his voice and manner, "a Certain Lady in disguise?"

§ 3

It became clear to Captain Douglas that if ever he was to get to Lord Moggeridge that day he must take his uncle firmly in hand. Without even attempting not to appear to shout he cried, "That is a little Boy. That is my Witness. It is Most Important that I should get him to Lord Moggeridge to tell his Story."

"What story?" cried the old commander, pulling at his moustache and still eyeing Bealby suspiciously....

It took exactly half an hour to get Lord Chickney from that enquiry to the telephone and even then he was still far from clear about the matter in hand. Captain Douglas got in most of the facts, but he could not eliminate an idea that it all had to do with Madeleine. Whenever he tried to say clearly that she was entirely outside the question, the general patted his shoulder and looked very wise and kind and said, "My dear Boy, I quite understand; I *quite* understand. Never mention a lady. *No.*"

So they started at last rather foggily—so far as things of the mind went, though the sun that day was brilliant—and because of engine trouble in Port Street the general's hansom reached Tenby Little Street first and he got in a good five minutes preparing the Lord Chancellor tactfully and carefully before the bicycle and its trailer came upon the scene....

§ 4

Candler had been packing that morning with unusual solicitude for a week-end at Tulliver Abbey. His master had returned from the catastrophe of Shonts, fatigued and visibly aged and extraordinarily cross, and Candler looked to Tulliver Abbey to restore him to his former self. Nothing must be forgotten; there must be no little hitches, everything from first to last must go on oiled wheels, or it was clear his Lordship might develop a desperate hostility to these excursions, excursions which Candler found singularly refreshing and entertaining during the stresses of the session. Tulliver Abbey was as good a house as Shonts was bad; Lady Checksammington ruled with the softness of velvet and the strength of steel over a household of admirably efficient domestics, and there would be the best of people there, Mr. Evesham perhaps, the Loopers, Lady Privet, Andreas Doria and Mr. Pernambuco, great silken mellow personages and diamond-like individualities, amidst whom Lord Moggeridge's mind would be restfully active and his comfort quite secure. And as far as possible Candler wanted to get the books and papers his master needed into the trunk or the small valise. That habit of catching up everything at the last moment and putting it under his arm and the consequent need for alert picking up, meant friction and nervous wear and tear for both master and man.

Lord Moggeridge rose at half-past ten—he had been kept late overnight by a heated discussion at the Aristotelian—and breakfasted lightly upon a chop and coffee. Then something ruffled him; something that came with the letters. Candler could not quite make out what it was, but he suspected another pamphlet by Dr. Schiller. It could not be the chop, because Lord Moggeridge was always wonderfully successful with chops. Candler looked through the envelopes and letters afterwards and found nothing diagnostic, and then he observed a copy of *Mind* torn across and lying in the waste-paper basket.

"When I went out of the room," said Candler, discreetly examining this. "Very likely it's that there Schiller after all."

But in this Candler was mistaken. What had disturbed the Lord Chancellor was a coarsely disrespectful article on the Absolute by a Cambridge Rhodes scholar, written in that flighty facetious strain that spreads now like a pestilence over modern philosophical discussion. "Does the Absolute, on Lord Moggeridge's own showing, mean anything more than an eloquent oiliness uniformly distributed through space?" and so on.

Pretty bad!

Lord Moggeridge early in life had deliberately acquired a quite exceptional power of mental self-control. He took his perturbed mind now and threw it forcibly into the consideration of a case upon which he had reserved judgment. He was to catch the 3.35 at Paddington, and at two he was smoking a cigar after a temperate lunch and reading over the notes of this judgment. It was then that the telephone bell became audible, and Candler came in to inform him that Lord Chickney was anxious to see him at once upon a matter of some slight importance.

"Slight importance?" asked Lord Moggeridge.

"Some slight importance, my lord."

"Some? Slight?"

"'Is Lordship, my lord, mumbles rather now 'is back teeth 'ave gone," said Candler, "but so I understand 'im."

"These apologetic assertive phrases annoy me, Candler," said Lord Moggeridge over his shoulder. "You see," he turned round and spoke very clearly, "either the matter is of importance or it is not of importance. A thing must either be or not be. I wish you would manage—when you get messages on the telephone—.... But I suppose that is asking too much.... Will you explain to him, Candler, when we start, and—ask him, Candler—ask him what sort of matter it is."

Candler returned after some parleying.

"So far as I can make 'is Lordship out, my lord, 'e says 'e wants to set you right about something, my lord. He says something about a *little* misapprehension."

"These diminutives, Candler, kill sense. Does he say what sort—what sort—of *little* misapprehension?"

"He says something—I'm sorry, my lord, but it's about Shonts, me lord."

"Then I don't want to hear about it," said Lord Moggeridge.

There was a pause. The Lord Chancellor resumed his reading with a deliberate obviousness; the butler hovered.

"I'm sorry, my lord, but I can't think exactly what I ought to say to 'is lordship, my lord."

"Tell him—tell him that I do not wish to hear anything more about Shonts for ever. Simply."

Candler hesitated and went out, shutting the door carefully lest any fragment of his halting rendering of this message to Lord Chickney should reach his master's ears.

Lord Moggeridge's powers of mental control were, I say, very great—He could dismiss subjects from his mind absolutely. In a few instants he had completely forgotten Shonts and was making notes with a silver-cased pencil on the margins of his draft judgment.

§ 5

He became aware that Candler had returned.

"'Is lordship, Lord Chickney, my lord, is very persistent, my lord. 'E's rung up twice. 'E says now that 'e makes a personal matter of it. Come what may, 'e says, 'e wishes to speak for two minutes to your lordship. Over the telephone, my lord, 'e vouchsafes no further information."

Lord Moggeridge meditated over the end of his third after lunch cigar. His man watched the end of his left eyebrow as an engineer might watch a steam gauge. There were no signs of an explosion. "He must come, Candler," his lordship said at last....

"Oh, Candler!"

"My lord?"

"Put the bags and things in a conspicuous position in the hall, Candler. Change yourself, and see that you look thoroughly like trains. And in fact have everything ready, *prominently* ready, Candler."

Then once more Lord Moggeridge concentrated his mind.

§ 6

To him there presently entered Lord Chickney.

Lord Chickney had been twice round the world and he had seen many strange and dusky peoples and many remarkable customs and peculiar prejudices, which he had never failed to despise, but he had never completely shaken off the county family ideas in which he had been brought up. He believed that there was an incurable difference in spirit between quite good people like himself and men from down below like Moggeridge, who was the son of an Exeter chorister. He believed that these men from nowhere always cherished the profoundest respect for the real thing like himself, that they were greedy for association and gratified by notice, and so for the life of him he could not approach Lord Moggeridge without a faint sense of condescension. He saluted him as "my *dear* Lord Moggeridge," wrung his hand with effusion, and asked him kind, almost district-visiting, questions about his younger brother and the aspect of his house. "And you are just off, I see, for a week-end."

These amenities the Lord Chancellor acknowledged by faint gruntings and an almost imperceptible movement of his eyebrows. "There was a matter," he said, "some *little* matter, on which you want to consult me?"

"Well," said Lord Chickney, and rubbed his chin. "*Yes.* Yes, there *was* a little matter, a little trouble—"

"Of an urgent nature."

"Yes. Yes. Exactly. Just a little complicated, you know, not quite simple." The dear old soldier's manner became almost seductive. "One of these difficult little affairs, where one has to remember that one is a man of the world, you know. A little complication about a lady, known to you both. But one must make concessions, one must understand. The boy has a witness. Things are not as you supposed them to be."

Lord Moggeridge had a clean conscience about ladies; he drew out his watch and looked at it—aggressively. He kept it in his hand during his subsequent remarks.

"I must confess," he declared, "I have not the remotest idea.... If you will be so good as to be—elementary. What *is* it all about?"

"You see, I knew the lad's mother," said Lord Chickney. "In fact—" He became insanely confidential—"Under happier circumstances—don't misunderstand me, Moggeridge; I mean no evil—but he might have been my son. I feel for him like a son...."

§ 7

When presently Captain Douglas, a little heated from his engine trouble, came into the room—he had left Bealby with Candler in the hall—it was instantly manifest to him that the work of preparation had been inadequately performed.

"One minute more, my dear Alan," cried Lord Chickney.

Lord Moggeridge with eyebrows waving and watch in hand was of a different opinion. He addressed himself to Captain Douglas.

"There *isn't* a minute more," he said. "What is all this—this philoprogenitive rigmarole about? Why have you come to me? My cab is outside *now*. All this about ladies and witnesses;—what *is* it?"

"Perfectly simple, my lord! You imagine that I played practical jokes upon you at Shonts. I didn't. I have a witness. The attack upon you downstairs, the noise in your room—"

"Have I any guarantee—?"

"It's the steward's boy from Shonts. Your man outside knows him. Saw him in the steward's room. He made the trouble for you—and me, and then he ran away. Just caught him. Not exchanged thirty words with him. Half a dozen questions. Settle everything. Then you'll know—nothing for you but the utmost respect."

Lord Moggeridge pressed his lips together and resisted conviction.

"In consideration," interpolated Lord Chickney, "feelings of an old fellow. Old soldier. Boy means no harm."

With the rudeness of one sorely tried the Lord Chancellor thrust the old general aside. "Oh!" he said, "Oh!" and then to Captain Douglas. "One minute. Where's your witness?..."

The Captain opened a door. Bealby found himself bundled into the presence of two celebrated men.

"Tell him," said Captain Douglas. "And look sharp about it."

"Tell me plainly," cried the Lord Chancellor, "and be—*quick*."

He put such a point on "quick" that it made Bealby jump.

"Tell him," said the general more gently. "Don't be afraid."

"Well," began Bealby after one accumulating pause, "it was 'im told me to do it. 'E said you go in there—"

The Captain would have interrupted but the Lord Chancellor restrained him by a magnificent gesture of the hand holding the watch.

"He told you to do it!" he said. "I knew he did. Now listen! He told you practically to go in and do anything you could."

"Yessir." Woe took possession of Bealby. "I didn't do any 'arm to the ole gentleman."

"But *who* told you?" cried the Captain. "*Who* told you?"

Lord Moggeridge annihilated him with arm and eyebrows. He held Bealby fascinated by a pointing finger.

"Don't do more than answer the questions. I have thirty seconds more. He told you to go in. He *made* you go in. At the earliest possible opportunity you got away?"

"I jest nipped out—"

"Enough! And now, sir, how dare you come here without even a plausible lie? How dare you after your intolerable tomfoolery at Shonts confront me again with fresh tomfoolery? How dare you drag in your gallant and venerable uncle in this last preposterous—I suppose you would call it—*lark*! I suppose you had prepared that little wretch with some fine story. Little you know of False Witness! At the first question, he breaks down! He does not even begin his lie. He at least knows the difference between my standards and yours. Candler! Candler!"

Candler appeared.

"These—these *gentlemen* are going. Is everything ready?"

"The cab is at the door, m'lord. The usual cab."

Captain Douglas made one last desperate effort. "Sir!" he said. "My lord—"

The Lord Chancellor turned upon him with a face that he sought to keep calm, though the eyebrows waved and streamed like black smoke in a gale. "Captain Douglas," he said, "you are probably not aware of the demands upon the time and patience of a public servant in such a position as mine. You see the world no doubt as a vastly entertaining fabric upon which you can embroider your—your facetious arrangements. Well, it is not so. It is real. It is earnest. You may sneer at the simplicity of an old man, but what I tell you of life is true. Comic effect is not, believe me, its goal. And you, sir, you, sir, you impress me as an intolerably foolish, flippant and unnecessary young man. Flippant. Unnecessary. Foolish."

As he said these words Candler approached him with a dust coat of a peculiar fineness and dignity, and he uttered the last words over his protruded chest while Candler assisted his arms into his sleeves.

"My lord," said Captain Douglas again, but his resolution was deserting him.

"*No*," said the Lord Chancellor, leaning forward in a minatory manner while Candler pulled down the tail of his jacket and adjusted the collar of his overcoat.

"Uncle," said Captain Douglas.

"*No*," said the general, with the curt decision of a soldier, and turned exactly ninety degrees away from him. "You little know how you have hurt me, Alan! You little know. I couldn't have imagined it. The Douglas strain! False Witness—and insult. I am sorry, my dear Moggeridge, beyond measure."

"I quite understand—you are as much a victim as myself. Quite. A more foolish attempt—I am sorry to be in this hurry—"

"Oh! You damned little fool," said the Captain, and advanced a step towards the perplexed and shrinking Bealby. "You imbecile little trickster! What do you mean by it?"

"I didn't mean anything—!"

Then suddenly the thought of Madeleine, sweet and overpowering, came into the head of this distraught young man. He had risked losing her, he had slighted and insulted her, and here he was—entangled. Here he was in a position of nearly inconceivable foolishness, about to assault a dirty and silly little boy in the presence of the Lord Chancellor and Uncle Chickney. The world, he felt, was lost, and not well lost. And she was lost too. Even now while he pursued these follies she might be consoling her wounded pride....

He perceived that love is the supreme thing in life. He perceived that he who divides his purposes scatters his life to the four winds of heaven. A vehement resolve to cut the whole of this Bealby business pounced upon him. In that moment he ceased to care for reputation, for appearances, for the resentment of Lord Moggeridge or the good intentions of Uncle Chickney.

He turned, he rushed out of the room. He escaped by unparalleled gymnastics the worst consequences of an encounter with the Lord Chancellor's bag which the under-butler had placed rather tactlessly between the doors, crossed the wide and dignified hall, and in another moment had his engine going and was struggling to mount his machine in the street without. His face expressed an almost apoplectic concentration. He narrowly missed the noses of a pair of horses in the carriage of Lady Beach Mandarin, made an extraordinary curve to spare a fishmonger's tricycle, shaved the front and completely destroyed the gesture of that eminent actor manager, Mr. Pomegranate, who was crossing the road in his usual inadvertent fashion, and then he was popping and throbbing and banging round the corner and on his way back to the lovely and irresistible woman who was exerting so disastrous an influence upon his career....

§ 8

The Captain fled from London in the utmost fury and to the general danger of the public. His heart was full of wicked blasphemies, shoutings and self-reproaches, but outwardly he seemed only pinkly intent. And as he crossed an open breezy common and passed by a milestone bearing this inscription, "To London Thirteen Miles," his hind tyre burst conclusively with a massive report....

§ 9

In every life there are crucial moments, turning points, and not infrequently it is just such a thing as this, a report, a sudden waking in the night, a flash upon the road to Damascus, that marks and precipitates the accumulating new. Vehemence is not concentration. The headlong violence of the Captain had been no expression of a single-minded purpose, of a soul all gathered together to an end. Far less a pursuit had it been than a flight, a flight from his own dissensions. And now—now he was held.

After he had attempted a few plausible repairs and found the tyre obdurate, after he had addressed ill-chosen remonstrances to some unnamed hearer, after he had walked some way along the road and back in an indecision about repair shops in some neighbouring town, the last dregs of his resistance were spent. He perceived that he was in the presence of a Lesson. He sat down by the roadside, some twenty feet from the disabled motor bicycle and, impotent for further effort, frankly admitted himself overtaken. He had not reckoned with punctures.

The pursuing questions came clambering upon him and would no longer be denied; who he was and what he was and how he was, and the meaning of this Rare Bate he had been in, and all those deep questions that are so systematically neglected in the haste and excitement of modern life.

In short, for the first time in many headlong days he asked himself simply and plainly what he thought he was up to?

Certain things became clear, and so minutely and exactly clear that it was incredible that they had ever for a moment been obscure. Of course Bealby had been a perfectly honest little boy, under some sort of misconception, and of course he ought to have been carefully coached and prepared and rehearsed before he was put before the Lord Chancellor. This was so manifest now that the Captain stared aghast at his own inconceivable negligence. But the mischief was done. Nothing now would ever propitiate Moggeridge, nothing now would ever reconcile Uncle Chickney. That was— settled. But what was not settled was the amazing disorder of his own mind. Why had he been so negligent, what had come over his mind in the last few weeks?

And this sudden strange illumination of the Captain's mind went so far as perceiving that the really important concern for him was not the accidents of Shonts but this epilepsy of his own will. Why now was he rushing back to Madeleine? Why? He did not love her. He knew he did not love her. On the whole, more than anything else he resented her.

But he was excited about her, he was so excited that these other muddles, fluctuations, follies, came as a natural consequence from that. Out of this excitement came those wild floods of angry energy that made him career about—

"Like some damned Cracker," said the Captain.

"For instance," he asked himself, "*now!* what am I going for?

"If I go back she'll probably behave like an offended Queen. Doesn't seem to understand anything that does not focus on herself. Wants a sort of Limelight Lover...."

"She *relies* upon exciting me!"

"She relies upon exciting everyone!—she's just a woman specialized for excitement."

And after meditating through a profound minute upon this judgment, the Captain pronounced these two epoch-making words: "*I won't!*"

§ 10

The Captain's mind was now in a state of almost violent lucidity.

"This sex stuff," he said; "first I kept it under too tight and now I've let it rip too loose."

"I've been just a distracted fool, with my head swimming with meetings and embraces and—frills."

He produced some long impending generalizations.

"Not a man's work, this Lover business. Dancing about in a world of petticoats and powder puffs and attentions and jealousies. Rotten game. Played off against some other man...."

"I'll be hanged if I am...."

"Have to put women in their places...."

"Make a hash of everything if we don't...."

Then for a time the Captain meditated in silence and chewed his knuckle. His face darkened to a scowl. He swore as though some thought twisted and tormented him. "Let some other man get her! Think of her with some other man."

"I don't care," he said, when obviously he did.

"There's other women in the world."

"A man—a man mustn't care for *that*...."

"It's this or that," said the Captain, "anyhow...."

§ 11

Suddenly the Captain's mind was made up and done.

He arose to his feet and his face was firm and tranquil and now nearer pallor than pink. He left his bicycle and trailer by the wayside even as Christian left his burden. He asked a passing nurse-girl the way to the nearest railway station, and thither he went. Incidentally, and because the opportunity offered, he called in upon a cyclist's repair shop and committed his abandoned machinery to its keeping. He went straight to London, changed at his flat, dined at his club, and caught the night train for France— for France and whatever was left of the grand manœuvres.

He wrote a letter to Madeleine from the Est train next day, using their customary endearments, avoiding any discussion of their relations and describing the scenery of the Seine valley and the characteristics of Rouen in a few vivid and masterly phrases.

"If she's worth having, she'll understand," said the Captain, but he knew perfectly well she would not understand.

Mrs. Geedge noted this letter among the others, and afterwards she was much exercised by Madeleine's behaviour. For suddenly that lady became extraordinarily gay and joyous in her bearing, singing snatches of song and bubbling over with suggestions for larks and picnics and wild excursions. She patted Mr. Geedge on the shoulder and ran her arm through the arm of Professor Bowles. Both gentlemen received these familiarities with a gawky coyness that Mrs. Geedge found contemptible. And moreover Madeleine drew several shy strangers into their circle. She invited the management to a happy participation.

Her great idea was a moonlight picnic. "We'll have a great camp-fire and afterwards we'll dance—this very night."

"But wouldn't it be better to-morrow?"

"To-night!"

"To-morrow perhaps Captain Douglas may be back again. And he's so good at all these things."

Mrs. Geedge knew better because she had seen the French stamp on the letter, but she meant to get to the bottom of this business, and thus it was she said this.

"I've sent him back to his soldiering," said Madeleine serenely. "He has better things to do."

§ 12

For some moments after the unceremonious departure of Captain Douglas from the presence of Lord Moggeridge, it did not occur to anyone, it did not occur even to Bealby, that the Captain had left his witness behind him. The general and the Lord Chancellor moved into the hall, and Bealby, under the sway of a swift compelling gesture from Candler, followed modestly. The same current swept them all out into the portico, and while the under-butler whistled up a hansom for the General, the Lord Chancellor, with a dignity that was at once polite and rapid, and Candler gravely protective and little reproving, departed. Bealby, slowly apprehending their desertion, regarded the world of London with perplexity and dismay. Candler had gone. The last of the gentlemen was going. The under-butler, Bealby felt, was no friend. Under-butlers never are.

Lord Chickney in the very act of entering his cab had his coat-tail tugged. He looked enquiringly.

"Please, sir, there's me," said Bealby.

Lord Chickney reflected. "Well?" he said.

The spirit of Bealby was now greatly abased. His face and voice betrayed him on the verge of tears. "I want to go 'ome to Shonts, sir."

"Well, my boy, go 'ome—go home, I mean, to Shonts."

"'E's gone, sir," said Bealby....

Lord Chickney was a good-hearted man, and he knew that a certain public kindliness and disregard of appearances looks far better and is infinitely more popular than a punctilious dignity. He took Bealby to Waterloo in his hansom, got him a third class ticket to Chelsome, tipped a porter to see him safely into his train and dismissed him in the most fatherly manner.

<h2 style="text-align:center">§ 13</h2>

It was well after tea-time, Bealby felt, as he came once more within the boundaries of the Shonts estate.

It was a wiser and a graver Bealby who returned from this week of miscellaneous adventure. He did not clearly understand all that had happened to him; in particular he was puzzled by the extreme annoyance and sudden departure of Captain Douglas from the presence of Lord Moggeridge; but his general impression was that he had been in great peril of dire punishment and that he had been rather hastily and ignominiously reprieved. The nice old gentleman with the long grey moustaches had dismissed him to the train at last with a quality of benediction. But Bealby understood now better than he had done before that adventures do not always turn out well for the boy hero, and that the social system has a number of dangerous and disagreeable holes at the bottom. He had reached the beginnings of wisdom. He was glad he had got away from the tramp and still gladder that he had got away from Crayminster; he was sorry that he would never see the beautiful lady again, and perplexed and perplexed. And also he was interested in the probability of his mother having toast for tea....

It must, he felt, be a long time after tea-time, quite late....

He had weighed the advisability of returning quietly to his windowless bedroom under the stairs, putting on his little green apron and emerging with a dutiful sang-froid as if nothing had happened, on the one hand, or of going to the gardens on the other. But tea—with eatables—seemed more probable at the gardens....

He was deflected from the direct route across the park by a long deep trench, that someone had made and abandoned since the previous Sunday morning. He wondered what it was for. It was certainly very ugly. And as he came out by the trees and got the full effect of the façade, he detected a strangely bandaged quality about Shonts. It was as if Shonts had recently been in a fight and got a black eye. Then he saw the reason for this; one tower was swathed in scaffolding. He wondered what could have happened to the tower. Then his own troubles resumed their sway.

He was so fortunate as not to meet his father in the gardens, and he entered the house so meekly that his mother did not look up from the cashmere she was sewing. She was sitting at the table sewing some newly dyed black cashmere.

He was astonished at her extreme pallor and the drooping resignation of her pose.

"Mother!" he said, and she looked up convulsively and stared, stared with bright round astonished eyes.

"I'm sorry, mother, I'aven't been quite a good steward's-room boy, mother. If I could 'ave another go, mother...."

He halted for a moment, astonished that she said nothing, but only sat with that strange expression and opened and shut her mouth.

"Reely—I'd *try*, mother...."

Milton Keynes UK
Ingram Content Group UK Ltd.
UKHW040701150224
437844UK00007B/702